Kiss Me If You Can

KISS ME IF YOU CAN

CARLY PHILLIPS

WHEELER
CHIVERS

This Large Print edition is published by Wheeler Publishing, Waterville, Maine, USA and by AudioGO Ltd, Bath, England.
Wheeler Publishing, a part of Gale, Cengage Learning.
The text of this Large Print edition is unabridged.
Other aspects of the book may vary from the original edition.
Set in 16 pt. Plantin.

LIBRARY OF CONGRESS CATALOGING-IN-PUBLICATION DATA

Phillips, Carly.
  Kiss me if you can / by Carly Phillips. — Large print ed.
    p. cm. — (Wheeler Publishing large print hardcover)
  ISBN-13: 978-1-4104-3281-0
  ISBN-10: 1-4104-3281-5
  1. Bachelors—Fiction. 2. Love stories. gsafd 3. Large type books. I. Title.
PS3616.H454.K57 2010
813'.6—dc22   2010037217

BRITISH LIBRARY CATALOGUING-IN-PUBLICATION DATA AVAILABLE
Published in 2011 in the U.S. by arrangement with Harlequin Books S.A.
Published in 2011 in the U.K. by arrangement with Harlequin Enterprises II B.V.

U.K. Hardcover: 978 1 408 49405 9 (Chivers Large Print)
U.K. Softcover: 978 1 408 49406 6 (Camden Large Print)

Printed in the United States of America
1 2 3 4 5 6 7 15 14 13 12 11

Dear Reader,

I'm thrilled to bring you the start of a brand-new series of books. The Most Eligible Bachelor concept isn't new, but I think my spin on it is both fresh and current — an online blog teams with a New York City newspaper with the sole purpose of helping the bachelor in question find the woman of his dreams. The stories are fun, sassy and of course sexy!

When jaded crime beat reporter and aspiring mystery writer Sam Cooper (Coop) stops a jewelry store robbery and is given a ring as a reward, he is labeled a hero and becomes the newest Bachelor in the infamous Bachelor Blog. Lexie Davis is a free-spirited Web designer with a love of travel who wants to purchase the ring for her beloved grandmother's eightieth birthday. But as Coop discovers, the ring is stolen property, and when his apartment is vandalized, it becomes obvious someone wants the ring back. As Lexie and Coop team up to uncover the ring's past, sparks fly between them. Add a cast of secondary characters working to derail the duo's efforts and drama ensues when Lexie's unorthodox family history is revealed. When all is said and done, can Lexie overcome her fear of settling down, especially when she discovers Coop wants to write a novel based on her grandmother's story as the big break in his burgeoning career?

Some books are hard to write — some are easy. Very few are pure unadulterated joy. *Kiss Me If You Can* surprised me, thrilled me and made me extremely happy all the way through. I hope you'll feel the same!

Visit my brand-new Web site, www.carly phillips.com, where you can write to me, track me on the Internet and join my new Club Carly fan club! You can also write to me at P.O. Box 483, Purchase, NY 10577.

Best wishes,
Carly

ACKNOWLEDGMENT

To Tracy Farrell — to the first of many more books together!

For Brenda Chin — extraordinary editor and most importantly a friend. You've brought me where I am today and for that I thank you!

PROLOGUE

THE DAILY POST
THE BACHELOR BLOGS

News flash! The *Daily Post* is happy to announce a partnership with the Bachelor Blogs, bringing you news of New York's hottest men, both online and in print!

Keep track of the city's most eligible bachelors: From single dads to firefighters to New York's finest, they're the ones who make a difference. Do you know an everyday hero? If so, write in! The next bachelor in the spotlight is up to you!

CHAPTER ONE

Sam Cooper's stomach grumbled at the sight of the blue-and-yellow umbrellas shading his favorite hot dog stand from the blazing sun. Fresh from a boring press conference, where the mayor and police commissioner had announced the long-awaited wrap-up of a string of apartment burglaries on the Upper West Side, Coop had his digital recorder in one pocket and cash in another.

The aroma of New York's finest hot dog had his mouth watering. "Hey, Dom. How's business today?" he asked the owner.

"Can't complain. Busy lunch crowd. Slow now but it'll pick up again during the commute." The older man, tanned from his days outside, lifted the metal lid, revealing Coop's belated lunch. "The usual?"

Coop nodded. "The works. Actually make it two. I haven't eaten since breakfast."

He glanced at his watch. Nearly 3:00 p.m.

Enough time for him to eat and get his story in before heading home for the day.

While Dom placed his hot dogs in their buns and began loading them up, Coop glanced around his city. On a hot August day like this one, few people wandered around outside. The smart ones hightailed it out of town, heading for the ritzy Hamptons or the Jersey Shore. Others holed up inside, with their AC blasting.

Coop's favorite hot dog stand was located on the corner of 47th Street and Park Avenue. A people watcher by nature — part of what led him to become a reporter, he supposed — Coop always studied the stores and buildings in the vicinity, and the people entering and exiting each.

As usual, the Vintage Jewelers caught his eye. Unlike most of the upscale stores in the area, it was rather ordinary. As if to compensate, the window changed often, rotating gaudy, elaborate pieces almost daily. Usually only women frequented the establishment — no big surprise — but today a man wearing a sweatshirt, hood over his head, stood inside.

"Strange," Coop muttered. The heat from the sun had him sweating in his shirt and the steam coming off the sidewalk blistered the soles of his shoes.

"Dogs are ready," Dom said, distracting Coop's attention.

But not before Coop caught sight of what looked like a gun in the man's hand. Coop's adrenaline kicked in and he focused on the store. There were two females behind the counter. If he barged in, he risked the guy shooting someone.

Inside the store, the man turned to leave.

Coop glanced at Dom. "Don't ask questions, just call 9-1-1," he said as he grabbed the metal lid off the cart and swerved back to face the store.

As the man exited, Coop acted on instinct. He stuck his foot out, tripping the guy before he could run. The man staggered but regained his balance and straightened up. Coop drew a deep breath and bashed the man in the head with the aluminum hot dog cover. His hood must have cushioned the blow or else the guy had a thick skull because he struggled to stand up a second time. Coop swung harder and the guy fell to the sidewalk, moaning in pain. The jewels spilled from his pocket onto the ground.

Before the other man could recover, Coop grabbed the gun from inside his sweatshirt and waited for the cops to arrive. His heart still beat hard, roaring in his ears as the sirens alerted him to the arrival of the police

15

and the cops quickly relieved him. While one cuffed the criminal and hauled him into their car, another took Coop's statement.

As he replayed the events in his head, Coop was almost glad his torn rotator cuff had forced him to quit the police academy and he had a newfound respect for his father and older brother, both career policemen. Wouldn't they get a laugh when they heard about his exploits. They'd rib him but good for trying to do their job.

"Hey, Mac, are you finished grilling me?" From his years working the crime beat, he was on a first-name basis with many of the detectives and cops.

The other man nodded. "We know where to find you. Go home and take it easy. You've had a rough day."

Coop shook his head. "I'm fine. I'll be at the office if you need me." At the very least, he could make sure this story had the right spin.

He turned to leave when two women came running out of the jewelry store. "Wait," the older one called. "I wanted to thank you!"

Coop strode toward the petite brunette who would have been no match for the robber, with or without his gun.

"I'm so grateful to you. Normally my father would be in the store with me, but

16

he's in Florida for the weekend. That man loaded up his sweatshirt with expensive items. You saved us a small fortune!"

Coop shifted from foot to foot, uncomfortable with her gratitude. "I was just in the right place at the right time."

She shook her head. "Don't be modest! Most people would have just walked away. I was in the store with my fifteen-year-old daughter, so I handed over the items because I didn't want her to get hurt. You must come inside. I insist on giving you a reward for your heroic actions. I've already been to the bank, so I'm going to have to offer you jewelry instead."

He shook his head once more. "No reward necessary."

"Reward?" A female television reporter Sam recognized shoved a microphone between Sam and the shop owner's daughter. "Go on! I'd love to get the exclusive on this for tonight's five o'clock news!"

"You mean you'd mention our store by name?" The store owner's eyes lit up at the idea.

The reporter nodded. "We can even shoot inside as you give your savior his reward."

Coop groaned. He recognized the runaway train and fought to avoid the inevitable. "I can't accept a reward. Like I told her, I just happened to be in the right place at the right time."

The reporter smoothed her hair, straightened her shoulders and motioned to her camera crew. "Roll tape," she said, ignoring him.

"This is Carolina Martinez, reporting from the scene of a robbery in midtown Manhattan, with the reluctant hero, crime beat reporter Sam Cooper, and the grateful store owner who is just about to present him with a reward." She glanced at her crew and said, "Cut!" before turning back to the stunned store owner. "It's your show. What do you intend to give him?" Carolina asked.

Coop found himself dragged into the shop by the insistent reporter and the store owner's daughter, followed by the camera crew. He wanted to get the hell out of here, but the woman, whose name he learned was Anna Burnett, had placed a tray of antique jewelry in front of him. Meanwhile, Carolina and her crew taped everything, leaving Coop with no choice but to go along with Anna's plea that he choose an item for his trouble.

Coop scanned the tray, looking for something that appeared inexpensive and that he could take without guilt.

"How about this watch?" Anna raised the

hammered gold men's timepiece, angled not for Coop but toward the camera.

Coop shook his head. "I couldn't. It looks too expensive and besides I don't wear jewelry."

"Then how about a necklace or a ring for your wife?" She lifted what appeared to be an emerald necklace, showing it off with a wide smile for the camera.

"Not married." *Anymore.* He forced a smile.

"Something for your girlfriend then!"

Before she could reach for something else, Coop chose the ugliest, most gaudy ring in the bunch, hoping it was also the least expensive. "I'll take this."

"I'm so glad you've accepted a memento for preventing our beloved store from being robbed. The ring is beautiful and there are many more lovely items at the Vintage Jewelers, located at 47th Street and Park Avenue." She swept the inside of the store with her hand, hamming it up as she took advantage of the free publicity.

Coop stifled a chuckle, if only because the damn cameras were still rolling. He waited for Carolina to yell, "Cut!"

Then Coop pocketed the ring, thanked Anna and Carolina, and got the hell out of the store before the intrepid reporter decided she wanted to interview him as well as humiliate him in front of the entire city.

A reporter by day and an aspiring novelist in his private time, even Coop couldn't have scripted anything like today.

As Coop walked into the newsroom, a round of applause greeted him, and his colleagues rose to their feet.

Coop frowned, waving away their whistles and comments, and headed for his desk. He lowered himself into his seat and leaned back, relaxing for the first time all day. He pulled the ring from his pocket and held the gaudy piece up to examine it more closely.

"You aren't going to see much in this dingy lighting." Amanda Nichols, the features editor at the paper, propped a hip on his desk. She leaned in for a better look at his ring and her long blonde hair fell in curls around her shoulders.

Coop liked Amanda. They'd had their moment, a brief fling after Coop's divorce, but there'd been no serious spark for either one of them. Luckily, she was the rare woman who could separate sex from friendship and they'd been able to remain on good terms ever since.

"It's ugly as sin, isn't it?" he asked.

"Let me see." Amanda held out her hand and he placed the ring in her palm.

Into glitz, glamour and shopping, she enjoyed material things. Clothing, jewelry, you name it — she knew its history.

She narrowed her gaze and peered inside the ring. "Ugly by today's standards, but by vintage ones, this is a collector's dream. It's Trifari. Look at the insignia." She drew his attention to the inside of the ring's shank, pointing with her long, painted nails. "You picked yourself a winner," she said, handing him back his reward.

"I didn't want something valuable. I wanted something I wouldn't feel guilty about taking," he said in frustration.

Amanda shrugged. "From what I heard, you saved the store owner a fortune. Don't feel bad. You can just give it to the special lady in your life." She not-so-subtly raised her gaze to meet his.

Coop cocked his head to one side. "Is that your way of asking if I'm seeing anyone?"

She grinned. "Actually, yes, it is. You work too hard. You're always pounding away at your computer."

Because he often pulled up his *other work* when he wasn't on deadline at the paper. Fiction writing was his real love, not that he shared that information with many people.

Lately though, the creative juices had dried up, causing him many hours of staring at a blank screen, both here and at home.

"I'm not seeing anyone," he said, hoping she'd leave it at that.

"I worry about you. A girlfriend would add some balance to your life."

So much for her dropping the subject.

Coop rolled his eyes. "I have enough balance and there's no need to worry. I'm fine. Now if we could stay on track?" He shot her a wry look and placed the ring on his desk. "Since it's worth something, I guess I'll store it in a safe place."

"Okay, but you know what they say about all work and no play . . ."

"I play enough," he lied.

"If you say so." She pinned him with a look that told him she was onto him.

What could he say? Lately, there'd been no woman who'd captured his interest. But if he admitted as much to Amanda, she'd start setting him up with her friends, and he shuddered at the thought. Blind dates were bad enough. Well-meaning friends trying to matchmake were even worse. Coop had an ex-wife and a healthy respect for being more careful with the women he chose. He certainly wasn't lacking for bed partners, if that was all he needed.

"I do. Now I need to get back to work."

She shook her head and sighed. "Okay, then. Catch you later, *hero.*" She winked and strode away, her hips swaying as she walked.

Coop turned to his computer.

Bringing up a Google search on the word *Trifari,* he spent a considerable amount of time researching until he finally found a photo of what looked like the ring he now had in his possession. To his surprise, it was part of a set that included a bracelet and necklace. Back in the 1950s the jewels had belonged to a wealthy family in Manhattan until they'd been stolen in a brazen robbery during a dinner party at the family home. The culprits had never been caught and the jewels had reportedly never been recovered.

Coop glanced at the ring on his desk. What the hell did he have in his possession? Did the jewelry store even know the value of the ring? How many times had it been passed on since the robbery over fifty years ago?

His journalistic mind wondered about the history of the jewels and he knew he had some more digging to do. But his novelist's mind began to spark with fictional spin-offs and possibilities. An unsolved crime dating back to the 1950s. A large dinner party, wealthy socialites, ongoing affairs between supposedly close friends and business associates, and a crime of passion. A murder and the theft of beloved family jewels.

Or . . . A new thought struck him. Did he want to move from genre fiction to true crime? Once he delved into this open case even further, he might find a treasure trove of information to work with.

Either way, Coop knew he was on to something. After months of writer's block, his adrenaline was pumping in a way that surpassed even the excitement of stopping the robbery today. He finally had the germ of an idea for his next book, with more characters and intrigue than he'd ever written before.

His first novel, published by a small press, had had a piddly print run and had barely sold enough copies to buy him dinner. But this story had definite potential.

His gut, which had never guided him wrong in his full-time career, told him he was finally looking at a book that could help him realize his private, lifelong dream of being a bestselling novelist.

Lexie Davis hovered over her grandmother, the scent of violets permeating her every inhalation.

"So let me make sure I understand you," Charlotte Davis said. "I click on the compass-looking thing and it brings up the Internet. Then I place the mouse —"

"The cursor —" Lexie corrected her paternal grandmother. Placing her hand over the warm, weathered one, she moved the mouse, guiding the cursor over the screen.

The older woman sighed, sounding put upon. "I place the *cursor* over here, click, and then I can Giggle anything I want to know about. Is that right?"

"Google not Giggle!" Lexie shook her head and tried not to laugh at her grandmother's innocent mistake.

These computer lessons were going to be even more challenging than she'd thought. Well worth her time and effort, since it meant Lexie could remain in constant contact with the grandmother she loved, but taxing nevertheless. Lexie figured her grandmother had a thirty-minute attention span, max. They'd only gone through half that time so far.

Her grandmother's old PC had died a natural death and Lexie, a Web designer and Mac addict had surprised her with a new computer. When the next wave of wanderlust hit and Lexie felt compelled to pick up and travel, she wouldn't have to worry about her grandmother's computer being on the fritz, leaving Lexie to wonder if she couldn't reach the aging woman because the computer had died — or because her grandmother had.

A glance at Charlotte reassured Lexie. Even with her upcoming birthday, her grandmother had aged well. She was still mentally fit and physically able. A healthy specimen, if Lexie discounted the older woman's self-dyed red hair and decades-old housecoat adorned by the antique jewelry Charlotte always wore around her neck and on her ears. Hopefully, Charlotte wasn't leaving this world anytime soon.

"Oh look, it's five o'clock. Time for *Eyewitness News!*" Charlotte reached for the television remote control and turned on the TV.

"Can't you wait another fifteen minutes? We're almost finished with the basics of surfing the Net."

"The news can run in the background. You know I like to keep up on local events."

Lexie nodded. She knew. If Charlotte Davis's stories were to be believed, Lexie's eccentric grandmother had lived a colorful life and had known many famous people. At the ripe age of seventy-nine and 330 days

— Grandma Charlotte counted off the boxes on her Derek Jeter wall calendar — Charlotte watched television and read the paper to see who she'd outlived this week. Lexie had long since stopped reminding her that the TV news only broadcast the more sensational deaths. Her grandmother's true interest in the Channel 7 news was —

"Bill Evans!" Charlotte exclaimed, pointing toward the handsome weatherman.

Lexie bit the inside of her cheek as she saw her hopes for more lesson time slipping away. "Grandma, pay attention."

"After this segment. Check out the dimples on this dude."

A glance at the screen told Lexie her grandmother was no longer referring to the weatherman.

"Of course he doesn't hold a candle to Bill Evans, but he's still hot." Charlotte pointed a wrinkled hand toward the large television screen in the corner of the room.

The words *Crime Beat Reporter Foils Robbery* caught Lexie's mental attention, but the man captured her female imagination. Dark hair, longer at his neck, he was tanned, dimpled and sexy. She couldn't tear her gaze away. His blue eyes showed his obvious discomfort as the store owner, whose jewels he'd saved, tried to reward him for his trouble.

"Would you look at that? He's too noble to take the reward!" Grandma Charlotte said.

"A true gentleman," Lexie said, impressed by the man's actions as well as his handsome face and toned physique.

An exasperated sound escaped her grandmother's throat. "A fool is more like it. Take the goods!" the older woman yelled at the screen.

Lexie laughed.

The man, whose name flashed on the TV as Sam Cooper, turned down a watch and a necklace before the grateful store owner shoved a tray of rings in front of him.

"Not married," he said in a deep voice that suited his rugged good looks. "I'll take this," he said at last, reluctantly choosing a ring from the assortment on the tray.

The camera panned in for a close-up of the ring. A large, gaudy, flowery ring.

"Grandma, look! That looks just like one of your necklaces!"

Charlotte rose from her chair and peered at the screen. "You're right! Holy shit-ake mushrooms!" her grandmother exclaimed.

Lexie rolled her eyes. "You've got to stop watching Austin Powers movies."

Charlotte ignored the comment. Instead,

her hand flew to her chest. She grasped not the necklace in question, but another one of her so-called treasures that she'd promised to leave to Lexie one day. Some of them were hideous, but in a world without her grandmother, Lexie would want any item that reminded her of Charlotte.

"I wonder if it's an exact match," Lexie mused.

"I hope Sylvia is watching this!" her grandmother said of her longtime friend and neighbor, Sylvia Krinksy, who lived down the hall.

Lexie's grandfather and Sylvia's husband had long since passed away, but the women's friendship had predated their marriages and had remained strong to this day. Sylvia was Charlotte's *person,* the one who was there for you in good times and bad. "Sylvia would bury the body for me," Charlotte liked to say, while Sylvia would sit beside her friend and nod.

Suddenly agitated, her grandmother began pacing the small apartment, muttering as she moved.

Lexie walked to Charlotte's side, placing her hand on her frail back. "What's got you so upset?"

"Nothing." Her grandmother waved her hand, dismissing Lexie's concern. "I'm fine.

Seeing that ring was a surprise that brought back memories. I'm okay now."

Not convinced, Lexie narrowed her gaze and studied her grandmother. Charlotte looked paler than she had earlier, though it was hard to tell beneath the heavy foundation and rouge she wore.

"Grandma? Was the ring part of the original set?" she asked.

Charlotte looked away. "I'm suddenly tired." Her grandmother let out a heavy, clearly forced sigh.

Lexie wondered what in the world was going on. Something about the ring on television had upset her grandmother, but she didn't want to discuss it. Not even with Lexie.

Hmm. "Well, we can pick up your lesson tomorrow," Lexie said. "Why don't you go lie down?"

"I think I'll do that."

Lexie started to gather her things together. "I have to go out and meet Claudia about our newest client," Lexie told her grandmother. "I may be late, so don't wait up. I have my key."

Claudia Milne, a self-taught computer genius, did most of the coding for the sites Lexie designed. She lived, ate and breathed HTML and Lexie thanked her lucky stars they'd met on the plane ride from Israel to New York after Lexie's first Middle East trip five years ago.

A wanderer by nature, Lexie had the enviable ability to do her job from anywhere. She saw no reason to lease an apartment in between travels when she could stay in her grandmother's spare bedroom whenever she was in town. Charlotte loved having Lexie over and Lexie appreciated being able to do things for her grandmother when she was around.

"What site are you working on now?" her grandmother asked. Charlotte was always interested in Lexie's client list, and often offered input on design. Most of which Lexie politely ignored.

"Athlete's Only. The Jordan sisters and Yank Morgan asked for an overhaul," she said of the sports and PR powerhouse agency — and Lexie's first client when she'd started her own Web design business.

"Isn't it late for a meeting? Do I need to call Yank and tell him they're overworking you?" Charlotte asked.

Lexie and Yank Morgan were old friends. They'd met during her childhood spent at the skating rink. And thanks to that friendship, Lexie had garnered her first major client in need of a high-tech Web site and entrée into the prestigious and lucrative sports world.

As a result, Lexie's portfolio now included an array of sports-oriented clients, from sport drinks to sports teams — much to the surprise of her parents, who had at one time tried to mold their daughter into a competitive ice skater.

To their never-ending dismay, Lexie had rebelled against the rigid, competitive world of schedules and conformity. The only good that had come from those years was her grandmother's friendship with Yank. Charlotte and Yank shared a love of unconventional eccentricity. They also understood the notion of being true to oneself, and together they'd convinced Lexie's parents to stop pushing their desires onto their daughter.

Lexie would be forever grateful to Yank for that, and for his belief in her Web-design talent. "Grandma, I never mind working late. Don't you dare say a word." Evening meetings suited Lexie's lifestyle perfectly.

When Charlotte didn't reply, Lexie turned toward her, but the older woman had already disappeared into the bedroom. To lie down? She'd been distracted since seeing the ring on television. Obviously, the piece had hit a sentimental nerve.

As Lexie gathered her laptop and her bag, she caught sight of her grandmother's wall calendar — and the date circled in red. August twenty-eighth, Charlotte's 80th birthday. Lexie had been racking her brain for something different and personal she could get her grandmother as a gift.

The matching ring provided the perfect answer, and her thoughts immediately turned to the reluctant if sexy man who currently held it in his possession. He'd clearly been hesitant to accept anything from the store owner. Maybe he'd be willing to sell the ring.

Lexie was excited by the prospect of being able to give such a personal gift to her grandmother for her birthday. Now all she had to do was meet the current owner and convince him to part with his new possession.

CHAPTER TWO

It was days before Lexie could even think of contacting Sam Cooper. The day after she'd seen the ring on the news, one of her clients had a huge update that they wanted to go live with, so she'd been holed up indoors. The next day, her grandmother had a dental appointment and she'd asked Lexie to go along.

Finally, this morning she'd made the newspaper offices her first stop, only to discover that a guard at the security desk refused to let her up without an appointment. The man said that that reporter had been inundated by women seeking to talk to him and that he had strict orders not to let any man-hungry, money-seeking women near him.

Sam Cooper was better protected than the president. Didn't make sense to Lexie, but not even her most charming smile did the trick.

She'd tried reaching Sam Cooper by phone at the paper, but her call went straight to a recording and instead of being able to leave a message, a digital voice told her the answering machine was full. Still, Lexie was on a mission and determined to meet the man. She just hadn't figured out how.

"What's got you so preoccupied?" Claudia, Lexie's right hand, asked as she joined her at her table in Starbucks for their weekly meeting.

Lexie glanced up from the laptop she hadn't been focusing on anyway. "Good morning to you, too."

Claudia, always the epitome of happy, sat across the table, smiling. Her light-brown hair had been pulled into a loose ponytail and soft curls escaped on either side. Although Claudia was five years younger than Lexie's twenty-nine, she was mature and the two had struck up a strong friendship.

Lexie folded her arms and leaned forward in her seat. Drawing a deep breath, she told Claudia the story of her grandmother's jewelry and Sam Cooper, hero, and his relationship to the ring. "So I want to buy it back, but I can't get near the guy to introduce myself, let alone broach the subject. Why would a reporter need such heavy security?" Besides the fact that he was masculine and hot enough to still be singed into her memory banks.

Claudia laughed. "A hero wouldn't need security but a *bachelor* would. I take it you haven't read this morning's paper? Online or otherwise?"

Lexie shook her head. "Haven't had time. What's up?"

"The *Daily Post* has a new feature called the Bachelor Blog. It's a column that highlights one of the city's bachelors and follows his exploits, hoping that by singling him out, the women will come out of the woodwork and he'll meet Ms. Right. Hang on. Let me find the blog to show you."

Lexie wrinkled her nose. "Sounds like *The Bachelor* from TV." Lexie had no patience for television shows where women lined up to compete to find a man.

Reality itself was no picnic, as she already knew firsthand. In her one and only serious relationship, she had let herself believe that a man could accept and even share her wanderlust — despite all the clues telling her otherwise.

Since Drew was a freelance journalist, it seemed a no-brainer that he'd want to see the world and use his experience as fodder for his work. But she'd had to twist his arm to get him to join her on her trips abroad.

She'd stupidly ignored the complaints about her vagabond lifestyle and convinced herself they were the perfect duo, until he'd reconnected with a woman he'd lost track of over the years. Just a friend, he'd said. Except he'd promptly dumped Lexie for that "friend," leaving her wiser when it came to men. In hindsight, Drew had been overly critical of more than just her travels, but she'd chosen to overlook that fact since almost everyone in her life criticized her for the same thing.

According to Lexie's disappointed parents, Drew was now living the suburban dream life they wanted for her. A dream she'd never shared. But Caroline and Grant Davis didn't understand — never would — and continued to remind her of that fact each time she saw them. Just one of the many reasons Lexie kept visits with her folks to a bare minimum when she was in town. Even though they lived a short half hour outside the city.

As for Drew, Lexie considered him a lesson well learned. Since then, she'd subscribed to a new philosophy: Love 'em and enjoy 'em until it was time to move on.

"Aha! Found it." Claudia rotated her laptop screen to face Lexie, who was happy to focus on something other than her pathetic past.

"This is today's Bachelor Blog. Your ring keeper is the new bachelor. And *that* explains why it's so difficult to get in touch with him," she said.

Lexie stared at a close-up photo of Sam Cooper, newspaper reporter and guardian of the ring. He was even more striking in the picture than he'd been on TV. His eyes were bluer and his hair was thick and straight, long enough for a woman's fingers to run through, but short enough to maintain his masculinity.

Claudia let out a slow whistle. "He is hot. But I see you've already noticed that," she said, grinning.

Lexie willed herself not to blush at being caught and scanned the article instead. "So women are just throwing themselves at him?" She tried to sound shocked, as if she couldn't imagine such a thing.

But she could. She just wouldn't admit as much out loud, nor would she be one of those desperate females. She was interested in a business transaction with the man, nothing more.

Claudia folded her arms across her chest. "If you want to corner this Sam Cooper, I suggest the backdoor method. You may have to wait a while, but my bet is he'll exit eventually."

Lexie narrowed her gaze. "Are you sure?" Because she couldn't imagine hanging out in an alley for hours based on hope alone.

"Do you doubt me?"

Claudia had street smarts and a knack for accomplishing any job she set her mind to, from complicated coding to even more complicated men.

Lexie nodded, conceding the point. "You're the master. Back door it is."

Coop lugged an enormous box down the elevator to the basement and out the back door of the newspaper offices to a huge blue Dumpster. He'd worked past dinnertime and the alley was shrouded in shadows as he dropped the box to the ground. The garbage bin was so high he couldn't lift the box and toss it in, so he had to empty the contents by the handful. Reaching down, he grabbed a double handful of perfume-scented letters from women extolling their virtues to the most recently crowned Bachelor in the ridiculously titled Bachelor Blog and dumped them into the trash.

To add insult to injury, the blog was published by his own damn newspaper! Upon discovering that *he* was the anonymous writer's newest victim, Coop had pleaded with the publisher of the paper to hold the presses. But nobody, not even their top crime beat reporter, could prevent the moneymaking machine that was the Bachelor Blog.

This was either retribution for something he'd done in a former life or proof of the old adage that no good deed goes unpunished. Either way, it was humiliating.

He'd had to instruct Chris Markov, the security guard in his building, to turn away any female without an appointment; he could no longer walk to work, as a few intrepid women had figured out where he lived and camped out on the doorstep like paparazzi hounding Britney Spears; and in this beautiful midsummer weather, he'd been forced to hire a cabbie to pick him up out back and drive him home. Which reminded him: he hoped Charlie was waiting at the corner when he finished here.

Coop tossed the last of the letters away. Bunches of flowers and boxes of candy came next. The wrapped stuff he'd sent over to local hospitals. If women were crazy enough to send him gifts, thinking he'd be interested in a desperate stranger, he wasn't about to taste-test anything they'd sent over unwrapped. His mother, may she rest in peace, had taught him well.

As he reached into the box for the last of the contents, his hand came into contact with soft cotton. He pulled the item out and, as he'd done when he'd opened the original packaging, Coop stared in disbelief at the ladies' thong underwear. At least a tag dangled off the back. This particular gift, he'd been too freaked out to worry about donating and had added to the trash immediately.

"Those are kind of cute. Maybe I could check the size before you throw them away?"

Coop froze at the sound of an unfamiliar female voice.

"I'm kidding. Can you get rid of those things before I introduce myself? The whole notion of Bachelor Blog and desperate, scheming women is giving me hives."

Coop caught the hint of amusement in the voice.

He tossed the panties back in the box and heaved his lightened load into the trash before turning to the woman who had intruded on his mission. She didn't look like any of the blond or brunette bombshells who'd included photos in their letters — the few he'd peeked at before a naked one taught him his lesson.

Instead, he found himself facing a striking

41

brunette with straight hair parted to one side and bluntly cut to her shoulders. Long, wispy strands framed a pretty face, partially hidden by funky black-framed glasses. Still, he detected high cheekbones and his gaze was drawn to her full, sexy lips. Besides her lush mouth, her eyes were her most outstanding feature, even behind the clear lenses. Her irises were wide and dark, color to be determined, thanks to the fading light.

The glasses lent an aura of intelligence to her otherwise seductive features. She presented a puzzle he wanted to take apart and put back together with a deeper understanding.

But just because he was attracted to her didn't mean she wasn't one of his stalkers. "Okay, I've lightened my load. So who are you and what are you doing back here?" he asked warily.

She flashed him a bright smile and he added nice teeth to her attributes. "I'm waiting for you," she said.

An unreasonable sense of disappointment filled him at her reply. "Well, I'm not interested." Shoving his hands into his pockets, he turned for the alley exit.

"How do you know when you haven't even heard what I have to say?" she called to him.

Despite himself, he paused midstride and turned. "Because you're female, you waited for me out back and you admitted that you're interested!"

"Not in you!" she corrected, sounding appalled at the notion, bruising Coop's ego in the process.

What was wrong with *him,* he wondered.

"I'm interested in your ring!" She lifted her hand to illustrate her point, showing him a flash of multiple rings on her fingers.

"You and every other husband-seeking female in the city," he muttered, even as he pondered where she'd put an engagement ring among the vast assortment of other jewelry she wore.

She pursed those seductive lips together and frowned. "Not in that way!" She dug into an oversize bag that hung from her shoulder and pulled out a photo. "Look. This is my grandmother and she's wearing a necklace that looks like a match to the ring I saw you accept on TV."

Surprised by her explanation, Coop took the photo, but the waning daylight didn't provide enough light for him to get a good look. "It's too dark to see," he said, handing the picture back to her.

"Well, trust me. It looks like a match."

He already knew the ring had once been

part of a set. Was her grandmother really in possession of the matching necklace or was the story just a ruse to get closer to him?

Coop's reporter's instincts told him she was sincere in her quest. And he had to admit that she wasn't acting like a woman who was interested in the city's newest bachelor.

Her admitted lack of interest bugged him. Especially since he was curious about her — and not just because of her supposed connection to his ring, which he had tucked deep into his front pants' pocket.

But he wasn't about to show her the ring until he knew more of her story. "Where did your grandmother get the necklace?" he asked, wondering if she'd come into possession of the item second- or thirdhand after it had been stolen.

"Look, do you think we could have this conversation somewhere else? Anywhere else would work for me. The stench of garbage is killing me." She waved her hand in front of her face, crinkling her nose.

Coop shook his head and grinned. "Smart as well as beautiful."

Behind her lenses, her eyes opened wide.

"Tell you what. I need to go home and shower. I can't tell you how many of the letters I just junked were covered in perfume. Would you want to meet up with me for a drink?" He invited her on a whim, but as he waited for an answer, his heart began pounding harder inside his chest.

She tipped her head to one side. "You'll bring the ring?"

He nodded. "You'll bring the photo?"

"Of course."

"Got a pen?" he asked, attempting nonchalance when in reality he was pumped at the notion of seeing her again.

She dug into her oversize purse and handed him something to write with. "Here. Use this." She turned over the back of the photo.

"How's eight o'clock?" he asked.

"Works for me."

He jotted down the name of his father's bar and grill, a place his old man had opened after retirement. Cops hung out there on their time off. The beer was good and the food better. It was casual enough for a business meeting and located on a well-traveled street where she'd feel safe with a virtual stranger.

Which reminded him. "I don't believe we've been properly introduced," he said.

"I'm Lexie Davis." She extended her hand and he took it.

"Short for Alexandra?"

"Alexis. My parents are pretty uptight. I changed it as soon as I was old enough to speak."

He laughed, enjoying the feel of her palm against his. Soft and feminine, her hand was small, yet he had no doubt this woman could stand up for herself. He liked her spunk and determination.

"And you're the infamous Sam Cooper," she said as she released her grasp.

He glanced at her curiously.

"The current Bachelor needs no introduction." She wrinkled her nose, dismissing his current status.

"So you're really not into the whole Bachelor Blog thing?" he asked, intrigued.

She shook her head. "No self-respecting woman would chase after a man just because he's single and in possession of a ring . . ." Her voice trailed off and she grinned, obviously catching her description of herself.

He laughed. "Relax, Lexie. We've already established you're not interested in me," he said, his voice gruffer than he'd intended.

"Says who?" She took back the photo and stuffed it into her bag. "See you at eight." With a brief wave, she turned and strode down the alley, giving him a chance to check out the rest of her lovely assets, encased in white jeans and a loose tank top as she walked away.

Lexie rushed back to her grandmother's apartment on the West Side and hurried to shower and change for her meeting with Sam Cooper.

"Sam Cooper." She let the name roll off her tongue, smooth and easy, like Kahlua and cream, her favorite drink.

She put her key in the door and entered the apartment. As usual, the smell of violets, her grandmother's fragrance of choice, assaulted her senses.

"Grandma? Are you home?" Lexie called out.

No answer. She figured Charlotte was down the hall at Sylvia's and headed for her bedroom, turning on lights as she walked through the apartment. Her grandmother preferred the dark, drawing closed the heavy draperies covering the old windows. Lexie flipped on a couple of lamps.

In her room, she ransacked her closet, looking for something appropriate to wear for a business meeting that wasn't a date, but was still with a man she wanted to impress. She wasn't someone who accumulated a lot of stuff, so the items she owned were those she truly loved and needed.

47

She'd never had to perfect the art of traveling light. It just came naturally to her. Making a fast perusal of her closet she chose a lightweight sundress and a pair of flowered thong sandals.

Half an hour later, she'd showered, put on a touch of makeup and blow-dried her recently cut hair. She added a thin orange headband that matched her dress, spritzed her favorite perfume and was ready to go.

Only the light butterflies in her stomach indicated that this evening suddenly meant more to her than a transaction in which she hoped to buy a ring.

When she'd gone to meet Sam earlier, she hadn't known what to expect. Sure he'd been good looking on the news, but he'd also been shy about accepting a reward and a little gruff with the TV reporter. She hadn't been prepared for his impact in person. Once he'd gotten past his wariness of her, he'd been downright charming.

And he'd called her beautiful. Heat rose to her cheeks at the memory. Then there'd been his touch. His hands weren't roughened from hard work, nor were they soft and manicured. In fact, his fingers felt just right as they'd wrapped around her hand and the jolt of awareness sizzled straight through to her toes, and other body parts she'd be better off not concentrating on too closely right now.

She hadn't heard any noise from the rest of the apartment and assumed her grandmother hadn't yet come home. Apparently, she was going to get lucky and slip out without having to answer any questions about where she was going. She wanted to surprise her grandmother with the jewelry at the party and the fewer opportunities her grandmother had to be nosy, the better.

She'd just leave the older a woman a note so she wouldn't worry. Lexie picked up her purse, double-checked that she had the photo of her grandmother with the restaurant name and address on the back and headed into the tiny hallway and through the den area leading to the door.

A catcall stopped her in her tracks and Lexie whirled around to see her grandmother sitting in the large club chair in the corner of the room.

"Where are you going dressed so pretty?" Charlotte asked.

"You scared me! I didn't know you'd come home." Lexie put her hand to her chest, covering her galloping heart.

Her grandmother placed her knitting on her lap. "I called out. You must not have heard me."

Lexie nodded. "Okay, well, I'll be home later. Don't wait up."

She took a step toward the door, only to have her grandmother say, "You didn't answer my question."

And she'd been so close to escaping, Lexie thought. "What question was that?"

"Don't play dumb with me. Do you have a hot date?" Charlotte asked, her eyes wide with curiosity.

Her grandmother would like nothing better than to see Lexie settled with a man, so there would be someone to look after her once Charlotte was gone. The ultimate in hypocrisy from a woman who, though she'd married, had also claimed to have been more like the independent, well-lived Rizzo in *Grease* than the demure and innocent Sandy. Minus the promiscuity. Lexie hoped.

She'd always idolized her grandmother and never took her push toward matrimony too seriously. She also knew better than to give Charlotte any real opening into her personal life.

"Sorry to disappoint you, but it's a work meeting, Grandma."

Charlotte raised a penciled eyebrow in disbelief. "Oh come on now. Don't kid a kidder. You are dressed too prettily for a client. So? Do I know him? Where is he taking you? Is this the first time you're going out with him? And is he a nice young man?"

Lexie let out a dramatic sigh, discouraged but not defeated. "Believe what you want, Grandma," she said, even as she couldn't help but laugh at Charlotte's enthusiastic rendition of twenty questions. "No, you don't know this client, we're going to a place called Jack's Bar and Grill, yes, it's our first time meeting, and of course he's a nice young man. I wouldn't agree to meet with any client otherwise."

"I'm not buying it."

Lexie glanced at her watch. "Well, that's up to you. I have to go or I'll be late." She blew her grandmother a kiss. "Love you."

Charlotte smiled. "Have fun! And remember, do everything I'd do . . . and more!"

Lexie rolled her eyes and headed out the door for the date that wasn't a date but a business meeting — with the sexiest man she'd met in quite a while.

Coop's cell phone rang before he reached the door of Jack's Bar and Grill. Since he was early to meet with Lexie, he paused to take the call outside where it would be quieter.

"Coop here," he said.

"This is Ricky Burnett. I own the Vintage

Jewelers. I hear you saved my daughter and granddaughter's life."

Coop wasn't sure he'd go that far. "I just happened to be in the right place at the right time, Mr. Burnett."

"Well thank you. I'm grateful," the man said in a gruff voice.

"You're welcome."

"But I need the ring back."

The abrupt declaration took Coop off guard and at the mention of the ring, his instincts went on high alert.

"Dad!" Coop recognized the daughter's voice in the background.

"Hang on a minute," Ricky said.

Coop kept the phone pushed against his ear, trying to hear what was being discussed on the other end. Considering that father and daughter were arguing, he didn't have any trouble eavesdropping.

"The nerve of you!" she scolded her father. "I told you that man saved our lives."

"And I'm grateful, but you had no right giving him something from my private box of stuff!" Ricky said.

"You're a pack rat, Dad. There'd be more stuff in the drawer than in the store if it was up to you. It's a good thing I clean up once in a while! At least I make us a profit."

"You've sold other things of mine?"

Sounding outraged, Ricky raised his voice.

"It's not like you've ever noticed! Classic hoarding, I saw it on *Oprah*. Now tell Mr. Cooper you're sorry and let him keep his ring in peace."

"You still there?" Ricky asked.

"I am." Coop wasn't sure whether he was more amused or intrigued by Ricky Burnett.

"Look, I'll give you another reward if I can just have my ring back," Ricky said, clearly ignoring his daughter.

So the ring meant something to the man. Did he know it was stolen? Had he played a role in the theft? Or was he just a hoarder, as his daughter said?

"You're impossible!" his daughter exclaimed. A loud slamming door sounded in the background.

Coop winced. "I'd really like to help you, Mr. Burnett, but I can't."

"Hey!"

"I'm sorry, but I've got to run." Coop disconnected, then patted the pocket where he'd placed the ring.

Sure he felt guilty about not returning it. Hell, he hadn't wanted to accept a reward in the first place. But armed with new information, Coop couldn't just turn it over to Ricky Burnett. Who knew if Ricky was the rightful owner? And Lexie Davis also had an interest in that particular piece of jewelry.

There was obviously much more to this ring, and Coop's reporter's curiosity pulled at him, while the story tugged at the fiction writer inside him. Until he unraveled the mystery behind the theft, the ring stayed put.

Chapter Three

Like its owner, Jack's Bar and Grill was vibrant and full of life. When Coop's mother died from a sudden brain aneurysm, not long after his father's retirement, Jack Cooper needed a substitute for the company and companionship his wife had provided. He'd found it in this bar and with his fellow cops who hung out here.

Coop walked into the place he considered his second home and was greeted by clapping and laughter, reminiscent of the newsroom immediately after the foiled robbery.

His brother, Matt, called out, "All hail the conquering hero!"

"Shut up," Coop said to his older sibling.

"Would you rather I said next time leave the crime fighting to us?" Matt asked, chuckling.

Not particularly, Coop thought.

"Dad, get the hero a beer."

Coop shook his head. He should have

known that picking Jack's as the place to meet Lexie was a mistake.

"Ignore your brother and come take a load off," his father said. "He's just jealous the paper didn't pick him for the Bachelor Blog." Jack slid a foaming glass across the bar.

"You read that crap?" Coop asked.

"On the way to the sports section," his father muttered without meeting Coop's gaze.

Coop took a seat.

"So how's it been, being the city's darling?" Matt asked.

Coop described the box of trash he'd dumped earlier.

"Sounds like a real hardship. You threw every last one of them away? You didn't save even one of those lady's numbers?" he asked, shocked.

"Can I help it if I like my women sane?"

Matt inclined his head. "Good point. To sane women. Like Olivia," he said of his wife of ten years.

Unlike Coop, marriage was another thing his brother had done well, following in their father's footsteps. Coop rarely dwelled on his failings, but sometimes it was hard not to compare.

Matt raised his beer glass and Coop met

him in a toast.

They both then tipped their beer and swallowed a large gulp.

"So when's your next shift?" Coop asked.

"Tomorrow morning. So I thought I'd keep Dad company tonight." Matt met Coop's gaze.

Both brothers ended up at Jack's more often than not under the pretext of wanting a drink. They were really checking up on their father, making sure he wasn't too lonely.

"In other words, his wife's sick of him," their father said, having overheard Matt's comment.

He had a point, but both Matt and Coop knew old Jack appreciated having his sons stop by.

"How's work going for you?" Matt asked.

"Same old," Coop said.

"Anything else new and exciting going on?"

Coop shook his head. "Except for the robbery and the damn Bachelor Blog, my life's pretty boring," he lied.

Until Coop knew more about Lexie and her grandmother's connection to the ring, he felt compelled to keep the information to himself.

"So life as a hero and famous bachelor is

boring, huh? Maybe you should'a taken the risk and become a cop," Jack joked.

His father might be teasing, but the joke hit a raw nerve.

Coop had torn his rotator cuff playing football in high school, injuring it again while training at the academy. After surgery, the doctors had warned him that most cops rarely recovered well enough from rotator cuff surgery to safely do the job required. Not to mention he'd be risking reinjuring the already weakened shoulder.

It nearly killed Coop to bail on the academy and the future his father had hoped both his sons would have. Joke or not, Coop didn't need the reminder that he'd disappointed his old man. He lived with the knowledge that he'd failed every damn day. So there was no way he'd admit to his father that, as much as he'd once loved his job as a reporter, he now found it too routine.

It was a sad commentary on life when the crime beat of muggings, robberies and stabbings became too ordinary to spark much interest. Coop had started out eager to report the news and make an impact in a way he never could have as a cop. He'd hoped that by reporting on crime he would increase public awareness and maybe spark outrage, eventually helping to save lives or catch criminals. Instead, it was a never-ending cycle of violence. A mundane repetition of the seedier side of human nature. He wasn't helping or changing things. He was just spreading the word.

Maybe that's why he enjoyed writing fiction so much. He could dictate the story arc, the plot, the characters and, most important, the outcome. He might not be making a difference in the world, but he couldn't duplicate anywhere else the satisfaction he got from writing.

Problem was, he'd yet to find the kind of public success and validation in writing fiction he'd found in journalism and reporting. And in a family of successful men, Coop refused to fail.

"If I weren't already married, I'd think I'd found the woman of my dreams," Matt said, his gaze suddenly glued to the front door.

Before Coop even turned around, he knew who had walked into the bar and a protective feeling he'd never experienced before washed over him.

A quick glance at Lexie, wearing a pastel-print summer dress, confirmed his hunch. The smart-girl glasses contrasted with the flirty outfit, making for an interesting contradiction. She was special. Unique.

"Maybe I'll welcome her to Jack's anyway." Matt started toward her and Coop planted a firm hand on his brother's shoulder. "She's with me."

Matt paused. "I thought none of the bimbos interested you?"

Coop stiffened. "Does she look like a bimbo to you?"

Matt laughed. "Relax. I'm happily married, remember?"

Coop loosened his hold. "Your next one's on me," he said to his brother, hoping to smooth things over without actually admitting he'd acted like an ass over a woman he barely knew.

"Sam?" Lexie called his name as she made her way toward them.

"You can go get that beer now," Coop said to his brother.

Matt grinned. "Not just yet, *Sam*."

Nobody called Coop by his first name except for his mother when she'd been alive.

"Sorry I'm late," Lexie said.

"Not at all. Why don't we take a table in the back?" Coop suggested. A quiet place where they could discuss the ring and her grandmother's necklace without being overheard.

"Sounds good."

"Aren't you going to introduce your date to your brother?" Matt interjected, a wide grin on his face.

Since there was no getting around it, Coop made the obligatory introductions. "Lexie Davis, this is my older brother, Matt Cooper." Feeling the heat of his father's gaze, Coop continued, "And the old guy behind the bar is my father, Jack."

"Nice to meet you both. I can see the family resemblance." Lexie's warm smile encompassed all three men.

"I'll take that as a compliment," Jack said. "So, pretty lady, are you one of those bachelorettes looking to hook up with the latest catch?" He nodded toward his son.

Coop cringed.

Lexie shook her head and laughed. "Oh, no. Not me. Sam and I have some business to discuss."

"Is that right?" Matt asked, sounding too pleased for Coop's liking. "Because my brother led me to believe there was something more serious going on between you two."

Coop had had enough. He placed his hand on the small of Lexie's back, leading her to a far booth, away from his prying family.

"I'm sorry. My father and brother seem to think everything is their business."

"You think they're bad? You should meet

my grandmother." She shook her head and laughed.

"Do you want something to eat or drink?"

She shrugged. "Maybe just an iced tea and some chips?"

"Easy enough in a bar." Coop excused himself, placed an order with his father, who promised to send the drinks and chips over.

He rejoined Lexie, easing into the seat across from her. Thanks to the small seating area, his knees grazed hers beneath the table.

"So, I have to ask." She paused and bit down on her lightly glossed lips. "What did your brother mean, you led him to believe there was more than business between us?" She rested both elbows on the table and leaned in close.

Her eyes, which he could now see were a golden brown, were full of curiosity and focused solely on him.

She was upfront. He liked that about her.

"Let's just say I let him know not only were you *with me,* but that yes, I'm interested in more than just business."

"I see." A smile curved her lips. A pleased smile.

"Tell me about yourself," he said, eager to learn more about her personally.

"Not much to tell. I'm a world traveler

and a Web designer."

The traveler part he could live without. The Web designer he definitely found intriguing. "What are some sites you've done, so I can check them out?"

A waitress who'd worked for Jack for years interrupted them only long enough to place their drinks and a basket of tortilla chips on the table.

"Let's see," she said when they were finally alone again. "I've designed quite a few small Web sites you might not know of, but I've also created the Hot Zone and Athlete's Only Web pages. Have you heard of them?" she asked.

"I'm a huge baseball fan. Renegades especially, so of course I know of the biggest sports agency in Manhattan. And I'm suitably impressed with your portfolio, I might add." He raised his glass and touched hers before taking a long sip of cold beer.

"Why, thank you," she said, obviously pleased. "But if you do take a look, you should know that both sites are due for an overhaul. We're currently working on them behind the scenes."

"We?"

"Claudia, my assistant. She frees me up for the design and creative portions of my work, and she also keeps updates going while I travel." Lexie adjusted her glasses. "So tell me more about you, Mr. Bachelor," she said, teasing him.

"Didn't you see enough of my exciting life out at the Dumpster?"

She laughed. "You've got a point. Although, I must admit, it's refreshing to see a guy who isn't a slave to the attention of fawning women."

They continued their easy banter. As they got to know each other, the tables quickly filled up around them. Luckily, the crowd would keep his father busy, and it appeared that Matt's partner had shown up, occupying his brother, too.

"So do you want to see the picture of my grandmother's necklace?" Lexie asked.

Before he could reply, she withdrew a photograph from her purse and handed it to him. The older woman in the photo had red hair and what could only be described as a mischievous gleam in her eye. As for the necklace, it definitely appeared similar in style to his ring.

Yet it was the rest of the older woman's outfit that captured Coop's attention. "I hope you don't think this is an odd question, but why is she wearing a housecoat with such an elaborate piece of jewelry?"

Lexie's laugh was infectious, and she used

it freely and often. "I've asked myself that question many times. Grandma never wears certain jewelry outside of the house. She says it's because it has more sentimental value than anything else. Does it look like a match?"

He pulled the ring from his pocket and held it out to her. She leaned closer, examining the ring he held between his thumb and forefinger. "Bingo!" she exclaimed. "Can I see it?"

"Of course."

She held out her hand for him to slip the ring on, which he did, then watched in amusement as she admired the ring on her finger. "A unique piece," she murmured. "Much like the necklace." She smiled and placed the ring on the table between them.

She didn't check out the insignia the way his style editor had, which told Coop that Lexie's interest was more personal than financial. "How long has your grandmother owned the necklace?" he asked.

Lexie shrugged. "She's had it for as long as I can remember. My grandfather gave it to her years ago," she said wistfully. "Did the store owner give you any information about the ring?"

Coop shook his head. "She didn't say a word. It was just sitting in a tray along with other items she didn't mind giving away."

Lexie folded her hands in front of her. Delicate hands with pale pink polish on her nails, and a grouping of bracelets dangling from her right wrist. "I suppose you're wondering why I sought you out."

"The thought has crossed my mind."

"I'd like to buy the ring from you as a gift for my grandmother's eightieth birthday."

He hadn't known what to expect from Lexie, but her wanting to purchase the ring caught him off guard. Another person interested in what had started out as a gaudy piece of junk.

Coop cleared his throat. "I'm sorry, but I can't begin to put a price on it. According to the style editor at the paper where I work, it's worth more than I thought or frankly hoped when I picked it from the tray."

Lexie cocked her head to one side. Even behind the glasses, she pierced him with her steady gaze, indicating that he'd pissed her off.

"Why didn't you just say that when I asked you what you knew about the ring?" she asked.

"You asked me what the store owner said about the ring and I told you." He just hadn't admitted he'd already discovered more.

He disliked being on the other side of questioning and squirmed in his seat. "Hey, it's not like I know you well enough to trust you with all my secrets," he said in an attempt at humor.

She frowned. "You know me well enough to decide you're attracted to me," she reminded him, leaning back in her seat, clearly waiting for him to say more.

She wasn't letting him off easily.

She also had a point. He *was* attracted to her. Especially the way her breasts pushed upward in the low-cut dress, revealing more than a sexy hint of cleavage for view.

He let out a low groan and forced himself to focus on the jewelry instead. "Apparently, the ring is part of a collection of jewels dating back to the 1950s." He'd been unable to find an exact date yet. But if he sold her the ring, as she requested, he'd lose his connection to the story.

The same way he'd lose his connection if he just returned the item to Ricky. He wasn't ready to reveal to Lexie Ricky Burnett's sudden interest in reacquiring the ring. Coop was still gauging her truthfulness and he didn't know how she'd feel about having competition for the piece. Besides, he wanted her focused while she revealed information to him.

"So it's worth more than its appearance suggests," Lexie mused. "The same probably holds true for my grandmother's necklace. Who would've thought it had value? Okay, so what if we have your ring appraised and then discuss a price?" Clearly she wouldn't be easily dissuaded.

She was logical. And smart. He liked that combination in a woman. It just didn't help his cause. Because if they brought the ring to a professional jeweler for an appraisal, the appraiser would probably identify it. Worse, he might realize that the ring was linked to an unsolved crime from years past and blow Coop's exclusive to this story. Coop needed to figure out all the angles before he made any decisions.

Something the logical beauty might understand. She might even possess pertinent information about the jewels and their past. He'd already learned the hard way that she preferred honesty.

"Your grandmother didn't know the necklace had value?" he asked.

Lexie shrugged her shoulders. "She never said and I never asked. I never had any reason to. Money's not important to me except as a necessity to do the traveling I love. Do you like to travel?"

He shook his head. "Not much."

Disappointment flickered in her eyes before she continued. "There are places in the world you can't possibly imagine. I love to see the beauty and the colors of different countries, people and heritages." Her cheeks flushed as she explained her passion.

A passion he'd like to see directed at him, not at foreign places that took her far away.

"Never mind," she said as if catching herself. "Back to business. I wonder how my grandfather came into possession of something that once was part of an expensive collection."

"I take it your grandmother never said?" he asked her.

"Nope."

He was curious about the same thing. There were many unanswered questions, leaving Coop even more intrigued by the jewels and their history. Not to mention by Lexie herself. At least now he had an avenue by which to learn more. He could uncover answers by getting closer to Lexie. Not a hardship, he thought, meeting her gaze. And something he'd want to do regardless of the jewels.

Her grandmother hadn't shared much about the history of her prized possession. Because she didn't know? Or because she had something to hide?

"Could you ask your grandfather?" Coop asked.

"He passed away fifteen years ago," she said softly, her eyes clouding.

"I'm sorry."

"Thanks. But Grandma's a survivor. She's been hell on wheels her whole life and she wasn't about to stop after Grandpa died. So she grieved and then picked herself up and went on."

Coop grinned. "She sounds feisty. Like you."

"Why, thank you!" Lexie drew up straighter, always pleased anytime someone compared her to her grandmother.

Her grandmother's unconditional love and understanding provided Lexie with the self-acceptance she didn't find within her immediate family. They were all overachievers, while Lexie had always been the one with her head in the clouds. They had goals; Lexie had dreams. Her free-spirited grandmother was the only one who accepted Lexie for who and what she was.

While Sam couldn't begin to understand how important it was for Lexie to be like the grandmother she loved, he'd picked up on the fact that she was like her. He didn't like travel, so theirs could never be a serious relationship. But a fling suited her just fine, and it had been too long since she'd had one of those.

She liked Coop, despite the serious side to his personality. But unlike her father and sister — both bankers — and her powerhouse attorney mother, whose life mission was perfect children, Sam didn't strike Lexie as uptight or unforgiving.

He interested her and he was unattached and single, another prerequisite Lexie demanded, thanks to Drew. Not that he'd been involved with someone when they'd started dating, but he'd obviously been too open to other possibilities. She tried to gauge men better now.

"Hello, Earth to Lexie." Sam snapped his fingers in front of her, calling for her attention.

"Sorry. I got lost in thought. I tend to do that." And get called out by her family for being ditzy.

"As long as it's not the company that's boring you," he said, a grin on his handsome face.

"Definitely not. It's more a function of my creative side." She wasn't about to admit that she'd been thinking about him. "I start to dwell on things and go off into my own world. Next thing I know, a new Web site idea's come to me. Sometimes I'm not even daydreaming about work."

"Looks like we have something in common."

She wrinkled her nose. "Insanity?"

He laughed. "No, creative daydreaming. You see, I'm a writer."

"I know. Crime beat."

He leaned closer. "I mean I also write fiction." He spoke softly, his words almost a whisper.

He was revealing a personal secret, making her, as the recipient, feel special. A warm feeling snuck up inside her and settled in her chest. "That's awesome! What kind of fiction?"

His shoulders relaxed. "Mystery. Sam Spade kind of stuff."

"I'm a huge reader and I love mysteries! In fact — want to know a secret? I'm an old-time Ludlum fan."

He nodded appreciatively. "A woman of complexity," he mused.

"Are you published?" she asked.

"Small press but —"

"You have big aspirations," she finished for him.

A mix of surprise and relief showed on his face. "How did you know?"

"Let's just say I recognize a kindred spirit." She reached out and placed her hand over his, wanting to impart under-standing.

Fireworks ensued instead. Touching him set off a spark of heat inside her body. The attraction, which had been simmering beneath the surface, exploded in full force.

Surprised, she started to pull away, but in a smooth move, he twisted his wrist and grabbed her hand instead. Liking the feel of him, she relaxed, letting him just hold on.

"Are you working on a novel now?" she asked, trying to keep some semblance of conversation going when all her focus had centered on the palm of her hand, where his thumb drew lazy circles on her skin.

"You could say something recently dropped into my lap." He drew a deep breath. "Which reminds me — before this thing between us goes any further, there's another thing you need to know."

"What is it?" she asked, suddenly wary of his intensity.

"The ring isn't just expensive — it's likely stolen property."

"What? Stolen? How?" she asked, her mind spinning with the implications. If the ring had been stolen, then what about her grandmother's necklace? A sick feeling settled in her stomach.

He shook his head. "I don't know. During

my quick Internet search, I discovered that the ring was part of a set that had been stolen back in the 1950s here in New York. I need to do more research. And that is another reason why I can't just sell you the ring."

She exhaled a slow breath and eased her hand out of his. She couldn't concentrate when he was touching her and she needed to think clearly. "I don't want you to do anything that's going to hurt my grandmother. I'm certain she knows nothing about this and it would devastate her."

"Are you?"

"Am I what?" She tipped her head to one side, unsure of his question.

"Are you sure she knows nothing about its history?"

"As sure as I am about myself," Lexie stated. "Look, I can talk to her about it, but I wouldn't get your hopes up that she has the answers. And before you ask — no, I don't think my grandfather was a thief," she said, acknowledging the next logical question.

He held up his hands in a gesture of defeat. "I wasn't about to suggest it. He could have come into possession second-, third- or fourthhand," Coop said, although he wasn't ruling anything out.

She nodded. "I don't want to upset my grandmother by even mentioning the fact that her necklace might have been stolen." Lexie drummed her fingers on the table, desperately trying to come up with a way to find out more without directly involving her grandmother. "Maybe Sylvia would know something."

Sam raised an eyebrow. "Who's Sylvia?"

"Grandma Charlotte's best friend. They're like Frick and Frack. The Thelma and Louise of their generation."

Coop shook his head and laughed. "The more I hear about your grandmother, the more I think I'd like her."

"Most people do." She paused, then met his gaze. "We need to find out more about these jewels. Maybe you're wrong and they aren't stolen property. Maybe they're a copy of the originals or something."

"Could be," he agreed. "Wait. What do you mean *we* have to find out more? I'm a reporter. I'll do the digging and get back to you."

"I'm the computer geek. I can find out more with a few clicks of the mouse than you can discover in a week's worth of questioning. Besides, if we work together we'll find things out that much quicker. Sounds to me like we need each other."

He groaned and looked a little put out at the notion. Just a little. Because that spark of attraction was still simmering between them. She could see it in his eyes and the way his gaze fell to her chest every so often in pure appreciation.

She wasn't above using it. Not when she felt the same way about him. "Oh, and Sam? There's one more thing you should know. If the ring turns out to be a fake, I still intend to buy it for my grandmother."

"I suppose we can add *stubborn* and *determined* to your list of attributes?"

She edged closer to the table, resting her elbows on top. "I can be very persuasive when I want to be."

"I'd like to see you in action." His gaze traveled from her lips to her chest and back up again. "So what did you have in mind?"

"Well, since we'll be working together, I think I can help you in other ways, too," she said.

"I'm listening . . ."

"For one thing, I'm very good at what I do and I was thinking, even with a book published by a small press, you need a Web site. Especially if you're going to make that jump to the big leagues."

His eyes opened wide in surprise, and knowing his mind had been on their sexual tension, Lexie let out a laugh. "While we're digging up information on the jewelry's history, I'll work up your Web site. If you like what I do, we can apply some of my charge toward the cost of the ring. So what do you say?"

"And if the ring's stolen and has to be returned?" he asked.

Lexie didn't want to think about that. "I'm an optimist. But if you insist on being more pragmatic and covering all bases, in that case, my work would be on the house."

"Why would you work for free?" he asked, skeptical.

"Truth? Because part of my designing any Web site involves me getting to know my clients. And I want to get to know you."

A ruddy flush darkened his cheekbones.

"I take it you're interested?" she asked, and before he could reply she added her standard client pitch. "You must realize that Internet presence is key today. In the case of an author like yourself, if I get to know not just you but also your product, I can convey the real you to your readers. Then there are the basic reasons for having a Web site. You need to connect with your readers through other social Web sites to bring traffic back to your site. And you need good S.E.O. I'm a pro at doing it all." She waved her hands animatedly as she described her reasons, hoping he'd see and understand them as clearly as she did. "Well?"

He shook his head. "I'm sorry, but you lost me at S.E.O."

She hadn't expected him to say no. Disappointment tasted bitter in her throat and her heart pounded hard in her chest.

"But you had me at, *I want to get to know you,*" he said in a deep voice.

Lexie exhaled in relief, picked up a paper napkin, rolled it into a ball and tossed it at him. "Not nice, setting me up that way."

He grinned. "Payback for setting *me* up with that little sexual innuendo first."

"Just so you know, I'm very good at follow-through," she said, gathering her purse. She pulled out a business card and handed it to him. "This has my e-mail and cell phone, so you can reach me any time. I'm guessing your work hours depend on what's going on in the city, so . . . you call me, okay?"

He accepted the card, his fingers deliberately brushing hers. "Okay."

"But just in case you're thinking of avoiding me and doing the research alone, give me a way to contact you, too."

"Smart girl." His lips curved upward in appreciation. "Don't call me at work. I want

78

to keep this separate." He grabbed a paper napkin and wrote his address and cell phone number on it, handing it to her.

She tried to pay, but he waved away the gesture. "It's on me. If not, my father will think he did a poor job raising me to be a gentleman."

"How can I argue with that? Thank you. I enjoyed myself, Sam." She rose to her feet.

He did the same. "One more thing. My friends call me Coop."

She nodded. "Friends. Is that what we are?"

He placed his hand on the small of her back. Weaving their way through tables and then the bar crowd, he walked her to the exit. As she reached the door, he leaned over and whispered in her ear. "I hope to be much more."

She turned back. Face-to-face, their breath almost commingling, she replied, "Count on it," before disappearing into the hot, summer night.

CHAPTER FOUR

Coop headed back to his apartment, whistling as he walked.

Whistling?

All from a first date with Lexie, if he could even call it a date, considering how much business they'd conducted. But he'd enjoyed her company and now he had himself a Web designer, a partner in his ring investigation and a romantic interest. There was no doubt about that.

He took the stairs to his walk-up two at a time. The dimly lit hall was quiet, letting him know his neighbors, a married couple on one side and a good friend of his who lived on the other, were probably still out.

He went to insert the key in the lock when he realized his door was ajar. The lock had been jimmied, deep gouge marks on either side of the handle.

Coop muttered a curse. He lived in a relatively safe neighborhood but, hell, this wasn't a doorman building and there was no security to be found. Silence and gut instinct told him that whoever had broken in was already gone. He kicked the door open and walked in slowly. Just in case. A quick look around confirmed his fear. Someone had broken in and tossed the place, leaving no couch cushion or piece of paper unturned.

For the second time in less than a week, Coop found himself on the other end of his own crime beat. He called 9-1-1 from his cell, hoping maybe something in this apartment held a clue to who'd broken in and why.

For the next few hours, New York's finest did their thing, dusting for prints, looking for evidence and taking his statement.

Coop had pulled out two bottles of Coke from the fridge and offered one to Sara Rios, the female officer on duty who just happened to be his neighbor and good friend.

Sara was pretty, with long blonde hair, big eyes and a good heart. In uniform she was a kick-ass cop. As a friend, she shared his taste in books and movies.

"At a glance, is anything missing?" she asked.

Coop bit the inside of his cheek. "Other than my laptop?" It had been the first thing he'd checked for and the only thing that seemed to be gone. "Everything else is here. Television, iPod, even my camera is still sitting where I left it."

"I'm sorry, Coop. But I did tell you to install better locks."

"Thanks for not saying I told you so," he muttered.

"You think it's work-related?"

He shook his head. Although work was the obvious reason someone would snag his computer, it didn't add up. "There's no current case I'm working on that's anything out of the ordinary. It's not like Son of Sam is sending me letters or anything."

She perched a hip on the arm of his sofa. "I hate to ask, but could it be a female stalker? One of your Bachelor Blog groupies?" She unsuccessfully tried to hide her smirk behind a notepad.

"Wiseass. The women in this city are desperate, that's for sure." He told her about the scented notes and panties he'd dumped in the trash earlier. "But if it was one of them, wouldn't I have found her waiting in my bed, not stealing my laptop?"

"You've got a point. We won't know anything more until we run some tests. The guys seem to be finishing up," she said, pointing to the forensic team, packing up. "If you realize something else is missing, call me. You know the drill. Sometimes it's the little information you don't think is important that can break a case."

He nodded. "I think I can handle it." He covered this crap on a daily basis.

"Now who's the wiseass?" she asked, treating him to a grin.

"I don't suppose we can keep this quiet? The last thing I need is more publicity."

She shook her head. "You know better. If your paper doesn't cover it, another one will. At this point you're the closest thing to a celebrity this city's got. Until another big thing comes along, the Bachelor Blog *is* the news." She slapped him on the shoulder, commiserating but not helping him in the least.

"What about the robbery you foiled?" Sara asked.

"You know as well as I do, that's an open-and-shut case. The guy couldn't make bail, so he's still sitting in lockup."

Sara glanced at her partner who was gesturing toward the door. "I'll check in when I get off duty in the morning. Call if you remember anything else."

He nodded. "Thanks, neighbor."

After the cops took off, Coop righted the sofa and table, ignoring the rest of the mess for now. He sat down, kicked his feet up and pulled on a long sip of soda. As he leaned back, something sharp jabbed him in the thigh.

The ring.

Why hadn't he thought of it sooner?

Coop took the object from his pocket and studied the piece of jewelry, letting the puzzle pieces add up. He'd just discovered that the ring had value. The same ring had been flashed all over the local news, the information regurgitated in the blog. And now both Lexie and Ricky were interested in the ring.

As for motive for breaking in here, Lexie had been with him, he'd shown her the ring and she'd had no reason to think he wouldn't work a deal with her to give the ring to her grandmother. Not only didn't she strike him as the thief type, but she'd been with him all night. And he couldn't envision her hiring someone to toss his place when he'd promised to bring the ring to their rendezvous.

Ricky Burnett, on the other hand, was a big question mark. Coop had already turned down his request to return the ring. But would a hoarder go to all this trouble just to reclaim any old piece? Or was his interest related to the ring's value? Or to its history?

Or had this been just a random robbery unrelated to anything going on in Coop's life at the moment?

Coop hadn't a clue about that, but he did know it was time to find out whether this ring was the real deal. First thing in the morning, he'd call in some favors. There had to be someone who could authenticate the ring without calling attention to the fact that it had once been stolen. Then he'd put the ring in a safe deposit box in the bank.

Just in case.

Lexie woke up to sun streaming through the window and the crooning sound of Perry Como coming from the CD player in the kitchen. Grandma loved Perry Como.

Somehow Lexie needed to broach the history of the necklace with her grandmother without arousing the older woman's suspicions that Lexie had an ulterior motive beyond curiosity about the past. Before she even thought about how, she needed caffeine.

Lexie padded to the kitchen in her T-shirt and bare feet, craving coffee before she could start her day. On her way, she passed her grandmother hunched over the computer in the den, Sylvia standing beside her.

"Morning," Lexie mumbled.

Both women jumped. "Mercy, you startled me!" Charlotte said.

"Good morning, darling," Sylvia said. "Go get your coffee so you'll be human, then we can talk to you."

The two women knew Lexie's morning routine as well as Lexie herself. In the kitchen, she poured her coffee from the pot her grandmother had waiting and added milk. All the while, she heard arguing in the other room. She couldn't make out the words, but given the way Charlotte and Sylvia bickered over everything from the brand of hair dye to use on each other, to which colored deck of cards they would break out for gin rummy, Lexie didn't strain herself to hear.

A few delicious sips of hot coffee later, the caffeine began flowing through her veins. She waited a few more minutes to savor her morning brew and let the jolt of awareness kick in before heading to rejoin her grandmother and her friend.

"Hi!" Lexie said, kissing first her grandmother then Sylvia.

"There she is, bright-eyed and bushytailed." Grandma Charlotte pinched her cheek. "I tried to wait up for you last night but I was too pooped."

Lexie smiled. "Sleep is good for you."

"Tell me about your date!" her grandmother said.

"I already told you last night it wasn't a date. It was just a business meeting. Web-design stuff," Lexie said, more truthfully this morning than when she'd fudged about meeting a client last night.

She *would* be working on designs for Coop's Web site. She also happened to have designs *on* him.

Vivid memories of his knee brushing hers came rushing back to her. His strong fingers wrapped around her hand, his thumb drawing lazy circles on her skin, making her tingle and burn. The man's effect on her had been so potent it was difficult to remember she also had to keep an eye on whatever information they discovered about the ring and the necklace, protect her grandmother and hopefully end up with the ring in her possession. That was her endgame. Even if the path there held the potential to be an extremely exciting trip.

"Look, Sylvia, she's blushing!" Grandma Charlotte said, pointing to Lexie's cheeks. "Just a client, my patootie."

"Keep eating that farmer cheese and your patootie will keep growing," Sylvia said to her friend before turning to Lexie. "Your grandmother is right about something else, too."

Sylvia pressed a finger to Lexie's cheek. "Yep. You're beet red."

Lexie rolled her eyes. "You both really need to get a life instead of worrying so much about mine." Lexie focused on the computer behind them. "So what were you two up to before I woke up? Practicing some of the things I taught you?" she asked her grandmother.

"Well . . . I . . ."

"We were just . . ."

Lexie looked over the stammering women's shoulders but a screen saver prevented her from seeing the actual screen. The words *Born Free* wound their way around the monitor in 3D.

Lexie narrowed her gaze. "I didn't set that up." And it would take someone pretty proficient with a Mac to know how to do it.

"Oh, I did," Sylvia jumped in. "I wanted to prove to your grandmother that I was smarter than she is, so while you're giving her private lessons here, I'm taking my own at the Apple store. And voilà!" She swept her hand toward the screen. "Try doing that, *Miss Giggle Me a Bachelor Blog*." Sylvia grinned, obviously proud of herself.

Lexie laughed at the women's one-upmanship. "Grandma, you're going to have to step up your game if you want to be able to keep up."

"I'll show you, Ms. Smarty-Pants," Charlotte said to her friend. "Watch how computer savvy I've become, thanks to my brilliant granddaughter. And speaking of my granddaughter, when did you start lying to your grandmother?"

"Lying?" Lexie crinkled her nose, confused by the accusation.

"The date that wasn't a date was actually something much more." Charlotte pinned her with the stare that used to have her confessing all when she was a teenager, attempting to avoid her parents' mandatory ice-skating practice sessions. Grandma would uncover the truth, then help Lexie ditch the routine of practice for side trips to museums in the city behind her parents' backs.

"Grandma, let's try being straightforward. What are you talking about?"

"Pictures don't lie. Not only did you have a real date last night, but it was with that sexy Bachelor Blog reporter." Charlotte waggled her already penciled eyebrows. An early riser, she always had on a full face of makeup before Lexie woke up.

"Pictures?" Lexie asked warily. Charlotte and Sylvia glanced at each other, then with a shrug, Sylvia pushed the mouse. The movement shut off the screen saver, revealing the Web page beneath.

Lexie adjusted her eyeglasses and leaned in for a better look. The caption on the morning edition of the Bachelor Blog read, *Newest Bachelor Works Fast. Is an Engagement Next?* and below it were two grainy photos. The first was of Coop showing Lexie the ring. And the other was of Lexie *wearing* said ring while Coop looked on with an adorable grin on his handsome face.

"Oh my God!" Lexie muttered. She hadn't seen anyone take a picture. Boy, people could be sneaky.

"Look how smitten he looks!" Sylvia said dreamily.

Smitten? Before Lexie could reply to that, her grandmother walked up to her and poked her on the shoulder. "How could you lie to an old woman?" She placed her hand over her heart.

Sylvia returned to surfing the Net.

"Cut the dramatics, Gran. I didn't lie. He's a client. I'm doing his Web site."

"And the ring?"

Lexie hoped she didn't blush more and

give herself away. "He was just showing it to me."

"Does it really look like my necklace?" Charlotte asked.

Two sets of eyes stared at her, waiting for an answer.

"Actually, there are similarities." Lexie didn't want to get her grandmother's hopes up, in case the ring was stolen and had to be returned. Until she knew more, she couldn't set the older woman up for potential hurt and disappointment. "But there are also differences. Seeing the ring got me wondering how the necklace originally came into Grandpa's possession."

Charlotte and Sylvia exchanged a long, pointed glance. Those two could practically read each other's minds, which often left Lexie struggling unsuccessfully to interpret the meaning.

Charlotte cleared her throat. "Your grandfather was given the necklace as a substitute for payment for services rendered."

"Driving services?" Lexie asked. Her grandfather had been a chauffeur to various wealthy families over the years.

Charlotte nodded. "So when can I see?" she asked.

"The ring?" Lexie asked.

"No, silly girl. When can I see your suitor?

I want to meet the man you are going to marry! Then *he* can show me the ring."

Lexie rolled her eyes and waved her empty left hand at her grandmother. "I'm not engaged, Gran."

"Pictures don't lie," Charlotte and Sylvia repeated in unison.

They each had a one-track mind and Lexie realized that until she humored them about Coop, her grandmother would keep changing the subject away from the necklace.

Lexie closed her eyes and silently counted to ten, breathing in deeply as her yoga instructor had taught her. "I'll see what I can do," she said, buying herself time.

No way was she bringing Coop over here. That would open up a can of worms she wasn't ready to deal with in more ways than one.

"Good! You let me know when and I'll plan a meal."

Lexie forced a smile. "Mind if I check out the news online?" she asked, hoping to end all discussion involving meeting Coop.

The two women stepped aside and Lexie lowered herself into the chair. Not even massive doses of caffeine could prepare her for the tornado that was Charlotte and Sylvia.

She clicked onto the *Daily Post,* Coop's paper, for a quick glance at the Crime Beat. She wanted to see more about his writing and his work — and was shocked to find another even more disturbing headline.

Crime Beat Reporter on Opposite Side of Beat — Again. Coop's apartment had been broken into last night, though the details were sketchy. The article went on to describe Coop's recent heroics, his status as the current Bachelor and some more speculation about his relationship with the as-yet-unnamed woman in the photo. At least she had anonymity for now.

But her mind wasn't on the Bachelor Blog, it was on the robbery and when it had occurred — before or after their date last night? If it was afterwards, there was a possibility the ring had been stolen in the break-in. The thought churned Lexie's stomach, but even more upsetting was the notion that Coop might have been hurt.

Lexie excused herself and ran for the shower . . . Next stop: Coop's apartment to check first on the man and then on the ring.

Coop's address wasn't too far from Lexie's grandmother's, and she hopped on the subway, arriving at his stop by 9:30 a.m.

She quickly glanced at the outside of the

walk-up apartment where he lived before running up the stairs, her flip-flops smacking against the floor with every step.

She rang his bell and waited.

No one answered, so she rang again. And again. Then she knocked loudly a couple of times for good measure. Just as she was about to give up and call his cell phone, as she probably should have done to begin with, the door next to Coop's opened.

An attractive woman dressed in a police uniform, stuck her head outside. "Looking for someone?"

Despite her petite stature, she had an air of authority Lexie couldn't deny. "Sam Cooper." Lexie pointed to his apartment.

The other woman looked Lexie over from head to toe, obviously assessing her before deciding to answer. "He stepped out early this morning and I'm not sure if he's back. Maybe he's in the shower." She yawned. "I worked the night shift and I was just about to try to get some sleep."

"Sorry." Lexie took two steps back. "I'll just call him later."

The neighbor leaned against her door-frame, arms folded across her chest, in no rush to get back inside, despite her claim. "Give me your name and I'll tell him you were here."

Before Lexie could answer, Coop's door opened wide. "Can I join the party?" he asked.

"You've got company," his neighbor said, over another yawn. She covered her mouth with her hand. "I'm going to bed. Let's get together later. It looks like we have a lot to talk about." Her too-perceptive gaze settled on Lexie once more before she inclined her head and closed the door on them both.

Confounded by the other woman, Lexie turned to Coop, intending to ask some questions, but one look at him and all rational thought fled. Wearing nothing but faded jeans, zipped but unbuttoned, she had a full-on view of his washboard abs, tanned chest and unshaven face. She forgot that she was curious about his neighbor, forgot why she'd come. Heck, she'd even forgotten her own name.

"Would you like to come in?" he asked.

Lexie nodded. She could handle a nod.

"Good. Better than talking in the hall."

"Or disturbing your neighbor," Lexie added.

"That's Sara. She's an NYPD cop and, as she said, she worked the night shift. She'll be less cranky in a couple of hours," he said, obvious fondness in his voice.

A frisson of jealousy crept through Lexie,

an unusual and unwanted emotion when it came to any man. She liked casual attachments. Not ones that elicited feelings of any kind.

Coop led her into his apartment and turned an obviously new lock, bolting the door shut.

He must have been up late into the night dealing with the police and the locksmith, she realized.

"So what are you doing here?" he asked. "Not that I mind, but I sort of expected you to wait a day or so to call."

She'd been panicked after reading about the burglary and rushed over here without thinking. Meeting his neighbor, who obviously knew he'd been up and out early, reminded Lexie that he had a life and she felt like an idiot for running over here uninvited.

And now here she was with a half-dressed man she'd just met yesterday. Who probably didn't want or need her concern. Lexie always operated on pure instinct and emotion, rarely stopping to think first, always asking questions later, but even for her, this turn of events was too much.

She cleared her throat. "I read about the robbery last night and I was worried. But since you're clearly okay, I should go. But before I do, can you at least tell me if the ring was stolen?"

He shook his head. "The robbery happened while we were out. I came home to this." He swept his hand through the air, encompassing the entire apartment, which had obviously been trashed.

"I'm sorry. And I'm glad you're okay. Since I caught you at a bad time, coming out of the shower and all, I should go. And call first next time." She turned to leave before she could ramble some more and make a bigger fool of herself.

"Whoa." Coop grasped her shoulder and spun her back around. "Don't run off. Please. You said you were worried about me." He sounded pleased about that.

She nodded, still tense and uncomfortable.

He smiled. "Then definitely don't run off. The cops took my statement last night, Sara checked in this morning, but I could use a friend," he admitted.

She raised her eyebrows. "Isn't that what Sara is?" As the jealous-sounding words escaped, déjà vu overwhelmed her and Lexie realized what was wrong, why she'd gone from needing to be here to her sudden urge to flee.

Lexie had already lost one important man

97

in her life to a woman whose importance she'd discounted. Just a friend, Drew had said of the woman in Paris. So while a trusting Lexie was enjoying the famous museums in the City of Love, Drew had gone for a quick lunch with his old female friend. Next thing Lexie knew, he'd stayed on in Paris with the woman he'd never gotten over.

And Lexie had continued on her travels alone, having learned two succinct lessons. No matter how temporary a relationship, any man she got involved with must truly be unencumbered by past relationships. And he had to respect, if not understand, her life. Drew had screwed her over on both counts and she'd been deeply hurt when he'd explained that Stacey, his *friend,* was much better suited to him than a wanderer like Lexie.

"Sara is a neighbor and a friend," Coop said, unaware of her feelings. And he didn't sound at all upset with her personal questions. "But you — I hope will turn into something more. So stay. Please."

His husky, compelling voice drew her in. "Sure," she said, relaxing a little.

He inclined his head. "Good. Because I'm worn out from getting no sleep and because for the second time this week, I'm on the wrong side of my own crime beat and I hate it."

Lexie sighed and adjusted her glasses. She wanted to be here for him, but she needed to explain her crazy reaction first. "I'm not normally so nosy, but I wanted to make sure you and Sara are *just* friends. She seemed to know a lot about your morning routine and looked at me like . . . I don't know."

"Like a cop whose neighbor had a robbery last night? Or like a friend who wanted to make sure she approved of the woman her neighbor was getting involved with?" He reached for her hand.

She let him.

"I feel ridiculous," she muttered. Although she'd had these rules for herself since Drew, she'd never grilled any man since about his personal relationships. Because none of the men since had affected her as strongly or as deeply as this one.

"Don't." Coop pulled her toward the messy living area and the couch in the center, settling onto the cushions.

"If it bothers you to think there's something between Sara and me, I'm glad. Just like I'm glad you came here because you were concerned." He brushed his hands over her bangs and slowly removed her glasses from her face, staring into her eyes.

"Are you okay?" she asked, reminded of why she'd come here in the first place.

"I never thought about what my job did to the people I write about, but I've been on the other side of the story twice recently and I can't say I like it much. It makes me feel raw and exposed."

"What would make you feel better?" she asked, leaning closer.

"This." He placed her hand on his chest, her palm centered over his heart. Then he lowered his head, capturing her lips in a soul-deep kiss.

He tasted like mint, he smelled like freshly showered man, and her entire body went into sensory overload. His tongue swirled inside her mouth, devouring what she gave, demanding what she didn't. He knew exactly how to kiss in order to engage all of her. He nibbled on her lower lip and a corresponding tug kicked in deep in her belly. He soothed the bite with his tongue and the swirls of need traveled lower and lower, winding into her abdomen. A trickle of desire dampened her underwear and she tightened her thighs together to prevent herself from climbing onto his lap and taking what she really wanted.

He thrust his hand into the back of her hair and tilted her head, giving him better access to the far reaches of her mouth and throat. In return, she curled her fingers into his chest, groping for something to hold on to, but finding only bare skin.

The far-away ring of a telephone penetrated her consciousness but she pushed away the intruding noise. He didn't seem to care who was calling either, because he'd lifted her shirt and cupped his big hands around her waist, letting his thumb trail up her sides. He paused beneath the strap of her bra. Still kissing her, he grazed her breasts over the fabric, teasing her nipples into tight, rigid peaks.

That's when his answering machine kicked on, a male voice sounding loud in the room. "Hey, bro, read the paper. *Is* an engagement next?" A loud chuckle followed. "By the way, good publicity for Dad's bar. The blogger mentioned it by name. Talk to you later."

Somehow Lexie managed to separate herself from Coop. He was breathing as hard as she was. His eyes were wide and glazed and she wondered if he was as stunned as she. They'd gone far fast. Normally, Lexie took her time before getting this close to any man, especially since Drew, but this thing with Coop seemed to have a life of its own, which meant it was only a matter of time before they . . . She shut her mind down, deliberately not finishing the thought. Her body was still tingling from that kiss. How far would they have gone if they hadn't been interrupted? She trembled at the thought.

But they *had* been interrupted and the message reminded her of the one thing they hadn't yet discussed.

"Did I mention that the blogger thinks we might be getting engaged?"

CHAPTER FIVE

"Engaged." Coop tried to process the word.

"Someone snapped some pictures of us last night at the exact moment when you were showing me the ring, so it looked like you might be . . . proposing." Lexie rose and tried to smooth the nonexistent wrinkles in her clothes.

He wasn't sure what had her more flustered, the reminder of the blog or that kiss. He sure as hell knew which one had hit him hardest. One feel of her lips and soft curves and he'd forgotten all finesse. His brother's call served as a reminder to slow down and Coop intended to heed the warning. He might want to run his fingers through her hair and pick up where they left off, but Lexie wasn't a quick lay. They had business together and dammit, he *liked* her. Wanted to get to know her better . . . even if he did want her in his bed.

"Do you want to see the blog?" she asked.

"I'll check it out in the paper later." He didn't need a visual. "I just can't believe the lengths people will go to. Someone must be following me," he said in disbelief.

"That or else someone at the bar recognized you, snapped the picture and e-mailed it to the blogger. Who knows?"

Since she didn't seem upset by the inaccurate news, he decided not to get worked up over it, either. There were worse things than to be paired with a beautiful woman. Besides it would keep the Bachelor stalkers at bay.

"The best thing to do is ignore it. Bigger news will come up eventually and replace me." He hoped.

Lexie laughed. "There won't be bigger news for my grandmother, I'm afraid." She picked up her glasses and slid them back on.

"She reads the Bachelor Blog?"

"Yep. And she's latched on to the idea that I could have a serious suitor."

"I take it she's happy with the notion?"

"Ridiculously so." Lexie placed her hands on her hips and walked around his apartment, eyeing the mess left by the burglar. "So are you working today?" she asked.

He shook his head. "I took the day off. After everything that's gone on, my editor didn't mind and I needed time to figure all this out."

"Not to mention the fact that you need to clean up?"

He groaned. "Please don't remind me."

"How about I help you instead?"

He hesitated, surprised by the offer. "I couldn't ask you to do that."

She smiled. "You didn't. Besides what better way to get to know the real you than by helping you sort through your personal effects?"

She scanned the items spread across the room and frowned, an adorable pout that brought back memories of her lips on his, her tongue deep in his throat.

"Unless you'd rather do it alone?" she asked, oblivious to his wandering thoughts, which he reined in.

"Are you kidding?" he asked. "I'd appreciate the help and the company. I can't say I kept the place in great shape before the robbery, so anything we do might be an improvement."

"Great. Let's get started." She walked over to the bookshelf and began picking up his hardcovers one by one, replacing them by height.

Joining her, he stacked the books, handing her one at a time. They worked in comfortable silence for a while, then started talking about the books he'd kept over the years.

"How about you?" he asked. "What's your place like? Are you a neat freak or do you prefer clutter?" He couldn't judge that part of her yet.

"Hmm. That's a complicated question because I don't have my own place."

He narrowed his gaze, wondering what she meant. "Do you have a roommate?"

"In a manner of speaking." She paused, turning to face him. "She's almost eighty years old, has lived in the same building for the last forty years and has a spare room she doesn't mind letting me use when I'm around."

"Your grandmother?" Coop recalled her mentioning that the older woman was spry for her age, but maybe she had other issues that necessitated aid.

Lexie nodded.

"Does she need live-in help?"

"God, no! She'd slap you for even suggesting such a thing." Her eyes twinkled at the thought. "Grandma is as independent as they come. But she has a spare bedroom and I figure what's the point of paying rent all year round when I'm not there on a consistent basis?"

A sick feeling settled in his gut. As much

as he'd like to ignore this subject, the more he knew the better prepared he'd be. "How often do you leave town? Or should I ask how long you stay around?"

"It all depends. I can go on short trips for a few weeks at a time or monthly journeys if I choose to. That's the beauty of my line of work. I can stay connected and do it from almost anywhere."

He shook his head, unable to understand the appeal of her lifestyle. "Why leave?"

She spread her hands in front of her as if the answer were obvious. "Sometimes it's a new venue I want to see, other times I just get antsy staying in one place for too long."

Just like his ex, Annie, who had loved her job as a flight attendant. Which hadn't threatened him at all at first. The insecurities came later, when she'd take on more flights, finding excuses not to come home.

He pushed the thoughts and similarities aside. Lexie wasn't his ex. He didn't know her well yet or even understand her motives for how she lived.

But he remained curious. "So those books we talked about your having read and liked? You don't own them? What about *stuff*? Don't you need a place to keep your things?"

"I own a few old books that I leave at my

grandmother's, and anything else I can download on my e-reader. Like I keep telling you, technology is a beautiful thing!"

"Do you miss having a place of your own?"

"But I *do* have a place. My grandmother has always been my refuge, so it's the closest to home I've ever had," she said simply.

Clearly, to her it made sense.

Walking over, he placed a hand on her shoulder. "What did you need refuge from?" he asked.

They'd long since stopped cleaning in favor of conversation, but he sensed that Lexie needed to keep busy, as she paused to rearrange some of the hardcover books they'd just shelved.

Then she pointed to the paperbacks. "Can you hand me those next?"

He did as she asked.

While she placed the books in order, switching them from upside-down to rightside up, she finally started to explain about her childhood.

"I come from a very *driven* family. Dad's a banker, Mom is a lawyer and my sister followed in our father's footsteps. I was more of an *oops* in their carefully planned life. I was unplanned and, to add insult to injury, I didn't act like them, either. They wanted me to follow their goals — I wanted to take things as they came."

"So you're unique." He'd sensed that from the first time they'd met.

She smiled. "And you're kind. My parents, once they realized they couldn't mold me into their image, came to see me as more of a . . . disappointment." Her voice cracked on the word.

And so did his heart, hurting for the little girl who couldn't please her family. Coop might not have lived up to his father's ideals, but it wasn't for lack of trying. And he'd always felt his father's love.

"It's their way or no way," Lexie went on. "Grandma always wonders how she had such a stick-in-the-mud for a son and she pushes his buttons whenever she can."

Coop laughed. "Hey, not all family members are alike. It's okay for you to be different."

Lexie released a wry chuckle. "I wish someone had explained that to my parents. Don't get me wrong — they loved me and wanted me to have every opportunity available — as long as they chose the opportunity. So at five years old when my ice skating talent became obvious, they started to push me toward competition."

"Let me guess," he said, continuing to

work with her on the cleaning. "You hated it."

"Actually, I loved skating. I just hated the rigorous schedules that came with their goals. I hated the conformity of the routines. And as I got older, I hated the competitiveness between skaters and even the adults in that world."

"Did you tell them?" He wondered if she'd felt comfortable enough with them to be honest.

She nodded. "I tried. But nobody listened. So throughout my teenage years, I was at the rink at 5:00 a.m., working with a coach and competing. Until finally my grandmother stepped in."

"How did she save you?" He was fascinated by this glimpse into her early life and the things that had formed the woman she'd become today.

"One day she picked me up after school for skating practice, took one look at my face and instead of going to the rink, she drove upstate. We went hiking at Bear Mountain. We watched the leaves turn colors and enjoyed the outdoors. It gave me a much-needed break."

As she recounted the memory, color flooded Lexie's cheeks, almost as if she were actually there, outdoors with the cool wind biting at her cheeks. There was no doubt this woman knew her passions, Coop thought.

"She obviously gets you," he said, meeting her gaze. "You're lucky to have her."

She nodded. "You sound like you understand. From experience?"

He inclined his head. "Yeah. My mom," he said gruffly. Coop swallowed hard and decided not to explain about the shoulder injury and being forced to drop out of the academy and stuck to the subject at hand. "She knew I loved writing, recognized my talent and guided me toward journalism. She got me."

Lexie smiled, her expression full of warmth and understanding. "Like my grandmother gets me."

"We were close. With my father and brother, I always felt like the outsider. I still do," he admitted. "So how did your grandmother fix things?" Because he had no doubt she had.

Lexie smiled. "She staged an intervention of sorts. She'd met Yank Morgan, the sports agent, at the rink and they'd become good friends. She and Yank sat my parents down and explained that championship skating wasn't only about talent but also desire. And desire is in someone's heart." She placed her hand over her chest. "Either you're born with it or you're not. And forcing me to compete might gain me medals but it would break my spirit. Which, in my grandmother's opinion, wasn't worth the cost." Her voice cracked slightly.

He brushed his hand across her cheek, grateful for the insight. "Did she win the battle?" Coop asked.

"At first Dad said only horses had spirits that could be broken and Grandma told him if he believed that then he was a horse's ass."

Coop snickered and Lexie grinned.

"Yank told them to let me be a kid and find my own way. Mom and Dad gave in, but to this day I can't say they understood why I was so unhappy doing something I was good at." Lexie rubbed her hands together as if warming herself. "So now you know. Nobody in my life gets me."

"Except your grandmother."

"Exactly." She nodded. "And you?" she asked hopefully.

He inclined his head, unsure of how to answer.

Traveling fed her spirit — that much he understood. It was ironic. After promising himself he wouldn't get involved with a woman who wasn't capable of putting down roots, he'd gone and done just that.

Gotten involved.

Too much to just walk away. But neither could he afford to invest more of himself because he already knew he could fall hard.

"Hey, are you hungry?" he asked, changing the subject to one easier to handle and that definitely placed distance between them. "We could break for an early lunch."

"I'm always hungry."

He laughed. "A girl after my own heart." His own skipped a beat at the thought.

Short-term, he reminded himself. They could hang out together for as long as it took to investigate the history of the ring and for her to build his Web site. She'd be here and gone.

At least this time he knew what to expect up front.

For Lexie the day passed quickly, cleaning broken up by lunch at a local pizzeria, but no more kisses. There was also a quick stop at a bank where Coop opened a safe deposit box. He stored the ring inside and together they worked for the rest of the day, putting Coop's apartment back in order.

She'd been fielding phone calls from her grandmother all afternoon, first asking where she was and then which client she was with. When her grandmother had realized Lexie was with Coop, Charlotte began sending her text messages.

When had her grandmother learned to text?

Invite ur yung man to dinner. Apparently, Grandma also thought she was young enough to send text slang. To which Lexie had replied, *he's not my young man.* But Charlotte wasn't about to be deterred. *Rest of city thinks U R engaged. Bring him to meet the parents. Aka me.*

And so it went. Lexie tried ignoring her, but the texts only piled up.

The best part of the day was that Lexie now had a glimpse into how Coop lived. The walk-up was cozy. A one-bedroom with purely masculine flavor and appeal. The centerpiece of the living room was a big-screen TV; a desktop PC sat in the corner, but the bookshelf held a prominent place as well. She could envision him stretched out at night, watching sports or reading, and relaxing after work. His home was as comfortable as the man himself.

Or at least as comfortable as the man she'd opened up to earlier today. Ever since they'd returned from lunch, she'd noticed a definite change in his attitude toward her. This, despite how much he'd seemed to understand her differences with her parents. Which meant he'd had more issues than he'd let on with her nomadic way of life. What else could have triggered the change in his mood?

She decided to tread carefully from now on and not read too much into that kiss. A kiss she still couldn't forget. Hours later and her body was still trembling. A quick look at his handsome face and a distinct tightening twisted inside her stomach. But he'd made no more sexy overtures and so neither did she.

By four o'clock, they'd finished their cleanup work and she glanced around, pleased with all they'd accomplished. "We make quite a team." The words slipped out before she could stop them.

He stretched his arms overhead, groaning as he moved. "I couldn't have done this by myself," he admitted.

"So imagine how much we'll get accomplished when we start working on the stolen jewels." She pointedly reminded him that they had another goal to start on as soon as possible. "What's your schedule look like?" she asked.

"Tomorrow I'm back to work, which leaves evenings, unless a big story breaks."

"Sounds good to me. I have an appointment at the Hot Zone tomorrow and I wanted to get a head start on some ideas I had for their new site. I can meet up with you later in the day or early evening. So what's the plan?" she asked.

He raised his eyebrows. "Plan?"

Why did he have to look so stupefied? It was a simple question. "I watch *Cold Case*. And this is as cold as they come, but you're an intrepid reporter who digs up stories all the time. So I'm sure you have a plan of action for us, right?"

He shook his head and laughed. "One step at a time, Sherlock. I haven't had a chance to think that far ahead. I've been a little preoccupied with this." He swept his hand around the apartment.

Her cell phone vibrated and Lexie let out a groan. "My grandmother," she muttered, glancing at the incoming text. *Dinner. Bring him. 6 p.m.* She closed her eyes and prayed for patience.

"What's wrong?" Coop asked.

"She wants you to come over for dinner tonight, but don't worry about it. I'll take care of it."

"I'll go with you."

Lexie narrowed her gaze. "Why in the world would you want to do that?"

"I want to meet the woman who's taken

such good care of you."

How could she refuse such a heartfelt declaration? "On one condition."

He raised his eyebrow. "And what would that be?"

"Help me convince her we're not really engaged."

"Done." He shook her hand to seal the deal. Sizzling electricity crackled between them, reminding her that as much as he'd tried to place distance between them, there was chemistry that would not be denied.

"Do you have allergies?" Lexie asked Coop as they stepped off an old elevator and strode down the dark hall.

That was an strange question, he thought. "No. Why?"

She inserted her key in the lock, opened the apartment door and the heavy smell of violets nearly bowled him over.

"Whoa." He waved his hand in front of his nose.

"That's why." Lexie laughed. "Don't worry. You'll get used to it. Ready?" Before he could answer, she stepped inside, pulling him along with her. "Grandma, we're here!" Lexie called out.

"I'm in the kitchen. I'll be right out!"

"Come on in," Lexie said, leading him

into the dimly lit apartment.

He glanced around, taking in the dark décor accentuated by varying shades of gold. Heavy, closed draperies covered the windows and large paintings with brassy frames and matching sconces hung on the walls.

"Be it ever so humble . . . Grandma has lived here since she married my grandfather." Lexie swept her arm around.

"Raised my son here. Lexie now uses his old room," Charlotte said, joining them.

The photograph hadn't done the older woman justice. She beamed happiness and radiated life. Everything about her was *more*. Her hair was redder, her makeup bolder. Her housecoat was colorful, more kimono than pajamalike, making him feel like he was facing Auntie Mame in the flesh. But his biggest surprise was the necklace around her neck. *The* necklace, which in person, looked exactly like his ring.

Coop hadn't been able to sleep much last night and early this morning. While tossing and turning, he'd searched for a way to authenticate the ring without bringing the cold case to anyone's attention. He'd finally figured out who to go to and, despite the early hour, he'd called in a favor.

A South African man Coop had met years ago was a highly respected jewelry appraiser. He'd also been a fence in his home country, something Coop had learned during an investigation. The tidbit of information wasn't relevant to any case at hand, but it had led to a mutual understanding between Coop and said appraiser. Anything he heard about what was happening in the black market, he fed to Coop first.

Before Lexie even arrived earlier that morning, Coop had met him at his store and had the ring appraised. At least Coop had confirmation of the ring's identity. Something he still had to share with Lexie when the time was right.

"I'm Charlotte Davis." She grasped his hand, pumping it in a firm shake. "And you must be Sam Cooper, Hero, Bachelor and now my granddaughter's fiancé!"

"Grandma, cut that out! I've been telling you all day we're not engaged." Lexie shot Coop an *I told you so* look, and, as if to prove her point, Lexie held out her left hand, revealing her ringless fingers to her grandmother.

"Well, I wouldn't wear the ring out in public, either, if I were you. Too valuable." In a not-so-subtle gesture, she fingered the gaudy piece of jewelry around her frail neck. "You have good taste, young man." She winked at Cooper.

"She doesn't take *we're not engaged* for an answer," Lexie said, her frustration mounting. "Coop, tell her we're not engaged."

"Can I get you two a drink?" Charlotte asked too quickly.

Coop shrugged. Obviously, the older woman didn't want to hear it. "I'd love something to drink, Mrs. Davis."

"Call me Charlotte. After all, we're practically family!" She paused. Her golden eyes, so similar to Lexie's, lit up. "Which means you can actually call me —"

"Charlotte!" Lexie jumped in before her grandmother could come up with a more familiar term.

The other woman inclined her head. "I suppose Charlotte will do for now. I'll go get the champagne, so we can toast and celebrate!"

She darted out of the room and he caught a glimpse of her slippers, red with fur trim, which matched her dress. Housecoat. Kimono. Whatever it was she was wearing.

"She is a piece of work," Coop said, truly admiring her spunk.

"I tried to get you out of it, but now that you're here she's reveling. And you promised to help me convince her we're not engaged, so stop humoring her." But Lexie grinned, finding her grandmother amusing despite it all.

"Does she try to make a permanent match with all the men in your life?" Coop asked, a stab of jealousy striking him in the heart at the thought.

"No. This is unusual even for her," Lexie mused. "What can I say? You're special and have been from the minute she saw you on television picking out the ring."

Charlotte returned with three glasses of champagne on a small tray, balancing them with ease.

Once everyone held their glass, Charlotte raised hers. *"L'Chaim."*

"That means, 'To Life' in Hebrew," Lexie whispered.

"I didn't know you were Jewish."

She shook her head. "We're not. Grandma's best friend Sylvia is, and she picked up some Hebrew and Yiddish over the years."

The toast seemed safe enough, and Coop touched his glass first to Charlotte's, then to Lexie's. "And to beautiful women and good company," he added.

"He's a keeper," Charlotte said, nudging Lexie in the ribs. "Let's move this into the kitchen. It's time to eat!"

The kitchen was a brighter room than the

rest of the apartment, cozy and comfortable. As she served, Charlotte chatted about everything and anything, from Lexie's amazing Web design talent to her own attempt to learn how to navigate the Internet.

She'd served the food, a pale-looking meat loaf, gravy on the side, mashed potatoes and green beans, piling each plate with generous portions.

"What's wrong with the meat loaf, Gran? Did you forget to season it?" Lexie asked, pushing the meat around her plate while eating the side dishes instead.

"I've been experimenting with lower-cholesterol foods. It's ground turkey, not chopped meat," the older woman explained.

Lexie narrowed her gaze.

Even through the dark frames on her glasses, Coop noticed the worry lines between her brows.

"Since when do you have to worry about high cholesterol?"

"Since my doctor called with my latest blood tests, but there's nothing to worry about, so eat!" Charlotte proceeded to follow her own words.

"How high?" Lexie asked.

"Not as high as my blood pressure." Charlotte covered her full mouth as she spoke. "So, Coop, tell me about your family," she said, in a clear attempt to change the subject.

Lexie lowered her fork to the table. "We're not finished discussing this."

"There's nothing to discuss. I'm watching my diet and taking new pills. My blood pressure will go down even more when I'm certain you are happily settled with your new man." Charlotte waved her silverware at Coop. "So, back to your family — is your father retired?"

Coop shot a worried glance Lexie's way. She'd set her jaw, but she gave Coop a small nod, indicating he should just humor her. Obviously, she'd deal with her grandmother's health issues later.

"My father's a retired cop," Coop said.

"Ooh, I love men in uniform!"

Lexie slipped off her glasses and placed them on the table, pinching the bridge of her nose.

Coop decided to keep the easy subject going. "These days my dad owns a bar downtown. It keeps him busy since my mother died."

"Got any siblings?"

Lexie rolled her eyes. "It's like the Grand Inquisition."

Coop laughed. "One brother."

Charlotte placed her knife and fork on her

plate. "So your mother went for two, huh? One was all the domesticity I could stand, especially since my son was practically born wearing a three-piece suit. How someone like me ended up with a stuffed shirt for a child, I'll never know. I love him, but he's not a load of laughs, that one. Speaking of your father, he called for you earlier."

Lexie sighed. "I hit ignore on my cell phone," she admitted. "I'll call him back later."

"How often do you speak to him?" Coop asked.

She shrugged. "I call my parents once a week out of obligation. It always ends up in an argument about something. We just can't see eye to eye on anything."

"It's their way or no way," Charlotte said, echoing Lexie's description.

"They live about forty minutes from here, but in reality the distance between us is much further. I see them about once a month. Now can we please change the subject?" Lexie asked.

Coop glanced down at his plate, realizing that during the discussion he'd finished his entire meal. "Your turkey meat loaf is delicious. Thank you," he said.

Charlotte beamed. "You're welcome. Now let's get down to the nitty-gritty. If I'm going to trust you with my granddaughter's future, I need to know all about you. Any skeletons in your closet?"

This was the point where he should remind Charlotte that they really weren't engaged, but with her health revelation, he didn't want to upset her. What harm was there in letting her push her agenda? He and Lexie knew the truth, while Charlotte merely appeared to be amusing herself, more than putting too much stock in their words.

He was about to answer that, no, he had no hidden skeletons, when he realized there was something he hadn't told Lexie. Since they were sharing information, he figured, why not reveal it now?

"There's an ex-wife in my closet."

Lexie coughed, then met his gaze, clearly intrigued by the information.

Charlotte perched her chin in her hand. "Do tell."

"Yes, do," Lexie murmured.

"Why would any woman let you become an ex?" Charlotte stared pointedly at her granddaughter.

"She was a flight attendant whose travel was everything to her," he said without meeting Lexie's gaze.

Charlotte leaned in closer. "What happened to make her an ex?"

Lexie groaned.

"She left me for one of her coworkers." And with that revelation, Coop was finished with the personal inquisition. "Time to turn the tables, Mrs. Davis."

"It's Charlotte, remember?

He grinned. "Charlotte. Tell me about the necklace you're wearing. The one that matches my ring."

CHAPTER SIX

Coop was a sly one, dropping a bombshell then expecting them all to switch gears, Lexie thought. Well, fine. She wanted to know more about the necklace as much as he did, but she wasn't going to drop the subject of his ex-wife, either.

Cheating flight attendant, she thought in frustration. Was it any wonder he had an aversion to Lexie's lifestyle choices?

"The necklace?" Coop prompted Charlotte, bringing Lexie back to the matter at hand.

"My husband and I had been married for about three years and my son was a year old when he gave me the necklace," Charlotte said in a wistful voice.

"Did he say where he got it, Grandma?"

Charlotte's gaze slid to the photograph of her husband, Henry Davis, in military uniform that she kept on the table by her favorite chair. "He received it as payment for work done. You see, before the draft for the Korean War, he was a chauffeur for a wealthy family, but they'd fallen on some hard times. Your grandfather, bless his soul, agreed to accept jewelry instead of cash." She lovingly fingered the necklace around her neck.

"Do you happen to know the name of the family who gave it to him?" Coop asked.

Lexie hadn't thought of that question. Then again he was the reporter.

"Heavens, no. My memory isn't that good anymore."

Lexie frowned. Her grandmother was still sharp and she had fantastic recall for most things.

Suddenly, from somewhere long ago, a memory surfaced for Lexie. "I remember Sylvia once mentioning that Grandpa drove for the Lancaster family. Remember when they filed for bankruptcy? Because they owned a lot of real estate in the city, it hit the news." She glanced at her grandmother.

Charlotte shook her head. "No, I don't remember that at all," she said and turned to Coop. "What about the ring the store owner gave *you?* Did she say where it originally came from?" Charlotte asked.

Lexie had already asked Coop the exact same question.

He shook his head. "She didn't say any-thing about it."

And since they'd agreed not to mention that the jewelry had been stolen, he left it at that.

"Well, is there any chance I can see the ring? I didn't know it existed, but now that I do . . ." She turned to Coop with pleading eyes.

"It's in a safe deposit box."

Charlotte let out a disappointed sigh.

"Well, maybe one day," he hedged.

To Lexie, it seemed as if he were putting her grandmother off.

But his ploy went over Charlotte's head, because without warning, she wrapped her arms around his waist. "Oh, thank you!" she exclaimed.

He awkwardly patted her back, all the while sending SOS signals to Lexie.

"Okay, Grandma, you can let Coop go now. It's time for him to leave."

Charlotte peeled herself off him.

"Why don't you go lie down," Lexie sug-gested, still unnerved by the news that her grandmother had high cholesterol and high blood pressure. "I'll walk Coop out and then I'll clean up for you."

"If you're sure you don't mind . . ."

Lexie pulled her grandmother into a hug,

trying to convince herself that she didn't suddenly feel frailer just because Lexie now knew about her medical issues.

"Thank you for dinner, Mrs. — I mean Charlotte. The food was delicious, but the company was even better." Coop pressed a kiss to the back of Charlotte's hand.

The gentlemanly gesture sent shivers of awareness coursing down Lexie's spine. Although she thought she could read people pretty well, he'd had her baffled since this afternoon. From that sizzling kiss to the way he'd pulled back after lunch, to his surprising willingness to come for dinner, she didn't know where she stood.

She was his jewelry investigation partner — that much she knew for sure. As for anything romantic, she hadn't a clue. She'd spent the better part of the evening tamping down any desire he aroused in her. Yet once her grandmother had disappeared into her bedroom and they were alone, every inch of her was keenly aware of the man. He studied her with those piercing blue eyes and she wanted to melt into his arms.

Instead, she folded hers across her chest. "So much for helping me convince her that we're *not* engaged."

"I tried! But she's pretty damn stubborn. Like someone else I know." Amusement danced in his expression. "I would have fought the good fight, but she mentioned her health and I didn't want to upset her."

Damn. Why did he have to be so sexy, sensitive, caring *and* have issues with women who liked to travel? Which brought up another bone of contention she had to pick with him. "Ex-wife?" she asked.

"It's not like I was holding out on you. Technically this is only our second date." He reached out his hand and pulled her toward him until her body aligned with his.

He wrapped his arms around her waist and met her gaze. "We are very different people."

She nodded. "Who want very different things out of life."

He paused, staring into her eyes until she felt the pull of his desire straight through to her stomach. "Are you getting on a plane anytime soon?" he asked.

She shook her head. "Not until after my grandmother's birthday at the end of the month."

She didn't have her destination chosen yet, either. By then the restlessness ought to take over and she'd be out of here, but for now she was exactly where she wanted to be.

"The question is, can you live with that?"

She looped her arms around his neck. "Because if so, until then, I'm yours."

He replied quickly, sealing his lips against hers in a kiss that was extremely delicious and way too short. He didn't slip his tongue inside her mouth, but he lingered long enough to tantalize her with his warm touch.

"I'll take that as a yes," she murmured.

"That's a yes. But I'm leaving before I do something extremely inappropriate in your grandmother's living room," he said, a seductive gleam in his eyes.

"I wouldn't mind."

"Neither would I," he murmured. "I have a full schedule for the next few days, but how about you come by my place around eight Friday night?"

"For work or play?" she asked as she walked him to the door.

He grinned. "If you're lucky, maybe a little of both."

Coop returned home to a clean apartment, his brain flying with ideas and ready to write. Something about being with Lexie and her grandmother had rejuvenated him. Instead of going to bed, he sat down in front of his desktop computer, which luckily the thief had left, and got to work.

He spent a long time outlining a story

loosely based on the theft of a valuable ring by the family chauffeur. Then he logged another hour researching the jewels and the Lancaster family, from whom the jewels had been stolen.

Lancaster.

The same name Lexie had remembered. Coop's gut clenched, but he kept digging until he unearthed another mention of the Lancaster theft, which detailed how everyone at the party had been questioned by the police and later exonerated. Except for the temporary staff, leaving a cold trail. One of them had been a chauffeur who'd driven friends to and from the party for the evening.

His neck and shoulders ached and he stood up and stretched. But it wasn't the physical pain that bothered him most. Lexie recalled the Lancaster family despite Charlotte's claim not to remember. And Charlotte admitted the necklace had been given to her husband in exchange for work done. Chauffeur work. Could all the similarities be a coincidence? Or *could Lexie's grandfather have been a thief after all?*

Coop shook his head, knowing that he couldn't bring this to her until he'd dug deeper. Maybe his father could get him access to the cold case files and he'd find something fresh the police had missed. Something that exonerated her grandfather. Until he had something definitive, he wasn't about to burden Lexie with mere speculation.

Coop glanced at his watch, surprised by the time. Three hours had whizzed by. He couldn't remember the last time he'd been able to get lost in his writing and research for so long. He knew he had Lexie to thank for igniting his muse, which led to more guilt over where his research might lead.

Coop groaned and headed for bed. He had to be at the paper early tomorrow and knew he'd have a fitful sleep as it was.

He managed to grab a few hours and woke up with the same renewed energy he'd had last night. But he didn't have time for personal research. The news never stopped and once at work, he checked the police blotter, noting that last night there had been a benefit for an AIDS charity with local bigwigs. A bracelet had been stolen, at least according to the owner. According to the police, however, a broken clasp or another accident might have been at play, since there was no way the item could have been taken off the victim's wrist. Coop eliminated the item from the news of the day. There were more valid thefts overnight that would make the paper.

A few minutes later, he received a phone call informing him that there had been a brutal rape near Central Park, the victim currently en route to the hospital.

Coop hit the ground running, arriving at the emergency room at the same time as the ambulance. The next few days passed in a flurry of interviews and activity, leaving him no time to investigate the ring's history or Lexie's grandfather's possible involvement.

Finally, Friday evening arrived. He had one last article to pull together for the evening edition, then he was off for the weekend, unless something big cropped up that he didn't want to miss out on.

Coop entered the lobby in the recently remodeled building. The news offices were on the seventeenth floor. Mirrored walls and trees lined the side walls and people were already leaving for the day.

As usual, Coop stopped by the security desk in the center of the lobby to say hello to his buddy, Chris Markov, the uniformed guard at the desk. The same age as Coop, the two had been friends for over five years and now played on the same summer softball league.

"Hey, man. How are you?" Coop asked.

Chris lifted his hat and scratched his head. "Not bad. Yourself?"

"Hanging in. Are you off duty soon?" Coop asked.

"Sure am. I'm taking my son to the Renegades' home game."

The mention of the team reminded Coop of his date with Lexie tonight. His mood, which had taken a beating with the depressing stories he'd been covering over the last few days, shifted gears and lightened.

"Great weather for a baseball game. The little man ought to have a blast," he said of Chris's seven-year-old son, who he'd been raising on his own since his wife walked out when the boy was three.

"He loves the Renegades," Chris said, laughing.

"I hear you. Have fun. I've gotta go write my story so I can get out of here. Catch you later."

Coop turned to leave, when Chris called out, stopping him. "I've been tossing the obvious gifts from the single ladies in this town, as you requested. But this came for you earlier today and it doesn't look like female lingerie." He pulled out a large brown box with the word *Fragile* stamped in red on the top and bottom.

Chris had been happy to take over handling the Bachelor's goodies. But he was right. This package looked more legitimate. Coop wasn't expecting any deliveries, but in his line of work you never knew who'd send you something they thought could be a lead on a crime. Although this was a little larger than anything he'd received before.

"Doesn't look like the fancy blogger stuff from last week." Chris, who'd gotten way too much enjoyment out of ribbing Coop about the gifts, chuckled yet again. "I imagine the fact that you're *engaged* has something to do with the women backing off."

Chris knew damn well Coop wasn't engaged, but persisted in giving him a hard time anyway. "Back off," Coop muttered good-naturedly. "And quit reading that garbage."

But it still boggled the mind how many people in this city read the Bachelor Blog. Throughout the day, at the hospital where the rape victim had been brought, everyone from nurses to candy stripers to the woman who worked reception had recognized Coop as the Bachelor. Some had merely stared and whispered to their female friends. Others had tried their best to convince him outright to date them instead of staying with his current girlfriend. Humiliating, yet he had no choice but to suck it up.

And he wasn't about to give Chris any more ammunition.

The other man laughed. "Of course I read the blog. Hey, I sit at a desk for eight-plus hours a day. What do you expect? Even if you're not engaged, at least you're getting some action."

"I take it you're not?" Coop asked his friend. From Chris, Coop knew how hard it was to date women when you had an impressionable kid around, not to mention the fact that Chris's mother practically lived with them to help out.

"Nah. You're definitely getting more than me if that photo is anything to go by."

Oh, no. "What photo?" Coop asked warily.

"You haven't seen today's paper?"

Coop shook his head. "Been a little busy."

Chris handed Coop today's edition, already folded open to the Bachelor Blog page. *Bachelor Gets Lucky,* read the headline and beneath it, a photograph of Lexie and Coop kissing.

"You live an interesting life," Chris said.

"Only recently." Since Lexie had come into it.

Coop stared at the grainy photo of the kiss. There were only two places that had happened, one when they were alone in his apartment and again when they *thought* they were alone in her grandmother's foyer. Apparently, Charlotte had a sneaky side.

He shouldn't laugh, but he couldn't help it. The old lady had guts, nabbing a photo and sending it off to the Blogger. Lexie would probably kill her.

The rest of the Bachelor Blog went on to mention how Coop had been seen entering Web designer Lexie Davis's grandmother's building, leading to speculation that he was already meeting the family. Nothing but truth in the facts reported. But the insinuation in the words, that Lexie and Coop were engaged and moving quickly toward marriage, couldn't be further from reality.

Coop felt a sudden sympathy for celebrities who were hounded, followed and roasted by the press, giving him a new appreciation of celebrities' resentment of the news media. He'd take gritty crime reporting over glitz, glamour and innuendo any day.

"Do me a favor," Coop said to Chris. "Don't believe everything you read in this particular section. Have fun at the game and say hello to Junior for me." Coop picked up the heavy box and headed for the elevator bank and his office upstairs.

At his desk, he slit open the package,

shocked to discover his laptop inside, well protected in bubble wrap.

"Well, well, well." Instead of touching it, he immediately called the cops, hoping the police would find evidence that might lead them to the culprit. Sara was off, but the officer on duty promised to send someone over. Like Coop, however, he doubted they'd find any clues in a plainly wrapped package that had been through the postal service and God knew how many hands.

By the time he finished up with the police and sat down to write his article, Coop realized he'd be late getting back to his apartment to meet Lexie.

When she didn't answer her phone, he called Sara and asked her to let Lexie in with his spare key. The whole idea of Sara and Lexie together put him on edge. Sara was closemouthed on the job, but off was another matter. And he could only imagine the tales she'd tell. Unfortunately, with a deadline looming, Coop didn't have a choice.

Lexie spent the morning on a call with Claudia, working on implementing ideas for the Hot Zone and the Athlete's Only sites. In the afternoon, she toyed with ideas for Coop's author Web page, but she'd struggled with how to approach Coop's site. Her lack of knowledge about Coop and his work made it hard for her to nail down any sort of theme for the site.

She needed to immerse herself in his world, something she looked forward to doing tonight. Not that she'd grill him, but she needed to learn much more about the author and his work — and the man behind them both.

Lexie arrived at Coop's on time, only to find that he wasn't home. Her stomach twisted for a moment. Had he forgotten? Neither of them had spoken this week, but she hadn't thought anything of it. Holding back disappointment, she knocked on his door one last time.

Sara peeked her head out of her apartment as if on cue. "He's running late and asked me to let you into his place."

"Thanks," Lexie said, relieved that he hadn't forgotten about her.

"He said he'd tried your cell phone but no one answered, so he called me."

Lexie frowned and pulled her cell from her oversize work bag, which held not just her personal things but her mini-laptop and notes as well. She glanced at the screen and poked at a few buttons before meeting Sara's curious gaze.

"Dead," Lexie explained. "I must have forgotten to charge it. It happens when I get wrapped up in work." It happened more often than she liked to admit.

Sara nodded. "Interesting. Coop's the same way. He tends to get involved in a story and forget what time it is. Frankly, I was surprised he remembered to think about his plans tonight. Which means they must be important to him."

Lexie wasn't normally the type to get tongue-tied, but this woman's bluntness caught her off guard.

"Hey, why don't you come in and hang out here until he comes home?" Sara offered.

"Thanks, but I don't want to bother you. And I really don't mind waiting by myself."

Sara waved her hand through the air. "No bother. It's my day off."

"Okay then, sure. Why not?" She didn't want to insult Coop's friend and neighbor.

Once inside, Lexie glanced around. Sara's apartment showed all the personality that the woman in uniform had lacked on their first meeting. Lexie stared at the frilly, lace décor, shocked at how feminine Sara's taste was. Then again, her choice of clothing on her day off, a summer skirt and tank top, which showed off voluptuous curves, should have given Lexie her first clue.

"What's wrong?" Sara asked, staring at Lexie in that coplike way she had, in a blatant attempt to understand what was going on in her mind.

Suspects probably broke under that stare, Lexie thought, drawing a deep breath. "Nothing's wrong. I was admiring your furnishings. I'm surprised. I have to admit I pegged you wrong."

"Thought I'd be a tomboy, huh?"

"Guilty," Lexie said, laughing.

As if to reinforce the point that she was no such thing, Sara pulled her long blonde hair back and wound it into a knot on top of her head like a true girl. "My AC doesn't always blow cold enough. I have a call into the super and I'm waiting for him to come up and take a look."

"I'm dressed lightly enough, so I'm comfortable." Lexie's grandmother didn't exactly keep the apartment like a refrigerator, so Lexie had learned to adjust.

"Can I get you a cold drink?" Sara asked.

"No, thanks."

"Then just take a load off." The other woman pointed to a comfortable-looking chair and Lexie did as she suggested, settling in.

Sara chose the sofa across the way. "I'm

sorry I was so rude the other day. I'd worked a double shift and I was exhausted."

"You weren't rude at all," Lexie lied.

"Liar."

"I'm sorry if I'm keeping you from anything," Lexie said again.

Sara shook her head. "You're no trouble. Any friend of Coop's is a friend of mine. Unless you're really one of those Blogger groupies looking to snag the man and his ring into holy matrimony?" She leaned closer, her defenses clearly up on Coop's behalf.

Instead of feeling threatened, Lexie was able to laugh at the accusation. "God, no. Anything but."

Sara visibly relaxed, her shoulders dropping low. "Then you can stay as long as you like. I just wanted to make sure if Coop got serious about anyone, it wouldn't be someone after him for the wrong reasons."

Lexie and Coop weren't getting serious, but she didn't see the need to confide in Sara about that.

Sara stretched her bare feet out onto the couch across from Lexie. "He deserves better than some female looking for the catch of the day."

Lexie nodded. "Agreed." Coop did deserve someone genuine and real.

"Just as long as you realize that Coop's not a guy you can toy with and walk away from, we understand each other."

Lexie shifted in her seat, straightening her shoulders and looking Sara in the eye. She could go toe to toe with this woman and not back down. "You seem very protective of someone who's *just a friend*."

Sara paused, clearly digesting Lexie's comment. Then she cracked a grin for the first time, taking Lexie by surprise. "You actually feel threatened by me!"

Lexie opted not to comment.

As if the ice had been broken between them, Sara's easy laughter suddenly filled the room. "There's no reason to be worried. I'm just protective of people I care about. Even friends," she said pointedly. "I know Coop pretty well. Unlike me, he isn't into revolving-door relationships," she said, another warning to Lexie. "He's more the steady kind of guy."

"What do you have against relationships?" Lexie was more than ready to turn the conversation away from herself and Coop, and since Sara didn't mind discussing Coop's personal life, Lexie decided Sara's was fair game.

"That's easy. I'm a cop who walks into danger daily and I come from a long line of cops with failed marriages because of the strain of the job. I'm not looking to repeat past mistakes. Then there's Coop, who likes the idea of one woman, one man. A relationship." Sara shuddered at the thought.

"Somehow I can't see Coop appreciating your telling me his secrets." She held her hands tightly in her lap, determined not to fidget under all this scrutiny.

"Maybe not, but someone has to look out for the man."

And Sara had definitely appointed herself Coop's guardian. Though the other woman's words were intrusive and blunt, Lexie still respected her candor. Good, solid friends — friends who understood you — were hard to come by and she was glad he had found one in this tough yet feminine cop.

Even if Lexie hadn't liked what Sara revealed.

Just when Lexie had managed to convince herself that she and Coop could enjoy a fling that lasted until their mutual interest in the ring and his Web site ended, his close friend was warning her not to put too much of herself into this relationship if she wasn't able to commit, should things between them work out.

A firm knock on Sara's door prevented

any further conversation, but couldn't stop Lexie's thoughts. It wasn't commitment Lexie had a problem with, it was staying in one place — something she knew Coop had definite issues dealing with.

Coop hoped Lexie liked Chinese food. He stopped by his favorite take-out place on the way home, thinking that if he had dinner in his hands when he finally got there, she wouldn't be as upset with him for being so late. When he put in his usual order, he realized he didn't even know the basics, like her tastes. As a result, he had a huge brown bag with enough food for an army, but at least she'd have a variety to choose from.

His plan was to mix work with pleasure tonight. As for whether he'd tell her about the chauffeur connection, he remained uneasy, wanting to be able to cushion the blow by looking into it further first.

By the time he arrived home, he was wound tight and ready for the evening to begin. But Lexie wasn't at his place, as he'd expected and he had to make small talk with his neighbor before they could be alone. And Sara, being Sara, was in a chatty mood.

He waited until she paused for a breath, to take Lexie's hand. "We really need to get going," Coop said pointedly.

"Reservations you're already late for?" Sara asked.

"Funny. Actually, I brought dinner home."

"You did?" Lexie asked.

He met her gaze and nodded. "Yep. And I'm starving." And after a look at her in a loose-fitting halter top, her long tanned legs peeking out from delicate white shorts, he was hungry for much more than food. Their one kiss had whet his appetite and fed his dreams at night, but hadn't been nearly enough to satisfy him.

"Me, too," she said, her words bland. But her eyes darkened behind the frames, revealing her understanding of his meaning.

"Go get a room," Sara said, laughing as she headed around them, toward the door to walk them out.

Coop placed his hand on the small of Lexie's back, letting her precede him.

"Thanks, Sara. I appreciate the company," Lexie said.

"Ditto," Coop said to his neighbor. "You won't take it personally if I don't invite you to join us?"

She shook her head and grinned. "Enjoy yourself," she said, patting him on the cheek.

He winked at her. "I intend to."

"Good, because this one passed inspection."

Which meant Sara must have interrogated Lexie the whole time they'd been together. Coop groaned and shot her a warning look. "You really need a guy of your own to focus on," he muttered.

"Good night, Coop," she said, shutting her door behind him.

Lexie waited patiently at his door. She didn't look like a woman who'd gone through something akin to the Spanish Inquisition, but in case Sara had been rough, Coop looked forward to making it up to her.

Ricky used to be a thief, but after fifty-plus years of retirement, the old tricks didn't come back easily. His bones were weary and the rush of adrenaline just didn't drive him the way it used to. But fear was a strong motivator. So when he realized his prized possessions, his *trophies,* had made an appearance on live TV, Ricky knew he had a problem.

If the old accomplices he'd betrayed got a gander at the jewels and recognized the loot, they'd raise holy hell and come after him. His accomplices were scary bitches and there were certain items he'd never gotten around to turning over to them as promised. Ricky had no doubt that all these years later, if they found him they'd make him pay.

Not that he blamed them. He'd whispered sweet nothings to each one, making promises he'd never truly meant to keep until the one night he'd slipped up and gotten caught in bed with one by the other.

That incident had broken up their little group, ended relationships, and the three had spread far and wide. Ricky had high-tailed it to California for a few years, where he'd met his wife. Once he figured that things had cooled off, he'd returned to New York, opened his store and lived quietly . . . until that damn robbery and his daughter's reward threatened to blow his world sky high.

Ricky had believed all the mementos of his former life had remained under wraps. Now he discovered that his daughter had been quietly selling things out from under him. So far none had come back to haunt him. But now that the ring had made a public appearance, Ricky had to get the piece back into his possession before that damn reporter tried to sell it. If a jeweler identified the ring, it wouldn't be long before the unsolved crime pointed straight back to him.

He'd tried asking for it nicely, or as nicely as he knew how, but he'd been rebuffed. Which scared him even more. Why would a guy who'd showed little interest in accepting a reward suddenly want to hang on to it so much? That's when he'd returned to his old ways, breaking into the reporter's apartment. He hadn't found the ring, but he'd taken the laptop, hoping the cops would think it had been a simple robbery.

But an unexpected thing had happened afterwards. He'd looked into his daughter's and granddaughter's eyes and realized that he wasn't the same man who'd stolen from the rich all those years ago. He'd raised his family with morals and decency and, dammit, he felt guilty now for taking something that didn't belong to him.

Wearing gloves, he bundled up the laptop in plain brown wrapping, protected it in bubble wrap, boxed it and headed to the busiest post office in Manhattan. He disguised himself with a toupee, which gave him a full head of hair again, a walking stick and sunglasses. He'd asked a stranger to address the box for him. Paying cash, he mailed the laptop back to the reporter, alleviating his guilt somewhat.

Then he returned home with the same two problems he'd had when he started.

The ring was still out there, waiting to lead some smart person back to him. And so were his accomplices.

CHAPTER SEVEN

"It was nice of Sara to let me stay with her until you came home," Lexie said as they walked into his place.

He tossed his keys onto the console table and locked the door behind them.

"I hope she didn't make you too uncomfortable." He knew how Sara could get when she was in an inquisitive mood.

"I'm a big girl. I can handle myself." Lexie treated him to a smile he recognized as forced.

In the short time he'd known her, he'd come to expect her relaxed grins and easy laughs. She wasn't feeling at ease now. "Meaning she grilled you mercilessly, like the cop she is?"

Lexie paused a beat. "Let's just say she saw fit to lay down the law." She glanced away, her gaze falling on the table by the couch in the living room. "Is that a new laptop?" she asked, obviously changing the subject.

He'd have to find out what Sara said another time. "That's *my* laptop. Stolen the other night and returned in the office mail today. Another reason I was late. I had to wait for the cops to dust it for prints and check it over. Not that they expect to find anything."

She glanced back at him. Behind the frames, her eyes opened wide. "Get out. Whoever stole it sent it back?"

He nodded. "Sounds strange to me, too, and I write this stuff for a living. I thought for sure the hard drive had been wiped clean or the whole thing taken apart piece by piece and sold for scrap."

She strode over to the table where he'd put the computer. "Do you mind if I take a look?"

"Of course not, but why?"

Lexie sat down on the couch and popped open the top. "Because I want to make sure nobody installed a Trojan horse or hidden spyware of any kind while it was out of your possession."

He cocked an eyebrow, impressed with her way of thinking. "Never thought of that."

She grinned. "That's what you have me for."

The impact of her words and her genuine sunny smile kicked him in the gut. She was so easy to be around, so happy and adorable, he couldn't believe how fast he was falling. Deadly for him in the long run, but he couldn't bring himself to worry beyond now if it meant giving her up before he had to.

"You do your thing and I'll put the food out for us. I hope you like Chinese."

"Love it," she said without looking up from the computer. Already engrossed in her task.

As he set the table with the plates he'd put together from his father's bar, he realized this was the first time he'd had any woman over for dinner — and he couldn't even serve the meal on a matched set. Though the guest in question didn't have an apartment of her own and he figured she wouldn't mind, it bugged him anyway. Wait till she realized his sheets and pillowcases weren't much better, he thought wryly, and decided the only solution was to keep her too busy in bed to care.

"How's it going over there?" he asked when he'd finished arranging the white boxes on the kitchen table.

She muttered something he couldn't hear.

"Say that again?"

"I said, why can't the world all convert to using Macs? Everything takes longer and is harder on a PC."

"So I'm a PC and you're a Mac. Is that a deal breaker for you?" he teased.

She blew out a breath of air, lifting her hair, which had fallen over her face. "Nah. I think I can live with it. At a glance it looks like your computer is clean, but I'm letting it run a full check just to be sure, which will take a while."

"Thanks. I never remember to do that stuff on my own."

"I figured. I'm also updating your virus software and installing some other free programs to keep this thing running well."

Listening to her explain, he couldn't control a laugh. "Did anyone ever tell you you're cute when you talk geek?"

She grinned. "Not in so many words, no."

He waved her away from the computer. "You can finish that later. Come eat. I've kept you waiting long enough."

She jumped up and joined him at the table. As it turned out, Lexie loved Chinese food. He'd clearly chosen well and her eyes danced with delight as she opened each white box and took a sampling of each. She even ate with the chopsticks provided, while he used a fork.

She devoured the meal with a gusto that impressed him. She had quite an appetite and wasn't embarrassed to show it. A refreshing change from the women around the office who picked at steamed vegetables for lunch or those he'd had relationships with who'd order an appetizer and call it dinner. Cheap dates, but annoying to be with.

Lexie insisted on helping clean up and they continued the small talk that came so easily to them both. He'd already filled her in on his long three days and she'd done the same. Since she hadn't mentioned the blog, he figured she hadn't seen the photo of them kissing. No time like the present to break it to her, Coop thought.

"So how's your grandmother?" he asked, leading into the subject.

She perched her hip against the counter near the sink. "Odd," she said.

"Odder than usual?"

Her lips pursed in a wry smile. "Believe it or not, yes. She and Sylvia always seem to have their heads together over the computer. She barely knows how to use it when I'm around, yet she's always on the thing. And they're whispering. A lot more than usual."

She passed him the plates to rinse and put in the dishwasher.

157

"I'm not surprised."

Lexie hesitated. "Why?" she asked, meeting his gaze.

"Seems we're making headlines again." He described the picture of them in the blog and waited for her to draw her own conclusion.

"Kissing," she said, her cheeks taking on an adorable flush. "So that would be alone here or . . . at my grandmother's. I'm going to throttle her!" Lexie said, her voice rising.

He shouldn't laugh, but couldn't help it. "Come on, you have to admit it's funny. Your grandmother's got nerve."

Lexie shook her head. "She's got me teaching her how to use the computer while she's snapping cell phone pictures and e-mailing them like a pro!"

He chuckled again. "At least she keeps herself busy."

Lexie rolled her eyes. "She's still in for a lecture about minding her own business and respecting my personal life," she muttered.

"Go easy on her." This time he held back the laugh.

"Maybe I ought to call her now." She glanced toward his telephone on the counter corner.

"Or maybe you should wait until you've calmed down?"

She moved her lips as if she were counting to ten. "You've got a point," she said at last. "I'll talk to her tomorrow. By the way, did you know your answering machine light is flashing?" she asked, tipping her head toward the phone and attached machine.

He hadn't noticed. He'd been too preoccupied with thoughts of finally seeing Lexie again. "I must have forgotten to check when I came in earlier. I guess I was too caught up looking for you," he said, hoping to take her mind off her troublemaking grandmother and put it back on them.

He stepped in front of her, reaching over and hitting the play button on the answering machine. His hand not-so-accidentally brushed her chest, grazing her breast through the light cotton shirt.

She sucked in a surprised breath.

Mission accomplished, he thought, pleased with how her eyes dilated, awareness and desire shimmering in their depths.

He'd spent dinner trying not to think about sex with Lexie, focusing instead on learning more about her and just enjoying. But now the leashed desire had been brought to the surface and he could barely breathe from wanting her.

Suddenly a male voice from the answering machine interrupted the sizzling moment.

"This is Ricky Burnett calling again," the gravelly voice said. "Did ya change your mind about returning my ring? I'll give you a cash reward for saving my daughter instead. You can find me at the store most days so stop by any time. It's got sentimental value and I want my ring back!"

"Don't hold your breath." Coop frowned at the man's words.

"He asked if you changed your mind," Lexie said, processing the message. "Has he bothered you about giving back the ring before?"

"Just once. Obviously, I said no."

Lexie narrowed her gaze. She couldn't think clearly with him standing so close, but with her back against the counter and his big body blocking hers, she couldn't step away. Nor did she want to. Every nerve ending inside her thrummed in anticipation of the kiss she'd been sure he was about to give before Ricky Burnett's message interrupted them.

Still, she wasn't about to let sexual desire fog her brain. "When was this?" she asked of Ricky's request for the ring.

"The day you and I met up at my father's bar. And before you get all righteously angry, I wasn't holding out on you. Back then I barely knew you. And I didn't think about it until after the robbery and we were interrupted by hurricane Charlotte," he said, rushing the words, clearly on the defensive.

He'd anticipated her complaint and she relaxed a little more. He wasn't deliberately trying to shut her out of things.

"So it was before this place was broken into?"

"Yeah, which makes him my number-one suspect, since he obviously couldn't know I had the ring in my pocket the first time he called and asked for it back. Maybe when I said no he decided to try to retrieve it himself."

"And when he didn't find the ring here, he took the laptop . . . Why?" she wondered aloud.

"To make it look like a legit robbery is my best guess," Coop said.

"Then why return it?"

He shrugged. "Beats me. That part makes no sense."

She pursed her lips, racking her brain for motive and finding none. Of course, with Coop's hard thighs pressed against hers, pushing her into the counter and arousing her more, it was difficult to focus on the robbery.

"What did the police say when you told

them about Ricky and the ring?" Lexie managed to ask.

"I didn't tell them. At least not yet." He shifted positions and she felt the swell of his erection against her stomach. His irises darkened, too, telling her he was every bit as aware of his actions as she was.

Lexie swallowed hard. "Why not?"

He braced one hand on the counter behind her. "Because I had the ring appraised and it *is* stolen property."

"Then why didn't the appraiser jump to call the police?"

"Let's just say he owes me."

Lexie nodded slowly. "Okay, and if you tell the police?"

"Then they'll begin to look into the history of the ring, find out it's stolen property and we'll both lose it before we ever figure out the mystery," he explained.

"Aah. Makes sense."

"I thought so." He wrapped the other hand around her waist.

Her heartbeat picked up rhythm and her breasts grew heavy beneath her light halter. But somehow she retrieved the thought that had been niggling at the back of her mind.

"You know, when Ricky was speaking, I thought it was odd that he didn't mention that your apartment had been broken into.

162

For all he knows, maybe the ring had been stolen, yet he didn't say a word! It's the first thing I asked about — after inquiring if *you* were okay, of course."

"Yes, I remember your worrying about my welfare." He grinned. "As for Ricky, maybe he didn't know about the robbery."

"It's been all over the news. You're the Bachelor!" she said, unable to control a laugh. "And his store has been mentioned in every recent article about you. I can't imagine him missing the break-in."

"True." Coop nodded slowly. "So if we play this out, if Ricky is the culprit, then he wouldn't mention the robbery because he wouldn't want to bring it up and have me link him with it in any way."

"That's what I'm thinking. I'm also thinking we need to go talk to this guy in person," Lexie said. She still held out hope that somehow the ring would end up in her possession as a gift for her grandmother. But she couldn't think beyond the here and now.

Her entire body tingled in anticipation of his first real touch.

"How about we go check out the store first thing tomorrow when it opens?" Coop asked.

She nodded. "I'm in."

"Yeah. I thought you would be." He

tipped his head until his forehead touched hers. Behind her, his thumb brushed lazy circles on her bare back. "The question is, What are we going to do with ourselves until tomorrow?"

"Oh, I can think of plenty of things to keep us busy," Lexie murmured.

Because she was finished talking, thinking or doing anything except this. She cupped her hands around his face and sealed her lips against his, effectively ending all conversation, hopefully for a good, long time.

Coop hadn't meant for the answering machine message to be foreplay, but that's exactly what happened. While he and Lexie bounced ideas off each other as if they'd worked together before, he'd driven himself into a heated frenzy. And judging by the way she'd beaten him to the first kiss, he'd done the same to her.

She threaded her fingers into his hair and pulled him against her, nibbling at him with her delicate mouth and tongue, urgent and insistent yet utterly feminine.

He groaned, unable to hold back the sound, then slid his hands around her waist, picked her up and settled her onto the clean countertop.

"What are you doing?" she asked, her

cheeks flushed and her lips damp.

"Giving myself easier access," he said in a gruff voice he barely recognized.

"To what?"

"You. This." He thanked the good Lord for the easy tops women wore in the summertime as he pulled the sides of her halter toward the center, revealing her bare, *braless* breasts for view.

His entire body shuddered at the unexpected sight. She was bigger than he'd imagined, her breasts full and white, her nipples rosy tight buds that had his mouth watering for a taste.

She leaned her head back against the cabinets and watched him with eager eyes. Unable to wait, he stepped into the vee of her legs and lowered his lips to one waiting breast. He cupped his hand beneath the heavy mound and began a leisurely exploration. Starting outward, he laved her creamy soft skin, inhaling her fragrant scent as he worked his tongue over her flesh, inching his way toward the center. He finally closed his mouth around her tight nipple, drawing the bud into his mouth and tugging insistently.

Lexie let out a low moan. She locked her legs around his waist, pulling him tight between her legs. She obviously liked it and he wanted to give her more, make her shudder, shake and beg for him to enter her. He quickly learned what she enjoyed, and he palmed her breast in his hand, while nipping at her bud first with his teeth, then with his tongue.

She bucked against him, arching her back, thrusting her core upwards, seeking relief he wasn't ready to give.

Not.

Just.

Yet.

He transferred his attention to her other breast, giving it the same lavish treatment, tormenting her — and himself — for a long while. When her breasts were finally so sensitive she was whimpering and begging him to stop, he listened, undoing the button on her shorts and pulling down hard and fast on the zipper.

"Lift up," he instructed.

She braced her hands on the counter and levered herself up so he could yank her shorts down over her thighs, making sure he took her barely-there panties along with him.

She settled back against the counter, with a squeal. "It's cold!"

"Not for long," he promised, and without waiting another second, took his fingers, parted her feminine lips and knelt so he could warm her with his mouth.

At his first touch, she leaned back, thrusting her pelvis up and he heard her head hit the cabinets.

"Are you okay?" he asked.

"Fine as long as you don't stop," she said in a breathless voice.

"Not a chance." He lifted her legs and placed them on his shoulders, giving himself complete access.

A part of him wondered if she'd pull away, but she hadn't been shy with him so far and she didn't start now. She relaxed her legs and didn't put up a fight.

She certainly trusted him and he intended to make it worth her while. With his tongue, he stroked her center. She moaned, writhing against him. He thrust inside her, she pulled him in deeper.

God, she was hot and sweet and so damn sensual, he thought, his lips finding the hidden bud that would, he hoped, show her heaven. He alternated long slick laps of his tongue with shorter licks. Her breathing came in uneven gasps and moans and he knew she was close.

Unfortunately, dammit, so was he.

He decided to move things along. Lifting his mouth, he pressed his palm against her damp, wet sheath, sliding one finger deep inside her. He kept the pressure strong, inside and out until she broke, convulsing around him in a hot, steamy orgasm that nearly stole his breath.

He let her ride out the storm, then slowly lowered her legs and made certain she was steady.

Lexie forced her heavy eyelids open and found herself face-to-face with the man who'd just given her extraordinary pleasure in a most intimate way. "Wow."

"You're amazing."

Lexie's cheeks burned. She wasn't inexperienced, but she'd never . . . in the kitchen . . . and been so uninhibited about it.

She wondered if she ought to be embarrassed, but when he cupped her face in his hands and pulled her into a deep kiss, she forgot to worry. His mouth told her exactly how much *he'd* enjoyed it, too. But as good as her body felt now, she was still achingly empty and she couldn't imagine he was feeling any better.

"I think we ought to move this to the bedroom," he said, as if reading her mind.

She nodded.

He caught her off guard by scooping her into his arms.

"I can walk," she felt obligated to point out.

He kissed her on the forehead. "But this way is faster."

She figured, why not enjoy the ride? She looped her arms around his neck and proceeded to nibble his earlobe, inhaling his masculine scent and arousing herself all over again.

He eased her onto the bed and she pushed herself against the pillows while he proceeded to strip off his clothes, his hurry to feel skin against skin matching hers. Lexie pulled her gaze off him only long enough to rid herself of whatever clothing remained.

When he slid onto the mattress, Lexie was naked and ready, and she propped herself onto her elbow to take her first look at him in all his glory. She wasn't disappointed. For a reporter who spent his days behind a desk or investigating stories, he was a finely built specimen. Tanned with a liberal sprinkling of dark hair on his chest, and muscles he'd hidden beneath his shirts, Lexie was beyond impressed and compelled to touch.

Reaching out, she drew a finger down the center of his chest, grazing lightly with her fingernail as she made her way lower, marking her territory as she looked him over. When her gaze and ultimately her finger finally hit the mark, she watched in admiration as he twitched and hardened beneath her hungry stare.

He studied her intently, but didn't say a word, letting her touch and learn his rigid yet smooth shape and feel. As she curled her fingers around his velvety hard erection, he stiffened in her hand and released a low, raw groan of pleasure.

Lexie smiled and continued her exploration, stroking him in her hand. Something about Coop made her feel comfortable enough to act first and worry later. Something about him emboldened her, allowing her to be very unLexie-like.

She realized now that, in the past, she'd gauged her actions in bed according to whether she felt she measured up to the current man in her life. Drew, being the longest relationship, had been the yardstick by which she'd reacted to the men who'd come after. Not that there'd been all that many. But those who'd passed through hadn't truly known who she was deep inside and Lexie had held back, afraid that, like Drew, they ultimately wouldn't even like — forget *love* — who she really was. So she'd always moderated her actions.

"You're killing me," Coop said in a tight, desire-laden tone.

Lexie glanced down to see her thumb gliding over the head of his penis, spreading the hint of moisture glistening on top. There was no moderation with Coop and she reveled in the fact that she could do this to him.

She grinned. "You can't die on me now. There's so much more for us to do together," she murmured.

Coop slid his hands around the back of her neck and pulled her into a long, thorough kiss. Then, he gently reached out and slid her glasses off her face. "As much as I love these on you, they've got to go or they might break."

He loved her glasses? Lexie's heart squeezed a little at his words. Her eyeglasses had been yet another thing about her that Drew wanted to change. Another way she hadn't measured up to someone's hopes, dreams or expectations. He'd constantly pestered her to do Lasik, belittling her fear of the surgery. All he'd cared about was that she would no longer have to wear the *damn things,* as he'd called them, as if they were an embarrassment.

"Where do you keep disappearing to?" Coop tapped her head.

"Nowhere," she promised him and herself. She pushed all thoughts of anyone or anything in her past back where they belonged.

Coop shot her an uncertain glance before turning to place the glasses on the night-stand.

"Before we go any further, you have protection, right?" Lexie asked. Because the one thing Lexie was meticulous about was protection. Not just because it meant she was smart and healthy, but because her traveling lifestyle didn't leave room for any unexpected surprises. She was on the pill, but it paid to be safe all the way around.

He answered by opening the top drawer and pulling out a box of condoms.

A sealed box that he quickly tore open and she nearly sighed in relief. "I bought them after that night at your grand-mother's."

He didn't keep them on hand just in case. Because, as Sara had said, he wasn't into revolving-door relationships.

Yet despite knowing she'd be leaving eventually, he'd invited Lexie in.

It went both ways. Coop wasn't like anyone who'd come before. And though she knew this relationship was destined to be short-term, she wanted to give — and take — everything she could while she was with him. And she trusted that he would not only do the same, but would never betray her, as her ex had.

Scary thought, investing that kind of trust. Yet it was there.

He put the foil wrapper beside them and turned his focus back to her. "Top or bottom?" he asked, with a wicked grin.

She ran her finger over his cheek. "You choose."

"Neither," he said in a gruff voice and pulled her against him. Lying on his side, he eased his body around hers, spoonlike, her backside pressed against his erection.

She swallowed hard, but relaxed into him, allowing his arms and his body heat to cocoon her in a haze of growing desire.

"You're so damn sexy," he whispered in her ear.

She'd never been called that before. Never thought of herself in quite those terms, yet around Coop she felt that way. Saw herself as he did.

"Bend your knee."

She did as he asked, parting her thighs, giving him complete access. He slid his hand between them and slipped his finger inside her. She was hot and wet and ready for him, and the pressure from this backward angle was intense. With his lips on her neck, his breath hot against her skin, he opened her sheath and pushed himself deep inside, expelling a harsh groan of pleasure, and holding her tight.

It had been a while for Lexie and it hurt for an instant, but as if he sensed her discomfort, he thrust in and stopped, waiting for her to adjust.

"You okay?" he asked.

The pressure eased and pleasure slowly consumed her. She shifted slightly and sighed. "Oh, yes."

He cupped her breast in one hand, his fingertips toying with her sensitive nipples, torturing her and yet pleasuring her at the same time. Lexie felt the pull from her chest all the way to between her thighs, causing her to squeeze herself around him and seek harder, deeper pleasure.

Coop took the hint. He grabbed on to her waist and began to move inside her, sliding in and out, pumping his hips against hers and all the while, whispering how damn good she felt in her ear.

The position was new to her and the angle increased his penetration. Each thrust took her higher until she couldn't stand it. She grabbed on to the headboard with one hand and held on as he moved into her over and over again, until she was whimpering with need and close to coming.

Without warning, he pulled out and rolled

her onto her back, coming over her and thrusting back inside before she could think or even breathe.

"I need to see your face when you come," he said between long kisses.

God, even his words made her burn hotter.

She wanted to see his face when he came, too, and she wanted it now. She lifted her legs, pulling him in deeper, her gaze never leaving his. He began to move, gliding his body out then in, making certain he stayed long enough to grind hard against just the right spot. He brought her closer and closer to the edge, keeping up the pace and the pressure, watching her each time he thrust deep.

Lexie felt full to bursting and yet it wasn't enough. "I need —"

"What?" he asked, his eyes gleaming with heat.

"You. Harder. Now." She forced the embarrassing words out and a pleased, aroused smile tipped his lips.

He paused long enough to take her hands and raise them over her head. "Hold on to the headboard."

She reached back and wrapped her hands around the cold metal bars. He inclined his head with a brief nod and leaned forward to kiss her once more. Then, he braced his hands on either side of her head and did as she'd asked — drove inside her faster and harder than before, not stopping to breathe, taking her higher and higher, just as she'd wanted.

Their breath mingled, harsh sounds that only served to heighten sensation until she couldn't think, could barely breathe and white-hot flashes sparkled in her head and pleasure consumed her entire body in a blinding, spectacular release that never seemed to end.

"That's it," he said, his voice rough and sexy in her ear. "Keep coming."

And somehow she did, taking him right along with her.

CHAPTER EIGHT

Coop returned from the bathroom and collapsed on top of Lexie. She accepted his weight, enjoying the feel of his hot skin against hers, even if she could barely breathe.

"Coop." She tapped his shoulder and he rolled to his side, taking her with him.

"Sorry. Didn't mean to crush you. Are you alive?" he asked, his breathing still labored.

"Barely." Lexie flexed her toes, feeling sore all over. "But in a good way. In an amazing way, actually." She curled against him and, to her surprise, his body twitched in response.

"So fast?" she asked, unable to hold back a laugh. Damn, she had some effect on him, she thought with no small amount of feminine pride.

"I knew we'd be good together, but that was beyond."

Pleased, she relaxed into him and inhaled

deep, taking in the musky scent of man and sex lingering in the room. Coop held her, his groin twitching against her back, but clearly his thing and his brain weren't on the same page, because his limbs grew heavy and his breathing deepened.

After a few minutes, she realized he'd fallen asleep.

So he was one of those men, she mused. Sex relaxed him. Not so for her. Sex wired her. She lay staring at the ceiling and decided she needed to work off her excess energy.

Getting up from the bed she contemplated whether she ought to leave and immediately decided against it. Coop hadn't given her any reason to think he didn't want her here when he woke up. She glanced over at the bed where he lay sprawled on top of the covers. His tanned skin stood out in contrast to the white sheets and she couldn't help but be drawn to him.

He was so handsome, generous, sexy and caring. No, Lexie thought as she listened to the sound of his breathing, she wasn't leaving because she wasn't finished with him yet.

Instead of her halter and shorts, she pulled her underwear and his T-shirt on, comfortably happy when it fell to midthigh. Then she headed to the other room. From his bookshelf, she pulled a copy of his novel, *Street,* the murder mystery he'd had published, and settled onto the couch to work. Unfortunately, she wasn't able to get an Internet connection on her machine because he had a locked modem and she'd need his password to get in. And she wasn't about to wake him to ask for it.

His laptop sat on the table where she'd left it and she couldn't imagine him minding if she worked there, considering he'd let her play around with it earlier. But a quick check told her the darn thing was still running the defrag program, so she couldn't work there.

She glanced around and caught sight of the desktop PC in the corner. She'd noticed it the other day when she'd helped him clean his apartment. She decided he wouldn't mind if she used it for a little while.

She sat down on the chair, glad it was covered in fabric and not cool leather. A quick shift of the mouse and the large screen came into view.

"Excellent," she said aloud.

But instead of the desktop screen, Lexie came face-to-face with a Word document.

Notes on the Ring, the top line of the page read.

Lexie bit down on the inside of her cheek and continued reading. The page detailed a famous jewelry designer, Trifari, known for the insignia inside the shank of its rings. She scanned farther down and noticed a reference to a robbery known as the Lancaster jewel heist. Probably an inside job, accomplished during a dinner party given the same evening as the theft. Probable suspects originally included anyone in the home that night, but the entire staff had been questioned by the police, their whereabouts accounted for, and all had been exonerated.

The police suspected a ring of highly skilled thieves who posed as staff for the evening, including the chauffeur. All three had disappeared without a trace. *Coincidence,* Coop had written. *Or could the chauffeur be Lexie's grandfather?*

And then another question jumped out at her from the bottom of the page. *True crime or fiction story — which will hit bigger?*

Betrayal coursed through her.

Well, to hell with not waking him. Lexie stormed into the bedroom, turned on the bedside lamp, picked up a pillow and tossed it at Coop.

"What the — ?" He bolted upright in bed.

"What's wrong?"

Lexie perched her hands on her hips and glared at him. "You are, if you think you can use my grandparents as fodder for your career or a stepping-stone to bestseller status!" She swallowed over the tears that always formed when she was blinding mad.

She wouldn't let herself be distracted by his hard body or sexy, sleepy good looks or by the fact that they'd just shared incredible sex. And to think she'd told herself she could *trust* the man.

"Well? Talk to me," Lexie demanded.

Coop forced his mind to focus on what she was saying. One minute he'd been fast asleep and the next she'd slammed him with a pillow and begun hurling accusations and demanding answers.

She didn't bear even a passing resemblance to the pliant sensual woman who had shared his bed earlier.

He pulled the covers over his naked body, not because he was embarrassed but because he even found her anger sexy, and he doubted she'd appreciate seeing the evidence.

"Exactly how did you come to these conclusions?" he asked.

"I couldn't sleep and decided to start working on your Web site. When I couldn't get an Internet connection on my laptop and yours was still running scans, I decided to use your desktop instead."

He exhaled a long groan. He couldn't accuse her of snooping. He'd left his notes up on the screen. "If you'll calm down, I can explain."

"I'll bet you can," she said, her tone laced with sarcasm.

"Lexie?" he asked, deceptively calm.

"What?"

"Sit down and be quiet for five minutes." He pointed to the edge of the bed.

Glaring, she flopped onto the side of the mattress, far from him.

He wanted her to calm down and think clearly, something she wouldn't do if she were steaming mad and working up a snarky answer to everything he said.

"You knew I was going to be looking into the history of the jewels, remember?"

She folded her arms across her chest. "And sharing what you learned. I don't recall your mentioning that I was right about the Lancaster family or that they were the ones who owned the jewels. Especially not before you slept with me!"

He clenched his jaw. "Because I wanted to find out more first. I was hoping I'd discover something that exonerated your grandfather so that by the time you found out there'd be nothing for you to worry about." Surely she'd understand his looking out for her.

Her scowl told him otherwise. "I don't need you babying me. I can handle whatever you find as soon as you find it."

"Stubborn woman." He shook his head and leaned back against the headboard. "Fine. Next time I find out something I'll tell you. Are you satisfied?"

She raised an eyebrow. "Are you kidding? We haven't even gotten to the part about how you're planning to write this story!"

Coop pinched the bridge of his nose. "Lexie," he said, holding on to his patience. "I'm a reporter. What did you think I'd do with an unsolved crime mystery?"

"I sure as heck didn't think you'd use my family to build your career!" Her voice cracked with emotion, but she clearly refused to show any weakness. Instead, she remained at the edge of the bed, stiff with anger.

A part of him didn't blame her. This was her family he was talking about and of course she'd be protective. But the rational part of him still wanted to get through to her.

"My reporting career is fine with or without this story," he felt compelled to remind her.

"But your novelist career isn't."

He winced. "Low blow."

"So is this!" She gestured wildly toward the outer room, but not before he'd seen the flash of guilt in her eyes.

She hadn't meant the hurled insult, after all. Which was not to say it didn't sting. "Let's just get some sleep," he suggested before either of them said anything else they might later regret.

She turned to face him. "Promise me you won't write the story if it involves my family."

He finally had an idea that not only clicked for fiction work, but also might be a huge crime revelation. "I can't. I need to see this thing through before I make any decisions."

She glared at him.

"I'm being honest, which is what you want from me, right?"

Lexie sighed. "What I want is for this mess to go away."

He understood her feelings. "I didn't create it."

She merely inclined her head.

"I think we should get some sleep and deal with things in the morning." He patted the space beside him.

Despite his clear invitation, he expected her to get dressed and go home. To his surprise, she climbed into the free side of the bed, punched the pillows and curled into a ball, facing away from him.

As he shut off the lamp, Coop didn't know whether to call it progress or not, and decided he'd find out in the morning.

Lexie woke up long before Coop thought she did. She wasn't a morning person and no good could come of another argument when she was more likely to act on emotion than fact. As she'd done after reading his personal notes last night.

Of course she'd known he was a reporter and a writer and he'd use whatever he discovered. But that didn't mean she had to like it or that she wouldn't do whatever she could to prevent him from doing so. One step at a time, she thought.

The first step was to pull herself together. So when she first opened her eyes and sensed him beside her, she feigned sleep until he rose, showered and walked out of the room. Only then did she stretch and let her body come awake. She showered and dressed again in yesterday's clothes. Then, praying that Coop had made coffee, she drew a deep breath and headed into the kitchen to face him.

As soon as she stepped out of the bedroom, the smell of breakfast assaulted her senses. A quick glance told her he'd set the table and now stood at the stove flipping an omelet in a pan.

"He cooks as well as makes coffee," she said, taking in the full pot in the coffeemaker. "How did I get so fortunate?"

"Just lucky, I guess." Coop eyed her warily, judging her mood. "Have a seat."

One omelet waited for her at the table and Lexie eased herself into a seat.

He put the next omelet onto a plate, set it down on the table, poured two cups of coffee and joined her. "I'll take the one that's been sitting." Before she could argue, he reached out and exchanged his plate for hers.

"I would have eaten that one."

"I don't mind if it's cooled off some. You eat the hot one," he said and began to eat.

"Thanks." Lexie picked up her fork, but couldn't manage a bite over her queasy stomach. She'd had some awkward *morning afters* before, but none with a guy she really liked and had shared spectacular sex with.

The prolonged silence sliced through her until she couldn't stand it another minute.

"Sorry I woke you last night." Her gaze remained on the omelet he'd generously cooked despite her bad behavior.

"What about throwing a pillow at me? Are you sorry for that, too?"

Embarrassed, she raised her gaze only to find him grinning at her.

The knot in her stomach eased. "I guess you don't hold a grudge?" she asked.

"Takes a lot to royally piss me off," he said, between mouthfuls. "Your not eating my food might send me over the edge." He waved his fork, gesturing for her to dig in.

She shrugged and started breakfast, surprised to find the eggs fluffy and delicious. "My God, you're good."

"I recall your saying something to that effect last night." He winked at her, then continued. "Actually, my mom taught me. She said it wouldn't kill me to learn to feed myself."

She caught both the affection and the wistfulness in his tone. "You miss her a lot, don't you?"

Coop nodded. "My family sort of divided in half in that my father understands my brother's mind-set a lot better than mine. My mom used to get me."

"What happened, if you don't mind me asking?"

"She had a brain aneurysm about five years ago. She died in her sleep. No warning, no nothing."

Lexie shuddered. She might not have a warm, fuzzy relationship with her own mother, but she did with her grandmother and she couldn't imagine his pain. "I'm so sorry."

"Thank you."

"You're welcome." She cleared her throat. "So what's on your agenda today?"

"I have to get to work, but I thought I'd pick you up from your grandmother's afterwards and we could go talk to Ricky together."

Lexie had finished eating and Coop rose to clear the dishes. She stood and waved him away. "Oh, no. I've got this. You can go get ready for work. I'll clean up and head out. I have to stop by the Hot Zone offices for a meeting and it's easier for me to leave from here than to go home — if that's okay."

Coop nodded. "It's fine." More than fine, he thought. He hadn't known what to expect from her this morning.

He'd sensed from her breathing that she'd been awake when he'd gotten up, but she hadn't wanted him to know, so he'd let her pretend to be asleep, giving her more time and space. Now, though the wariness hadn't left her gaze, she was speaking to him in civil tones and not rushing out of there.

He helped her bring the plates into the kitchen, but let her rinse and put them in the dishwasher, since she seemed to want to do her share. Either that or cleaning was a way of avoiding him. Whether or not they were discussing it, she was obviously upset with him. Coop didn't hold on to hope that she understood his driving need to dig into this story or even write about it, but at least it wasn't an overt source of contention between them.

"Is it okay if I take a copy of your book with me? I want to read it. It will help me design your site," Lexie said as she dried her hands on a towel.

He nodded. "Take the one on the bookshelf. I have extra copies in storage."

He tried not to squirm at the thought of her reading his work. After all, publication *meant* his words were out there for consumption. But Lexie's opinion of him and his writing mattered, probably more than it should.

"I've been thinking," she said, interrupting his thoughts. "Now that we know the ring really is stolen, there's a good chance that the necklace is, too. Which means my grandmother's in possession of stolen property. I need to talk to her and at least prepare her for the possibility that she might have to give the necklace back." She leaned against the same counter he'd sat her on last night.

He shifted, pushing those memories out of his head before his body reacted more than it already was.

Her grandmother losing her necklace wasn't something he'd wanted to bring up, and Coop was glad she'd come to the decision on her own.

"Let me come with you when you tell her. Maybe I can help soften the blow."

Lexie shook her head, her eyes sad. "The necklace's personal for her. Maybe she'll want to be alone when I break the news."

Coop narrowed his gaze. He'd met Charlotte and, despite her age, she wasn't frail; nor was she irrationally emotional. He had a hunch she wouldn't mind having Coop there, despite Lexie's claim. Which meant it was Lexie who didn't want him there.

Because she was trying to keep an emotional wall between them, something he refused to allow. "Come on, Lex. She likes me. Hell, she already considers me a member of the family," he said with a grin meant to disarm her. "I'm sure she'd appreciate the moral support."

Coop's words were one thing. His goal another. In reality, he wanted to be there more for Lexie than for Charlotte. He'd already hurt her by not giving up the story and as their research and questioning progressed, harmful information might arise. He wanted to be there to help her through.

He could tell from her stiff posture and the uncomfortable silences that she no longer trusted him the way she had before. And she probably hadn't completely forgiven him, either. But Coop was a journalist used to digging for information and working to get what he wanted. He enjoyed a challenge and he wasn't giving up on Lexie.

He missed the comfortable woman who'd twirled lo mein in her chopsticks and talked a mile a minute between mouthfuls, laughing and smiling the entire time. He craved the soft, pliant female who'd come apart on his kitchen counter and again in his bed.

Coop never gave up. Eventually, he'd get her to soften toward him again. "What's it going to be? I'll meet you at your grandmother's?"

She opened her mouth, ready to argue, then closed it again. "Fine, if that's what you want to do. Be there around noon. My meeting should be over by then."

He nodded, satisfied that she'd agreed.

Though he already had an interview scheduled at noon, he'd just push it up or back, making Lexie his priority. "Afterwards we can go back downtown together and stop by the Vintage Jewelers to talk to Ricky. Okay?"

A muscle worked in her jaw. "Sure," she said at last.

She wasn't throwing pillows or eggs at him, but she was nowhere near ready to let her guard down. Coop was equally determined to stick by her side during their free time until he'd gotten past her walls.

He glanced at the clock on the microwave and muttered a curse. "I need to get going." Without hesitating, he wrapped his hand around the back of her neck and pulled her toward him for a goodbye kiss.

And not a quick peck, but a long, drawn-out, lip-locking, tongue-dueling, *don't forget what we shared last night* kind of kiss.

Lexie was feeling closed in. Stressed by circumstances beyond her control, she needed time and space to think about her incredible night with Coop and the revelations she'd discovered afterwards. She also wanted to figure out a way to break the news to her grandmother about the stolen jewels and her grandfather's possible role in the theft. Normally, when she felt trapped, she hopped on a plane.

That wasn't an option this time, though she couldn't deny the desire to see wide-open spaces somewhere in the world. But not when she was so embroiled in this mystery and . . . yes, with Coop. She couldn't concentrate on work, so she canceled her appointment at the Hot Zone. Instead of heading home, she decided to do the next best thing to flying away.

Lexie found herself at the Empire State Building. She passed through security and purchased her ticket. Although early in the morning, the tourist site was already filling up, the lines beginning to form for the high-speed elevators. Lexie didn't mind. The hum of voices kept her company as she headed to the eighty-sixth floor observatory, a place she'd come many times before. It was always worth the wait and the price of admission.

Lexie used this place as her personal think tank whenever she was home and felt the world crowding her. The view through the windows provided a balm for her sanity. She knew the statistics by heart, but it never ceased to amaze her. On a clear day like today you could see for eighty miles. The sky was blue and seemed to flow endlessly over the rooftops, reaching out toward Connecticut, New Jersey, Pennsylvania, even Massachusetts.

She remembered her first trip here with her grandmother. As one of her "playing hooky" moments to avoid a skating lesson, they'd taken the fast elevators together. Her grandmother had held her hand and told her to lean her forehead against the cool windows.

Lexie repeated the action now, touching her head to the glass pane and closing her eyes. When she opened them again, she felt as though she were suspended in midair over the glorious city below. She inhaled deeply and waited for all her problems to float away. The breathless sensation she'd anticipated filled her for a little while, but soon her mind drifted to Coop and the feel of his lips on hers, the memory of his body deep inside her own and the uninhibited way she'd responded.

She couldn't allow herself to forget that he had an agenda of his own. The bigger the story about the ring turned out to be, the more invested Coop the reporter would become. Not to mention Coop the fiction writer. His interest was completely at odds with her own.

And that of her grandmother. Which led

to the next thing that preoccupied her thoughts. How to tell Charlotte that her beloved husband might have been involved in a house robbery and her precious necklace might have to be returned to its rightful owner. Suddenly, the endless blue sky and expanse of sun no longer held the same appeal.

Reality awaited her and Lexie had no choice but to deal with it the best way she knew how. Head-on confrontation. Which also reminded her that she needed to reprimand her grandmother for spying on her and Coop, snapping pictures like a voyeur and sending them off to the Bachelor Blog for public consumption.

She righted herself and stood for a few minutes, waiting for the light-headed sensation to end. Taking one last look at the incredible skyline, she turned and headed for the elevators.

She wondered what Coop would think of the view and realized she'd like to share her special place with him and watch his reaction to the city they both loved. A chill rushed through her, the idea leaving her shaken and yet giddy at the same time.

Lexie arrived back at her grandmother's with plenty of time to spare before Coop would show up for lunch. She needed to shower, change and maybe even sit her grandmother down and start the awkward conversation they needed to have. But Charlotte wasn't alone. Sylvia had just put hair dye onto her grandmother's scalp and it looked like Charlotte was about to return the favor.

Lexie glanced at the two women. "Didn't I call and say Coop and I were coming by for lunch?" She'd suggested that he pick up deli sandwiches from her grandmother's favorite restaurant on his way and he'd agreed.

Her grandmother nodded. "And we're getting ready!"

"I can see that." Lexie glanced at the purple dye in Sylvia's hair.

"Someone didn't come home last night!" Charlotte said, a twinkle in her eye.

Though she was an adult, Lexie flushed. Until now, living with her favorite relative had never caused a crimp in Lexie's social life. She'd always been thoughtful about checking in with her grandmother, just to keep her from worrying. Yet last night she'd been so consumed with Coop that all rational thought had fled from her mind. She'd never been so head over heels in lust before that she'd stayed out all night, forgetting about what her grandmother might think.

That, too, was telling.

"I hope you didn't worry," Lexie said, concerned that she'd stressed her grandmother.

Charlotte dismissed the notion with an unladylike snort. "Of course not. I knew you were in good hands!"

If her grandmother only knew how good. Thoughts of the kitchen counter immediately came to mind and another heated blush crept up her face.

"Grandma, I heard the Bachelor Blogger posted an interesting picture yesterday. Would you happen to know anything about that?" Lexie asked, changing the subject.

Charlotte and Sylvia exchanged fleeting glances.

"Of course not," her grandmother said.

Lexie raised a disbelieving eyebrow. "Oh, really?"

"Really. Your grandmother would never send a picture of you kissing Coop." Sylvia slapped her free hand over her mouth.

"Kissing? Was that yesterday's blog? I hadn't had a chance to check it out for myself." Charlotte shot Sylvia a disgusted look before attempting to cover.

"Me, neither, but that's what Coop told me, too," Lexie said. "What's interesting is we'd only kissed twice. Once here and the other time we were completely alone." She directed her pointed comment at her grandmother. "I don't appreciate you snooping or making my private life public. And on that note, I'm going to shower." Lexie stepped backwards out of the room, keeping a watch on the two women the entire time.

To Charlotte's credit, she didn't flinch. "Sylvia's staying for lunch, dear."

Lexie paused. As much as she adored her grandmother's friend, some news was better broken in private. "Coop and I have a lot to discuss with you," Lexie said to her grandmother, trying not to insult the other woman Lexie considered family.

"No worries. Whatever you have to say I'd just tell Sylvia anyway," Charlotte said.

In this case, Lexie wasn't so sure, but she forced a smile.

"But if you need a private lunch I understand," Sylvia said as she walked to the sink and rinsed her hands.

"Nonsense. You're my person. You know all my secrets, so you're staying," Charlotte said, hands perched on her hips.

Which meant there was no arguing, Lexie knew.

"You're more than welcome any time, Sylvia," Lexie reassured the other woman.

"Coop will be here around noon." Which gave them a couple of hours to finish their hair and get decent, and Lexie time to put her night with Coop into perspective.

As if such a thing were even possible.

Chapter Nine

Though Lexie had agreed to let Coop come over, it had been grudgingly and he felt pretty sure she wouldn't welcome him with open arms. He stopped not only for deli but for flowers, too, hoping to smooth things over between them. Coop wasn't a flowers and chocolates kind of guy. He'd never given much thought to the whole kiss-and-make-up thing, either, but in Lexie's case he wanted whatever time he had with her too badly to let her stay angry.

He arrived twenty minutes late, thanks to a long line at the deli, and rang the bell.

The large black door swung open and Lexie stood on the other side. She had on white walking shorts and a ruffled tank top. Her hair had been pulled into a short ponytail and cute wisps of hair framed her face. As expected, desire kicked him in the gut.

Also as expected, she didn't look pleased

to see him. "You're late" were the first words out of her mouth.

The same mouth he wanted to greet with a kiss, but he refrained. "But I come bearing gifts." He held out the flowers in one hand and the bag of food in the other.

"Thank you." A flash of appreciation lit up her face, but when loud cackles sounded from inside, the joy faded.

"I hope they're not too drunk to enjoy the food," Lexie muttered and stepped aside to let him pass through.

"Did you say *drunk?*" Coop asked.

Lexie sighed. "See for yourself." She waved a hand and he headed into the violet-scented apartment. She took the flowers and the food and said, "I'll put these in water and get lunch on the table. The sooner they eat, the sooner they'll sober up. You can go deal with them in the meantime."

Coop found Charlotte and another woman in the den with an odd-shaped bottle set on the table in front of them. "Oh, there he is! Isn't he even more handsome in person?" Charlotte said, more than asked.

"You flatter me." He stepped forward and leaned over to kiss Lexie's grandmother on the cheek. A streak of dark coloring ran from her temple toward her ear. Her hair appeared a darker eggplant color, instead of the bright red he'd seen the other day. "You look lovely. And who is your friend?" Coop asked.

"Sam Cooper, this is my best friend Sylvia Krinsky. Sylvia, this is *the* Bachelor."

"So nice to meet you!" Sylvia, whose hair was the same color as Charlotte's, rose to shake his hand.

"Same here."

"Sit." Charlotte patted the seat beside her. She hiccupped. "Excuse me," she said on a giggle.

"I see you started the party without me," he said, eyeing the bottle of Manischewitz, a brand of traditional Jewish wine.

"Yes, well what's deli food without a nice glass of vino to go with it?" Sylvia asked. "And Manischewitz is the wine of champions!"

"I don't think that's their slogan," Charlotte said, her words ending on another hiccup. "Excuse me."

"Well, it should be."

"Lunch is ready!" Lexie called from the kitchen.

"Did you hear that? Food is served."

And from the ladies' giggles between sentences, Lexie was right. It was none too soon.

Coop settled into the seat at the head of

the table, as Charlotte insisted. He decided to take his cues from Lexie about how much to reveal to the women and when. Apparently, Lexie wanted to eat first and talk later, hoping to sober them up, no doubt. But Charlotte and Sylvia continued to pass the bottle of wine back and forth between them. Coop figured the wine might loosen their lips about whatever they knew of the jewels.

Lexie didn't seem as certain. She eyed the women with concern and ate in silence. Not that either he or Lexie could get a word in anyway. Charlotte and Sylvia chattered non-stop.

"So, Grandma, I need to talk to you about your necklace," Lexie finally said, interrupting them when she saw an opportunity.

Charlotte's hand went to her empty neck. "Oops, not wearing it today. Today was hair day," she explained to Coop. "Sylvia and I do each other's dye jobs in order to save money on those expensive salons." She patted her hair with one hand.

"I completely understand," he said to the older woman before turning to Lexie. "Where do you want to start?" he asked.

"At the beginning. Grandma, remember how you were watching on TV when Coop received the ring?" Lexie clenched her hands together, her knuckles turning white under the strain.

"Oh, yes! I knew right then and there you'd be the perfect man for my granddaughter. I'm not getting any younger, you know, and it would be nice to have her settled before I pass on." Charlotte drew her hands to her heart in true dramatic fashion.

"Gran! Cut that out," Lexie said, appalled.

Coop wasn't sure what bothered her more, the fact that Charlotte was still pairing them up as a long-term couple or her talk of dying one day soon.

Lexie exhaled hard. "Let's try to focus, okay?"

Charlotte's head bobbed up and down.

Sylvia's did as well.

"Good. Coop, why don't you explain what you found out about the ring," Lexie suggested.

Charlotte and Sylvia closed their mouths and leaned forward in their seats, clearly interested in his story.

Just as he was interested in Charlotte's reaction. "After I chose the ring, I returned to my office and showed it to my style editor. She immediately recognized it as a valuable piece of a collection. Trifari, she said it was called." Coop never took his gaze off Lexie's grandmother.

Wide-eyed, Charlotte listened without comment.

"Go on," Lexie urged.

"Yes, do," Charlotte said.

"A little research turned up something very interesting."

"It was part of a set and my necklace is the match?" Charlotte asked, sounding proud of herself for making the connection.

"I wish it was that simple, Grandma. I need you to listen to what Coop says and please don't get upset. We need to watch out for your blood pressure." Lexie's warm eyes filled with concern.

"My blood pressure's fine. Medication's controlling it and you worry too much. Go on, Coop," Charlotte demanded.

A quick glance at Lexie confirmed that that's exactly what she wanted him to do.

"The ring appears to be part of a collection of jewelry that does include your necklace."

"Aha!" Charlotte pumped her frail arm in victory. "I was right."

Lexie groaned and rolled her eyes.

"But the entire set was stolen during a brazen house robbery in the 1950s. The set disappeared and the thieves were never caught," Coop explained.

Charlotte fingered the paper napkin on the table, crumpling it into a ball. "Then whoever stole it probably turned it over to a fence and I bet that's how my Henry got the necklace."

Lexie frowned and adjusted her glasses, something he noticed she did when deep in thought. "I thought you said Grandpa was given the necklace as payment for chauffeuring services."

Coop had been about to call the other woman on the same thing.

"Exactly. Whoever gave your grandfather the necklace probably got it from a fence," Charlotte said, amending her new story to suit the facts.

"Makes complete sense to me," Sylvia said.

They reminded him of a comedy pair. Laverne and Shirley or Lucy and Ethel came to mind.

Coop rubbed his eyes with his palms. Their banter was getting to him as well. "Ladies, that would work except for one important detail. The family who originally owned the jewels and from whom they were stolen was named Lancaster and lived in Manhattan."

Lexie nodded. "And I remember mentioning the other day that Sylvia once said

206

Grandpa worked for a family named Lancaster."

Charlotte's lips pursed in a pout. "As I recall, I said I don't remember that name or conversation. What's the point of all this?" She began fanning herself with the rumpled napkin. "Is it warm in here?"

"Grandma, are you okay?" Lexie rose from her chair.

"I'm fine. Just suddenly overheated from the wine."

"Which is why you shouldn't be drinking." Lexie began clearing the table, starting with the wineglasses and bottle, carrying them to the sink far from Sylvia and Charlotte's reach.

"The Surgeon General says one glass of red wine is good for your heart!" Charlotte said.

"I'm sure half a bottle of Manischewitz Concord Grape exceeds the recommended daily allowance," Lexie said.

"Get back to the point. I need to know what it is you're suggesting," Charlotte said, her eyes narrowed.

Lexie drew a deep breath. "That maybe Grandpa didn't actually get the necklace as payment. Maybe he just said he did. Maybe he —"

"You think your grandfather was a thief?"

Charlotte asked, her voice rising, clearly appalled at the notion.

Lexie rushed over and put a comforting hand on her grandmother's shoulder. "Grandma, I'm not saying that at all. Of course, I don't believe it. But if it appears that way on the face of things, then we need to dig deeper and clear his name!"

The pain in Lexie's face sliced through Coop unexpectedly.

"What's the point?" Sylvia asked. "Obviously, nobody has looked into that case in years. Why would they start now?"

Lexie's gaze fell to Coop and he squirmed in his seat. They both knew he'd be digging up the past and he waited for Lexie to out him.

She kept her hand on her grandmother's shoulder in support. "It turns out that, although Coop got the ring from a woman, the actual owner of the store is a man. And he's called Coop more than once trying to get the ring back."

Lexie didn't meet Coop's surprised stare. She hadn't told her grandmother that he was planning to write this story, and he couldn't imagine why she'd covered for him.

Before he could process the thought, Sylvia began to cough.

Charlotte jumped up and slapped her

friend hard on the back.

"Watch it. You'll crack a rib," Sylvia muttered.

"Are you okay?" Coop asked.

Lexie hovered on the other side of Sylvia's chair.

"I'm fine. Choked on my own spit." The older woman dabbed at her damp eyes with a napkin.

Coop glanced at the toasted older women and knew they wouldn't be getting any lucid information from them today. "I think you ladies should lie down and take a nap," he suggested.

"That's a good idea." Lexie helped Sylvia up from her chair, then Charlotte. "Coop and I will take care of things here."

As Coop watched the two women depart, he had the definite sense they knew more than they were telling. He just didn't know what. Or whether Lexie would see past her worry for her grandmother and believe Coop's instincts, which had never failed him before.

It didn't take long to straighten up the kitchen after lunch and Coop helped Lexie, respecting her obvious need for silence. Lexie was grateful for the short time to gather her thoughts. The pretty flowers he'd bought sat in a vase on the counter, reminding her that he wasn't a complete jerk. Just a self-centered one whose story meant more to him than her grandmother's feelings.

"I see you have your hands full with those two." Coop broke the silence, speaking of her grandmother and Sylvia.

"Tell me something I don't know." She blew her hair out of her face. "And I never got a chance to tell my grandmother that her necklace is stolen property and she'll likely have to return it."

Coop nodded. "There's time for that." He placed his hand on her back, the innocent touch immediately turning hot as awareness sizzled through her.

His eyes darkened to a hue she recognized from last night.

Lexie swallowed hard. How was it that this man had such an overwhelming effect on her?

"Let's sit," Coop said, his voice rough. "We need to talk."

His jaw was taut. Not a good sign.

"What's wrong?" she asked.

"Come." His hand still on the small of her back, he guided her toward one of the kitchen chairs.

"Would you rather sit in the family room where it's more comfortable?"

He shook his head. "It's more private in here. I don't want your grandmother to overhear."

Uh-oh.

Lexie lowered herself into her seat. "What's going on?"

Coop straddled the chair next to her, looking sexier than any man had the right to. "First things first. Why didn't you give me up? You could have told your grandmother about my story, but you didn't."

She'd wondered that herself. "Don't get the wrong idea. I wasn't looking out for you. I was looking out for her. I figured she'd have enough to deal with today without adding that to the mix." Which had been the initial reason she'd given herself.

There was another, more personal reason as well.

"Is that it?" Coop pushed.

Damn the reporter in him.

"Fine. My grandmother likes you." And that mattered to Lexie more than it should. "I didn't want to disillusion her."

Coop cleared his throat. "I don't think your grandmother has as many illusions about life as you think."

Lexie narrowed her gaze. "What exactly does that mean?"

"You said yourself that she and Sylvia have

been acting strangely lately, right?"

"So?" She locked her jaw, certain she wouldn't like the direction in which he was headed.

"Well, didn't you notice how quickly Charlotte came up with the fence story as an explanation? Before we even asked her how your grandfather would have come into possession of stolen goods, she offered an answer."

"She's a quick thinker."

Coop leaned in closer.

The masculine and oh-so-familiar scent of his aftershave sent her senses and her body into overdrive. Tamping down arousal in favor of rational thought wasn't easy, but she tried.

"And when we tied the robbery to the Lancaster family, she played dumb and claimed she didn't remember any such name."

Coop's satisfied expression made Lexie uneasy. "How do you know she doesn't remember? Maybe she's telling the truth. Ever think of that, Mr. Hotshot Reporter?" Defending her grandmother came naturally to Lexie. She'd done it often enough with her parents over the years, offering explanations for her over-the-top behavior. Now was no different.

Coop exhaled a frustrated groan. "Every time the Lancaster name comes up, your grandmother either changes the subject or gets sick."

"She said she was *warm,* Coop. Not sick."

"As a diversion maybe? I can't prove it or explain it, but I have a hunch that she knows more than she's saying."

Much as Lexie wanted to deny Coop's belief and continue in her defense, she wondered about the possible truth in his words.

Her grandmother *had* been acting odd lately. The woman had a memory like a steel trap for the most minute details from the past, and Lexie had seen no indications that Charlotte was getting forgetful. Except for this convenient memory lapse. And what were the chances Charlotte had forgotten the name of the family her grandfather worked for, let alone gotten her beloved necklace from?

Lexie shifted in her seat, uneasy but unwilling to admit as much to Coop, who had his own agenda. She had no intention of helping him build a case — or a book — about her family. Whichever member happened to be involved.

He cleared his throat, obviously waiting for her to say more. "How about we agree not to discuss this right now. Instead we just continue digging into *facts*." Lexie would deal with whatever she discovered, as long as it was truth and not fiction or a reporter's hunch.

"Fair enough." Coop braced his hands on the top of the chair.

"First stop the Vintage Jewelers?" she asked. "After we each work this afternoon."

He inclined his head. "And then we go to Dad's bar for dinner."

Lexie immediately shook her head. Dinner with Coop, alone time, intimate time, no longer seemed like a smart idea. Even if she wanted him as much, if not more than she had before, their competing agendas made any kind of relationship just plain stupid.

Coop stood. "Suit yourself. I just want to see if he can get us access to the old case files on the robbery."

Not a dinner *date*. She'd jumped to the wrong conclusion. Embarrassment warred with disappointment, even though she'd turned him down.

She didn't want him investigating without her. "Umm, I can move some things around and go with you." She bit the inside of her cheek hard.

"Great. I'll make sure Dad has a table

waiting." He winked at her.

And that's when she knew. He'd cornered her into exactly what she'd been trying to avoid. Intimate, alone time with a man she craved like crazy. She wasn't as annoyed as she should have been, which probably made her insane.

Ricky hid in the back of his own store, feeling more like a sneak than he had back in the day. He'd just come from the bank, leaving Anna in charge. He'd returned unannounced via the back entrance just as *they'd* walked in the front. He'd heard the chimes signaling customers and peered through the curtains separating the store from the office.

He hadn't recognized them right off. No, sir, they'd tried to disguise themselves, but he'd heard their voices when they'd asked about the ring Anna had given to that damn reporter and Ricky *knew.* He didn't have a plan yet, so he eavesdropped, watching and listening as his daughter fielded their questions.

"We saw the robbery on the news. It must have been so frightening for you."

Because he was named Ricky, the women had taken on nicknames when they'd all been a team. The one he'd nicknamed Lucy spoke first. Apparently, things hadn't changed. She was still the ringleader of the two. The other had been Ethel, the best friend and follower.

"I was just glad the robber didn't hurt my daughter," Anna said, her voice catching.

Ricky still broke into a sweat at the reminder that something could have happened to his daughter and granddaughter, the only things he'd done right in this lifetime.

Up front, the talk turned to families, seemingly normal conversation since most old people who came in to browse liked to chat about themselves. Not Ricky. He'd always been private, which had kept him out of trouble all these years. But he listened with interest, curious despite himself about his ex-partners' lives. Apparently, Lucy was widowed and had one child and Ethel was a widow without kids to keep her company in her old age. And, of course, they had each other, they explained to Anna, patting each other's hands. It was all Ricky could do not to puke.

He couldn't tell if the years had been kinder to them than they had to him, thanks to the scarves tied around their heads and the large black sunglasses covering half their faces.

Ricky almost laughed out loud and gave himself away.

"We're curious about the ring you gave that handsome reporter," Ethel chimed in, pulling Ricky's thoughts back to the matter at hand.

"You know, he's been named the latest Bachelor," Lucy said.

Still reading the gossip columns, Ricky thought to himself.

"He really didn't want to take a reward, but I insisted. He finally chose the ring. Whatever you want to know, I can't tell you much about it," Anna said.

Good girl, Ricky thought.

"Not even where you got it?" Ethel asked.

"You'd have to talk to my father. The ring was just one of many trinkets he collected over the years. I'm afraid he's something of a pack rat."

"I'll just bet he is," Lucy muttered.

"Excuse me?" Anna asked, surprised by her comment.

The old battle-ax. Still as feisty as ever.

"I said, I'll just bet he is. I saw on *Oprah* how more people than we realize have that serious psychological disorder. It can lead to hoarding," Lucy explained in a more serious tone.

Anna sighed. "I know. That's why I periodically sell things when Dad isn't looking."

"Is your father around?" Ethel asked, sounding nervous now.

"No, he went to the bank, but he should be back soon if you'd like to stay and talk to him," Anna offered.

Good thing Ricky had never remembered to put chimes on the back door as well as the front. Not even his daughter knew he'd returned.

"No, thank you," Lucy said. "We need to be going."

Ricky nodded. Yes, yes they did. Get out. Go away. Never come back.

"Oh, wait! Is that your father?" Ethel asked.

Ricky shut his eyes and swallowed a groan. On the wall behind Anna was a photograph.

"Yes, it is. That's my dad and Ed Koch, back when he was mayor of New York," Anna said proudly.

Ricky still recalled the night they'd met at a restaurant and his wife, bless her soul, had insisted that he and the mayor pose together. She'd later had the photo enlarged and framed. Then she'd hung it on the wall.

Ricky had forgotten all about it until now. The innocent picture gave Lucy and Ethel all the information they needed — that this was Ricky's store and the ring hadn't been passed around through the years, but had stayed in his hands.

The telephone rang and Anna excused herself to take the call. The phone was right behind her so she didn't have to come into the back, thank God.

"It was taken a long time ago," Ethel said. "But he was aging already." Ricky caught the glee in her tone.

"And not well. Look at that paunch. He's balding and that comb-over is laughable."

Lucy always was a bitch, Ricky thought, his hand going to the top of his now completely bald head. Behind those disguises he doubted they looked like cover models these days, either.

"I'm sorry for the interruption," Anna said, returning. "Did you like the ring? Maybe I can find you something similar."

"No, thank you. It was such an interesting-looking piece, we were just curious about its history," Lucy said. "But it was nice chatting with you, dear."

"Same here. Come back any time. You can talk to my father or maybe there will be something new that interests you!" Anna said in her cheery saleswoman voice.

Normally, Ricky was proud of her ability. Now, though, he cringed.

The jig was up.

He started to sweat, his mind whirling with scenarios of how to deal with the two women when the time came and they cornered him. And he knew for certain they would.

His gut — which had always told him when to do a job and when to get out — had warned him to be prepared for one of them to find him. Not both together. They'd been best friends until that night he'd gotten his kicks with Ethel. The last time Ricky had seen them they'd been rolling around the bedroom floor in what would be called a catfight these days.

Over him.

Coward that he was, he'd slipped out while they were still going at it. All these years he'd assumed they were enemies. Apparently, he'd been wrong, which made his situation even more precarious.

United, those two could make a grown man wet his pants.

CHAPTER TEN

Lexie and Coop struck out at the Vintage Jewelers. Anna told them her father had taken a sudden trip out of town. Gone fishing, she'd said, shaking her head, her annoyance clear. Until he returned, they'd get no new information on that end. Lexie hoped they did better asking Coop's father for a favor.

Only Coop had forgotten it was Ladies' Night at his father's bar. The place was crowded and the older Cooper was busy serving drinks. That meant Lexie and Coop had to hang out until things slowed down and Jack had time to talk. Thankfully, he had saved them the same table in the back.

Since she didn't know anyone at the bar and she had work to do, Lexie settled in. Coop went to order drinks and made the rounds, saying hello to people and chatting it up. Thanks to the preponderance of women hanging around and Coop's status as the Bachelor, all the ladies surrounded him, stopping to make conversation and gauge his interest. To his credit, his body language didn't lead any of the women on, but Lexie couldn't control the jealousy coursing through her anyway.

Deciding that the green monster didn't suit her, she pulled out her laptop and started to make notes on ideas she had for his site. Words that described him and his work. Though she still needed to read his novel, the *feel* of the site was something that came naturally to her. She always started with a color scheme, so she pulled up Pantone charts and from there it was easy to narrow down the ones that worked for her, but she picked a variety so he'd have a choice.

"You're back a second time. That's impressive. So my brother hasn't scared you away." Matt Cooper pulled up a chair and joined her.

She forced a smile, mostly because she was still stinging over the subject of Coop's next book. "Your brother and I have *business* together."

Matt raised an eyebrow. The inquisitive look gave him a resemblance to his brother, but not enough to eclipse Coop in the looks department. Matt was handsome, just not as drop-dead sexy as Coop. At least in Lexie's biased opinion.

"Personal business or private?" he asked.

Lexie rolled her eyes. "What is it with you Cooper brothers and asking questions?"

"It's in the blood." Matt grinned. "So?"

Lexie decided he wouldn't give up without an honest answer. "Both. But right now I'm working on his Web site." She didn't intend to reveal anything about the mystery of the ring. That was for Coop to do, not her.

"What kind of Web site does he need?" Matt asked, seemingly confused.

"He's a published author. Authors need Web sites." Wasn't that obvious? she wondered.

Matt's eyes opened wide and he let out a laugh. "Come on. His mystery writing is just a *hobby.* He's a crime reporter. That's what he does."

If Matt believed that, then he didn't know his brother well at all. Though she ought to bite her tongue, she couldn't. "Have you read his book?"

She should have bitten it harder.

"I'm not much of a reader." Matt glanced down at the scarred wooden table. At least he seemed embarrassed by his lack of interest.

"Did you buy a copy to support him?"

Lexie pushed.

He squirmed in his seat.

Clearly he didn't enjoy being on the other end of an interrogation, she thought, amused.

"They didn't print many copies. The book was hard to find," he finally replied.

Her amusement faded. "Not very brotherly of you." She reached into her oversize bag and pulled out the copy she'd taken from Coop's apartment. "Here. Read it." She shoved the book into his hand. She'd just have to get herself another one.

To her surprise, he burst out laughing. "I can see why my brother likes you. Beautiful, smart and loyal."

"You make me sound like a puppy dog!"

"Not at all. Just a step — make that an entire staircase — up from Coop's ex-wife. And not just because you're here in the flesh."

Lexie didn't want to get into a discussion of Coop's airline stewardess wife's traveling. "I'll take that as a compliment." She hoped Matt would leave it at that.

Coop walked over, joining them in what Lexie thought was just the nick of time. "Am I interrupting?" he asked, his gaze wandering from Lexie and landing squarely on Matt.

The flash of annoyance in his eyes told her he wasn't immune to the jealousy she'd experienced minutes earlier.

"I was just keeping the lady company. And now I need to get home to my wife." Matt took his time rising from his seat. He slapped his brother on the back, winked at Lexie and strode away laughing.

"Pain in the ass," Coop muttered. "I ordered burgers, fries and drinks. I hope that's okay."

Her stomach suddenly rumbled and she grinned. "Perfect, actually."

For the next few minutes, while they waited for the food to be served, Lexie and Coop discussed the tone he was looking for his Web site to convey. He took a brief look at the color combinations she'd come up with, but the bar lighting wasn't good enough for him to make an informed choice, so they tabled the discussion for another time.

Then they enjoyed dinner while talking about things in general, nothing about the ring or her grandmother or anything threatening. They confirmed they shared similar taste in music and movies, since Lexie preferred action thrillers to chick flicks and they each loved a good comedy.

Being with Coop was easier than being

with any man she could remember and the sexual tension was ever present. She might still be annoyed with him, but she couldn't deny how much she wanted him.

He pushed his plate away and leaned back in his seat. "I'm stuffed."

She laughed. "Me, too. Your father makes a delicious burger."

"Make sure you tell him that." Suddenly he reached down for his phone, which had obviously been vibrating. He checked the incoming number and took the call. "Coop here." He listened, his relaxed demeanor changing in an instant. "Be there soon," he said and hung up.

"Work?" she guessed.

He nodded. "Assignment. Big fire uptown. I need to go." He didn't try to escape his responsibility and she'd never think to ask him to.

"I can get myself home. I have plenty of reading to do to keep myself busy," she said, then caught herself. "Actually . . ."

"What?"

"I gave your brother my copy of your book."

"You what?" Coop asked, shocked by Lexie's words. "Why the hell would you do that?" And why the hell would Matt take it?

He'd never shown any interest in Coop's

writing before. And since Coop's first effort was hardly a smashing success, he hadn't exactly made a big announcement about it, either. But his family knew. His father had a signed copy at home that Coop had given him, but he doubted the old man had ever read it. And Matt had never shown any interest in his brother's *hobby,* so why bother setting himself up for ridicule?

And why was he even having this conversation with Lexie now when he had a story to cover? "Here." He pulled out the keys to his apartment. "Why don't you go back to my place? There's a box of my book in the hall closet. You can read one of those and wait for me while I'm gone. I'll talk to my father about access to the cold case files later or first thing tomorrow."

She hesitated, so he took her hand and placed the keys in her palm, curling her fingers around them. "You're not going to avoid what's a damn good thing between us because you're still upset with me."

She glanced down at her hand. "I'm not, huh?" A smile curved her lips, telling him he'd won this round.

"Nope. We'll discuss that — and the fact that you gave my brother my book — later. At my place." He brushed a kiss over her lips and ran out to cover the story.

■ ■ ■ ■

Lexie enjoyed nothing more than munching cookie-dough-flavored ice cream while she read or worked, so she stopped at the store for a pint on her way back to Coop's apartment. As she reached the entrance, Sara, dressed in uniform, was on her way out.

"Hey there." The other woman waved. "Coop's not home."

Lexie hesitated, then revealed the keys.

Sara's eyes opened wide. "Well, well, well." A genuine smiled crossed her face. "He must really care about you."

"You sound as if you approve."

Sara laughed. "Yeah, I guess I do."

Only because Sara couldn't see what was going on inside Lexie. Between the worry over her grandmother's blood pressure, the possibility that she was somehow involved in a years-old theft and Coop's intent to write a tell-all story, she felt as if the walls were closing in on her. Add Sara's wide smile of approval and the mounting pressure only increased.

A few more minutes of chitchat and Sara left for work. Lexie let herself into Coop's apartment, found the box of books and pulled one out.

Before she settled in to read, she took out her laptop and began browsing some of the places in the world she'd yet to visit.

Viewing potential destinations calmed her down somewhat. It helped that she now had places in mind for when this entire jewel-heist situation came to an end. By then, the Hot Zone relaunch would be done and Lexie would have a good chunk of cash to split between savings and travel. Hopefully, her grandmother's blood pressure would be under control, too, her computer knowledge solid enough for them to exchange e-mails, and Lexie could go in peace, even if she didn't stay away as long as usual. As her grandmother aged, Lexie had cut her trips shorter, coming back more often to see her.

And what about Coop?

Given his determination to write this story, she shouldn't care. But she was here despite that because he was right. Writer's wrote. She didn't have to like it, but she couldn't stop him, either. And she couldn't deny herself the pleasure of his company while they researched together. But she had no doubts that once she took off on her first excursion, he wouldn't be waiting for her when she came home.

A shiver took hold at the thought. But it wasn't stronger than the desire to go.

■ ■ ■ ■

Coop didn't get home until 2:00 a.m. Exhausted, he climbed the stairs to his building, fully expecting Lexie to be sound asleep in his bed. He couldn't think of a sweeter thing to come home to at night, and the thought pulled him up short.

He grabbed on to the handrail and paused, wondering how he'd gotten to this point so fast. He breathed in deep to calm his rapidly beating heart and reminded himself not to get used to having her around. Looking forward to coming home to Lexie was a sure path to heartache.

Enjoy the here and now. With that thought firmly in mind, he let himself into his apartment.

"Hey!" he said, surprised to find the light in the living room still on and Lexie curled up on the couch reading his book.

She barely glanced up as he walked into the room.

"It's late."

"I know. But I'm almost finished." She waved him away.

She'd changed into one of his V-neck T-shirts. It hung low on her smaller frame and her cleavage was visible. He wished she'd give him the attention she was focusing on his damn book, but a part of him was pleased that she was so engrossed in his story.

He turned into bed with the light still glowing in the other room, knowing she was drawn in but curious how she really felt about his abilities. Because in the one area of his life that meant the most to him, Coop was petrified of failing.

Coop woke up to find Lexie, hands cupped behind her head, staring at the ceiling. Morning was one of the few times he could look at her without her glasses and he savored the sight before she realized he was awake, too. She didn't spend much time in the sun and she had fair, porcelain-like skin with a hint of freckles over her nose and cheeks.

He reached out and ran his fingertip over the small bridge of her nose. "Been up long?"

"Not really." She smiled and rolled onto her side, propping herself up with one hand.

"What time did you finally turn in last night?"

"Not long after you, but you were already out cold."

He nodded. He'd crashed like a dead

man, exhausted from the hours on his feet and from inhaling the smoke from the deliberately set fire.

He was still feeling the effects this morning. "Why are you up so early?"

"I don't need more than six hours' sleep."

In his line of work, his hours were unpredictable so he'd learned to operate on less sleep, too. "So, are you going to tell me what you thought of the book?" He asked the question weighing on his mind since his eyes opened and his brain cleared.

A slow smile crossed her lips. "I couldn't put it down."

That much he knew. "And?"

"You write a really compelling story, Coop. The mystery kept me hooked, the characters were true to life, the tension incredible. It was a real page-turner!"

She said all the right things, but he sensed more going on behind those intelligent eyes. "What are you not saying?" he asked, wondering when he'd become a glutton for punishment.

He had a beautiful woman in his bed, complimenting his work, yet he was pushing for more.

She scooted into a sitting position facing him. "Okay, here's the thing."

He eased himself against the headboard

and braced for criticism he probably wouldn't like. Never mind that he'd asked for it.

"I had problems with the setting," she said hesitantly, clearly unsure of whether to go on.

"It's okay. I can take it," he motioned with his hands. "Give it to me."

She ran her tongue over her lips. His brain cautioned not to be distracted by the sight. His body didn't listen and a morning hard-on took hold.

"It's just that . . . Okay, well take that scene in East Harlem where the cop is looking for his prime suspect. We're in his head, we know how raw and emotional his feelings are and why. But what does he see on the street?" She waved her hands animatedly in the air as she spoke. "It could have taken place anywhere. It needs the color and the flavor of the place itself. The words need to jump off the page. Have you ever been there?" she asked.

"Of course." East Harlem was in his backyard. He was writing from firsthand experience.

"Well? Then you need to *show* the ethnic mix, the smells of all the nationalities of food wafting out from the various restaurants. The musical beat of salsa seeping onto the street from open windows." She snapped her fingers to an imaginary tune. "The chatter of words in a variety of languages and the differing ages of people mingling on the streets." Her eyes flashed with fire and excitement, dragging him into the world she created with her words and her energy.

Without even being there, he viewed East Harlem through her eyes, felt as if he were walking the steamy streets at night, experiencing the picture she painted.

Adrenaline rushed through his body and his brain in a way he'd never felt before. Just like the first night he'd spent with her at her grandmother's, she'd pumped him up to write once more.

He leaned close, sealing his lips over hers in a too-brief kiss.

"What was that for?" she asked, her pupils dilated, her voice husky. "Didn't I just insult your work?"

"You brought awareness to my work. And you know all that color and flavor you just had me experiencing?"

"Yes?" She cocked her head to one side and a lock of hair fell endearingly over her cheek.

"I'm going to return the favor for you now." He brushed her hair away with one hand.

Lexie smiled, more than eager to put aside critique for his hands-on experience. Whatever obstacles stood between them couldn't compete with the heat they generated under the covers. He reached for her, but she'd already decided that she wanted more control this time. Just to put them on equal footing.

She hooked her leg around his ankle and using him for leverage, she pulled herself on top of him.

"Check you out," he said, approval in his husky voice.

His pupils dilated, desire darkening his eyes.

"I think you've got this all wrong. I want to check *you* out."

"Please do." He spread his arms and legs, giving her his glorious body.

Starting with his mouth, she placed her lips over his, taking her time while she explored with her tongue, tasting, twirling, teasing and hopefully arousing him as much as she was arousing herself.

He wrapped one arm around her back and pulled her more tightly against him. She allowed him to direct that call only because it thrust her pelvis against his rock-hard erection, separated from her body by nothing but her thin silk panties and his cotton boxer briefs. And if he thought those were going to last long, she intended to teach him otherwise.

She moved from his lips to nuzzle his neck, inhaling his musky male scent. She trailed her tongue down the corded muscles of his neck, making her way to his chest and caught one nipple between her teeth, alternating between tugging on the distended tip and laving it with her tongue.

His grip on her back tightened and a rough groan of pleasure reverberated inside his chest. If she'd doubted her power over him, she had no doubts any more. They were equally caught up in this sensual haze. And she was consumed by it. Every ounce of pleasure she gave him caused her own body to react. Her breasts were now heavy, her nipples tight and her underwear damp with desire. And when he reached beneath her T-shirt and cupped her breast in his hand, the pressure felt so good that she arched her back, urging him on.

He pulled at her shirt and she yanked it over her head, tossing it onto the floor in a sudden desire to be completely naked, skin to skin. As if by mutual agreement, underwear came next, but when they met once more on the center of the bed, he returned to exactly what he'd started — her breast in his hand, only this time he was more determined. More focused.

So much for her being in control. When it came to Coop, she gave it up willingly.

He dipped his head and pulled her waiting nipple into his mouth. She arched her back, thrusting her breast deeper. He massaged with his fingers, laved with his tongue, and Lexie was gone. The sensations rippled straight to her core. She shifted against him, settling the place where she felt most needy against his erection.

She wasn't in the mood for foreplay, she wanted the real thing, Coop inside her, thrusting hard and fast until she couldn't think, only feel.

"Night-table drawer?" she asked, so aroused she was almost driven to skip this necessary step. Yet in this one area, Lexie was always extra cautious.

"Top one."

Lexie reached over to find a condom and Coop placed his big hand on her behind, kneading her flesh in an intimate way that was too erotic to be embarrassing. Finally, she came back over him, foil packet in hand.

She ripped it open and, with his help, slipped protection over his hard length. Her hands shook so badly she couldn't even take the time to enjoy touching him and promised herself there'd be time for that later. She positioned herself over him and he guided his shaft between her legs until the tip of his penis was enclosed by her heat. Then Lexie took over, gliding her body onto his, bringing him deep until he filled her at last. So tight she thought, and moaned at the perfection of their union.

Coop had died and gone to heaven. Or at least he was on his way there, as Lexie's damp hot body glided down over his, cocooning him in the most exquisite sheath.

Her eyes fluttered closed and another long, sexy moan escaped those lips, causing his body to react with an involuntary thrust of his hips. She worked her pelvic muscles in response, clenching tight around him and releasing, then repeating the motion. Each clamp of her walls increased his sensation and pleasure. She didn't even have to move on him to bring him closer to coming. But if she wanted to join him, she'd better get going fast. He didn't know how long he could hold out against those subtle but potent contractions.

Before he could warn her, she began a slow rocking movement of her hips and he could no longer think, let alone speak. He reached out and played with her sensitive breasts, rolling her nipples between his thumb and forefinger, knowing it would make her crazy.

And he was right. She began to ride up and down his shaft, grinding her pelvis into his with a downward thrust that ended in a rocking motion of her hips and a shuddering sigh. She knew just how to hit her exact right spot and bring herself higher and higher. He caught her rhythm, and thrust upward at the same moment she tilted against him, harder each time.

Their bodies ground together in unison, their sighs and groans mingled until Lexie's orgasm took hold. She cried out his name as she fell over him, her breasts crushing into his chest and the grip and release of her body taking him along for the ride.

A little while later, Lexie took her turn in the bathroom while Coop, who'd showered first, dressed for the day. She'd instructed him to open her laptop and pull up the color schemes she recommended for his Web site, so he could choose the one he liked best.

Though he'd rather shower *with* her, they'd agreed it would only lead to distraction. Yet Coop was definitely distracted anyway by the sound of the water and the images of a naked Lexie under the steady stream flashing through his mind.

He shifted until his jeans were more comfortable and opened her laptop. Not being a Mac person, he had no idea what all the icons at the bottom of the desktop screen meant. Some had dots below them; some didn't. Clueless, he clicked on one and brought up a program called iWeb.

He shook his head, unable to remember where she'd told him to look. Next he clicked on an icon that resembled a compass with a blue light beneath it. This time a Web browser opened.

He was about to close it out when he realized the program had already been open and he was just revealing a previously visited page. He found himself staring at a Web site about Australia. He blinked, but the image didn't go away. It was clear that this wasn't job-related, but a travel-oriented site.

Nausea filled him as he realized that at the same time he was settling in and enjoying Lexie, she was planning her next trip abroad. And though he'd known going in that this was her M.O., he had to admit that facing it head-on was harder than he'd anticipated. And it hurt a helluva lot more.

How could the woman who gave him such confidence about his writing and even himself be the same one who had one foot out the door?

Answers didn't matter.

Reality did.

He now knew how betrayed Lexie had felt when she'd found his story information on his computer. Knowing she was antsy and withholding those feelings from him was frustrating, painful and left him feeling raw.

But there wasn't a damn thing he could do to prevent her from leaving.

When Lexie stepped out of the shower, her body still tingled from Coop's lovemaking and she regretted their decision to put work first today, even if she understood the necessity. She dried her hair and slipped back into her outfit from yesterday. She really had to throw a change of clothes in her big bag or else stop sleeping here.

Not really a contest which one of those would be happening.

She walked into the bedroom, expecting to find Coop at her laptop poring over color ideas. Instead, her computer was open on the bed but Coop was nowhere to be found.

"Coop?" She headed into the small hallway leading to the living room and kitchen but they were empty.

Confused, Lexie made her way back into

the bedroom and settled on the mattress. "Maybe he went to pick up breakfast," she said aloud.

Then why wouldn't he have told her he was leaving?

She clicked the spacebar a few times and her laptop powered up. There, on the screen, weren't the color samples she'd told him to look over. Instead, she found herself staring at the Web site she'd glanced at earlier: *How to See Australia Like a Native.*

No wonder Coop was gone.

CHAPTER ELEVEN

Coop found his father at home. He still lived in the small house off the Grand Central Parkway that he'd shared with his wife. His morning routine hadn't changed. Cornflakes and milk along with black coffee and the news on TV.

Coop poured himself a mug and joined his dad at the kitchen table.

"So what brings you by so early this morning?" Wearing a worn pair of jeans and a white T-shirt, Jack leaned back in his chair and studied his son.

"I need a favor."

His father raised a bushy eyebrow. "Sounds intriguing."

Coop look at him, surprised. "How is that possible? I didn't tell you anything yet."

"You forget I'm a cop. I find intrigue everywhere," he said, deadpan. "Besides you never ask for favors, so this must be good."

Coop shrugged. The man had a point.

"You know the ring I got from the jewelry store?"

"Do I know the ring?" he asked wryly. "Cops foil robberies every day without fanfare but my reporter son steps up and he's not just a hero but the city's most famous bachelor."

"Way to show your pride, Dad." Coop took a long sip of his coffee. Good thing he knew his father was, in fact, proud of how he'd handled the situation or he'd take his words personally.

Jack cracked a smile. "So what about the ring?" he asked.

Coop set his mug down on the table. "It might be part of a cold case from the early '50s." Coop went on to explain the details of the robbery, excluding Lexie's grandmother's possible involvement.

At the mention of an unsolved case, his father's eyes opened wide. "What are the chances?" he said in awe. "So what's the favor?"

"Get me into the storage room with the cold case files. I want to dig around and see if I can put some pieces together."

Jack nodded. "Guess I can pull some strings and do that. Make sure you wear old clothes. You won't believe how filthy it is down there. The room's in the bowels of an old building."

Coop grimaced. "Sounds appealing."

His father laughed. "So now that we've got business out of the way, let's talk personal. Tell me about that pretty lady of yours."

Coop stiffened. He had no desire to discuss Lexie with his father. "I don't suppose I can just get up and leave now?"

Jack rose and headed for the sink, rinsing his cup and placing it in the dishwasher. A big change from the man who used to leave the mess for his wife to take care of, Coop thought, proud of how far his father had come.

"I like that gal. She's got spunk and brains. You need to bring her around when the bar's less busy. I want to get to know her better."

Coop groaned. "I wouldn't get too attached to her, if I were you. She's too much like Annie."

"She cheated on you already?" he asked, sounding outraged on his son's behalf.

Coop winced at the blatant reminder. "Hell, no. She likes to travel," he clarified. "She's got one foot out the door at all times. The woman doesn't even have a place of her own. Her home base is a bedroom in her grandmother's apartment."

Jack rubbed his razor-stubbled face. "So she's quirky. Doesn't mean she's unobtainable. Maybe you have to step up your game."

"I think you've been reading too many romance novels." Since Coop's mother passed away, Jack had been known to have a drink of scotch and dip into one of his mother's old paperbacks.

"Low blow, son." Jack actually flushed red.

Coop shook his head. "Are you seriously suggesting I invest more of myself in someone who's a sure bet to leave?"

"Is she worth the risk?" Jack walked over to his son. " 'Cause a good woman is hard to find and this one seems solid. She hangs around the bar even when she knows nobody. And the way she looks at you?" He let out a slow whistle. "Maybe you can't see the difference through the hurt."

"Easy for you to say, considering Mom was a keeper."

His father's eyes lit up at the mention of his wife. "If you're so sure Lexie isn't, what are you still doing hanging around with her?" Jack asked in that wise-father way he had.

"I have my reasons," Coop muttered. For one thing, she held clues to the ring's past.

But he could have researched the case

with Lexie and not gotten involved with her personally or intimately, a voice in his head reminded him. He'd chosen to go deeper.

No, Coop thought, he hadn't chosen. He'd been *compelled* to get to know her on every level, in every way.

Because apart from the sex being phenomenal, Lexie provided a positive jolt and boost to his mood, his work, his life. He enjoyed being with her in ways that transcended anything he'd experienced before.

In Annie, he'd found young love.

In Lexie . . . Coop shut down that train of thought, unwilling to go further. If he didn't think about his feelings for her, just maybe she couldn't slice out his heart the way Annie had.

If he were smart, he'd walk away now while he was still whole. But he wasn't ready to give her up until he had to. A time he now knew was approaching faster than he'd planned or liked.

"You know what your problem is?" Jack asked, interrupting Coop's dark thoughts.

"No, but I'm sure you're going to tell me."

Jack grinned. "You're always so damn afraid of failing that you don't take chances."

"Is this about dropping out of the academy instead of risking permanent injury?" Coop pushed his chair back and stood up.

Jack ran his hand over his face again. "You would have made a damn good cop. You have the head for the detective work, but the injury risk was real."

Coop exhaled a slow groan. At least he'd acknowledged that.

"But that doesn't change the fact that you're afraid of failing. Hell, yes, you're a fine reporter, but you haven't made it as a novelist. Why? Because you aren't putting your heart and soul into your books. If you did, you'd be at the top of that profession, too!" Jack's voice rose, carrying and echoing in the small house.

"How would you know?" Coop yelled back.

"I read your book, that's how."

His words took the weight out of Coop's argument, catching him off guard. "You did?"

His father nodded. "And though the procedural and the tension are good — better than good — there's a fire lacking everywhere else, because you're giving it a halfhearted effort."

Lexie's comments came back to him, but he couldn't focus on what she'd said. Not with his father's criticism bouncing around his head.

"Give me a break," Coop muttered.

"The hell I will!" Jack stood, walking toward his son. "I always tell it like it is and now's no different. You aren't giving it your all. This way you can fail and not be as devastated. Same as Lexie. If you don't invest your heart, you can't be hurt again. Afraid of failure," he said, nodding his head.

Son of a bitch. "I didn't come here for this."

"Tune me out. It won't make the truth go away."

Coop started for the door.

"When you get to the station, ask for Ed. You remember him, big guy. Stuck on desk duty after a gunshot hit a nerve in his leg. I'll make sure he lets you into the file room."

"Thanks," Coop muttered and stalked out, slamming the door behind him.

Ever since she was a little girl and her grandmother rescued her from skating practice hell and took her to state parks, Lexie had learned to pick up and run. As an adult, "Have laptop will travel" was her motto and when she was upset, she either took off on a trip or buried herself in work.

This morning she chose the latter and stayed in Coop's apartment to do it. Much as she wanted to be furious with him for leaving, she couldn't be angry. If he'd found the Web sites, he was probably upset and needed to be alone and sort things through. She just planned to be here when he returned.

When her cell phone rang, she grabbed it fast without looking at the number, hoping it was Coop. "Hello?"

"Alexis?"

At the sound of her given name and her father's authoritarian voice, Lexie's stomach cramped — as it always did when he spoke. "Hi, Dad."

"How are you? Or, should I ask, *where* are you?"

She rolled her eyes at the deliberate jab. "You know I'm in town. I checked in last week."

"I thought perhaps the urge to leave had struck."

She clenched the phone tighter in her hand. "I told you I'm here until Grandma's birthday."

He cleared his throat. "Yes. And will we have to wait until then to see you?"

Lexie had seen her parents when she'd returned to town the month before. Her father was right. They were due for a visit.

"Is that your way of saying you miss me?" she asked hopefully.

"It would be nice of you to stop by. Which is part of why I'm calling. Your grandmother is acting odd, even for her."

So he'd noticed it, too, Lexie thought.

"Your mother was hoping you'd bring her by for dinner this Saturday night."

A formal dinner at her parents' home. Just the stifling thought had Lexie's flight mechanism kicking into overdrive. "Did you ask Grandma if she's free?"

"When I do talk to her, she's been ridiculously hard to pin down to a day or a time. And sometimes she doesn't even answer her phone when we call."

Because she checks her Caller ID, Lexie thought, stifling an inappropriate laugh. Her father's ways wore on both Lexie and Charlotte, but they both knew his concern, however awkwardly expressed, was genuine.

"I'll talk to her and get back to you," Lexie promised.

"One last thing. Your grandmother mentioned that you've been seeing a nice gentleman."

Lexie closed her eyes and swallowed back a curse that would cause her father's already thinning hair to fall out completely. "I doubt she used those exact words."

To her surprise, her father laughed. "You're right about that. At any rate, it would make your mother and me happy if you brought him along."

No doubt because they hoped that a steady relationship meant Lexie would curb her wandering ways. Last time, *they'd* picked the man and Drew had been the result.

"I'm sure Coop's busy," she lied, not wanting to subject herself or him to dinner at her parents'.

At that moment, the sound of the key in the lock caught her attention. She turned to see Coop letting himself inside.

He strode in and stopped short, surprised to see her settled on his couch, her laptop and papers spread out around her.

She waved and pointed to the phone, turning her attention back to her father. "Yes, I'll mention it to him, but it's not like we're serious. There's really no need —"

"Just do your best, Alexis."

Lexie sighed. "I'll see what I can do."

"Okay, let us know. Your mother needs time to prepare."

"I will, Dad. 'Bye." She ended the connection and let out her first real breath of air since taking the call.

Coop sat across from her on his favorite club chair. He wore faded jeans and a navy NYPD shirt. And his posture was stiff, his expression unyielding.

Lexie stopped breathing all over again.

"What was that all about?" he asked.

She bit the inside of her cheek. "My father invited us to dinner Saturday night."

"Us?"

She nodded. "Grandma told them about you and they'd like to meet you."

"And you told them there's no need to bother." He set his jaw, but she caught the hurt flash across his face before he quickly masked it.

Lexie swallowed hard. "Because —"

"It's not like we're serious." He used her own words, tossing them back at her.

She swallowed harder. "Trust me, I was just trying to protect you. You really don't want to be subjected to a dinner where my father expresses his disapproval of my lifestyle choices and my mother keeps saying she wishes I could be more like my sister, Margaret. And, before you ask, no, they don't call her Meg, Meggie, Peg or anything else."

She thought she caught a glimmer of understanding in his eyes. A second later it was gone. "Does a reporter not meet their high expectations?"

Lexie laughed at his assumption, which couldn't be further from the truth. This wasn't about Coop. "I already told you, *I* don't meet their expectations. You're smart, successful, and you seem to act like a *normal* person. I'm sure they'll love you."

"Is that why you don't want me to meet them? Because it might send them the wrong signal, that you're changing to be more like them?" he asked, folding his arms across his chest in a clearly defensive pose.

"I just don't understand why you'd want to." She recalled making the same statement when he'd accepted her grandmother's invitation to dinner.

That time, he'd said he wanted to get to know the person she loved and admired so much. She wondered what his reasons were now.

"Let's call it curiosity. I want to see what makes you tick."

She should have guessed that was his motivation. And she would have still insisted he not attend, except he said the words with a definite challenge in his tone.

And her reply flew from her lips without the consent of her brain. "So, fine. Come. See why Lexie runs."

The minute the words were out of her mouth, she muttered a very unladylike curse because he'd set the trap and she'd taken the bait.

Coop grinned. "Just let me know what time. I'd be happy to pick you up and take you there." His Cheshire cat smile confirmed her hunch.

"Grandma's coming, too," Lexie warned him.

His smile widened. "The more the merrier."

"Great," Lexie muttered. "Just swell."

From the unintentional sexy pout on her glossed lips, Coop knew she was annoyed. He wasn't thrilled with himself, either. He'd gone from wanting to keep an emotional distance to insisting he meet the rest of her family. It was one thing for him to decide to pull back, but another to hear her minimize what they shared.

Hearing her tell her father it wasn't like they were serious had pissed him off. To the point where he wanted to rip the phone out of her hands and kiss her hard enough to make her eat those words. He wanted to touch all those sensitive spots on the body he knew so well, make her come and then let her tell him they weren't all that serious. He broke into a sweat just thinking about it.

Instead, he was going to meet her family. When she wanted nothing more than to get on a plane and leave as soon as possible.

Fucking swell.

His pride at manipulating her into agreement quickly turned to disgust with himself. Well, what's done was done. He'd deal with it tomorrow when dinner rolled around.

Right now it was time to change the subject. "My father said he'd get us into the file room where the cold cases are stored."

As expected, he captured her attention and her eyes sparkled with excitement. "That's great!" She jumped up from her seat. "When can we go?"

"No time like the present." He glanced at her white shorts and frilly top from the day before. "The file room is in the basement of an old building. You probably want to put on jeans and an old shirt."

She glanced down and frowned. "I hate for us to have to lose time by going to my grandmother's first, but I guess we have no choice."

"I don't mind."

He almost suggested that while she was at her grandmother's, she pick up some things to leave here. To make things easier in the future.

He bit back the words. He wasn't sure what worried him more. Her reaction to that suggestion or what his response would be if she said no.

Coop drove to her grandmother's so Lexie could change. He was quiet in the car ride over and Lexie remained silent, too. She wasn't sure how to broach the subject of the travel sites he'd seen or how to explain her need to pick up and go.

There were surprisingly few people in the world who understood — at least in Lexie's experience — and nothing she ever said or did made a difference. Too often she didn't understand it herself. What had started as a flight mechanism had grown into something she not only enjoyed doing but needed to do. She didn't always understand why, but she *accepted* that part of her. It hurt more than she'd anticipated to realize Coop couldn't do the same.

When they reached the apartment, to Lexie's surprise, her grandmother was nowhere to be found. She knocked on Sylvia's door, too, but the other woman wasn't home, either. Lexie figured they'd gone out for the day.

She wrote a note telling her grandmother she'd be home later and informing her that the three of them would be going to her parents' home for dinner Saturday night.

Which, Lexie realized, was tomorrow.

She called her father and left him a voice-mail message letting him know they'd all be there, prompting an unsettling feeling in the pit of her stomach. Suddenly all areas of her life seemed to be crowding in on her and she yearned for a trip to the top of the Empire State Building instead of one to the bowels of a NYC police precinct.

By the time they headed back downtown, stopped for a quick lunch and reached the station, it was late afternoon.

Once at the main desk, Coop asked to speak with a man named Ed Potter.

A few minutes later, a burly, older guy in uniform who walked with a cane strode toward them and shook Coop's hand.

"Who's this lovely lady?" Ed asked.

"Lexie Davis," she said, and extended her hand in greeting.

"Nice to meet you." He gripped her palm in a firm shake.

"How have you been, Ed?" Coop asked.

The older man smiled. "Can't complain. When it's not raining, the old injury doesn't bother me as much." He patted his left leg with his hand. "How 'bout you? It's been a while. Last time I saw you was at your mother's funeral. Quite a turnout for quite a lady."

Coop bowed his head. "Thanks. She was special."

Lexie heard the ache in his voice and her throat closed up a little. She wished she could have known the mother he'd been so close to.

"How's your dad doing?" Ed asked. " 'Cause I'm sure I don't get the truth out of him. Always claims life's great."

Coop grinned. "He's doing all right. Never moans and groans. I wish he'd meet someone to keep him company, but so far the right woman hasn't walked into his bar."

Ed nodded. "Whoever she is, make sure she's more understanding of guys' night than my wife, Gretchen."

Coop laughed — a deep, gruff sound Lexie always enjoyed, and one that never ceased to send shivers of awareness through her body.

"I take it that explains why we don't see you around Jack's?" Coop asked.

"You got that figured right."

Lexie glanced at the larger man, surprised he'd let his wife dictate who he saw and what he did. So much for judging a man by looking at him.

Ed led them toward a flight of stairs and Lexie shot Coop a surprised look.

"The cane's just in case the leg starts to

hurt. It don't stop me from getting around," Ed said, as if reading her mind.

She nodded and followed him as they descended lower and lower.

Coop hadn't been kidding when he said the file rooms were filthy. Dirt and grime that had probably once just been dust covered everything inside the room. Lexie, who'd slept everywhere from tents in Yosemite to outdoor huts in Africa, didn't mind dirt, but this kind of dust and mold was another story. Her allergies immediately kicked in and her nose began itching within minutes of reaching the depths of the old building.

"Okay, this is it." Ed stopped at a closed door, pulled out a set of keys and let them inside.

"Door locks behind you, but you're set on the inside. You can let yourselves out. Take as long as you need."

"Thank you," Lexie said.

"Thanks." Coop slapped the other man on the back. "Don't be a stranger. Bring Gretchen with you to Jack's if she won't let you out of her sight."

"Best burgers ever," Lexie said by way of incentive.

Ed grinned. "I might just do that." He

raised a hand in a wave goodbye and walked out.

The door creaked, then slammed shut behind them with a loud thud, leaving them alone in the dimly lit room.

An eerie silence surrounded them, settling on Lexie's shoulders and she shivered. "I wonder if this is what it feels like when prison doors slam shut behind you."

"No, that's worse. The sound of iron slamming shut is harder and more . . . final. My father took Matt and me when we were kids. He wanted to scare us straight *before* we did anything wrong." He paused for a moment. "It worked."

She shuddered once more. "I can't even imagine." Turning her sights to the task ahead of them, Lexie glanced around at the aisles filled with boxes stacked row after row on shelves. "Wow."

"They should be in chronological order," Coop said, and started walking past the most recent years.

They passed the 1960s and finally found the decade before. "The robbery took place during a holiday party, so let's start with December." He pulled out one huge file box and placed it on the floor, followed by another. Together they covered two years.

By unspoken agreement, they settled on

the floor to look through them.

Lexie took the year 1950 while Coop tackled 1951.

He pulled off the lid and began to flip through the cases. "September, October . . . It's pretty much in order."

Lexie followed suit. "Same here," she said, surprised. "I really thought this would take days. I never imagined this place could be as organized as you see on TV." Lexie shifted, getting as comfortable as she could on the hard, cold concrete floor.

"It's not the same as being computerized, but it's pretty damn good."

His tone was brusque and businesslike and Lexie couldn't stand it another minute. She couldn't be intimate with someone at night and be angry and distant during the day. She wasn't sure if the travel sites bothered him more or if it had been her description of their relationship to her father. She hadn't intentionally meant to hurt him with either.

"Listen, about this morning . . ." She decided to start with the Web sites. "I know you found the Australia travel site on my computer."

He glanced up, meeting her gaze. "It's no big deal."

"Then why did you leave without saying

goodbye or even telling me you had some-place to go?" As she spoke, the same pain hit in the pit of her stomach.

"Since we're not that serious, why should it matter?"

She was about to call him on the petty comment when she caught the twinkle in his gaze.

Now she was just plain confused.

"And I should have let you know I was going to my father's." A muscle worked in his jaw and she waited, giving him time. "Look, seeing your travel plans caught me off guard — even though I knew you wouldn't be staying long."

She appreciated his honesty. She might think about taking off and traveling, but she never connected those thoughts with leav-ing *him.*

She wasn't ready.

"They aren't actual plans. I was just look-ing at places I might want to see one day. Have you ever been out of the country?" she asked cautiously.

He shook his head. "Never had the op-portunity." And he turned back to looking through the files in the box.

Lexie let out a long breath, glad it wasn't dislike of the notion. But never having had the chance? She found that incredibly sad.

"Maybe you need to create your own opportunity," she suggested.

"Found it!" He pulled a file from the box. "Says Lancaster on the tab." Excitement fueled his voice.

Their discussion on the back burner, Coop opened the folder and she scooted in close so she could read over his shoulder.

She breathed in his delicious, familiar scent and sexual awareness kicked right in. The urge to run her fingers through his hair while they scanned the words on the page was strong, but she needed to concentrate on what they found. So she refrained.

For now.

"It says here all the party guests were questioned and released. Same for most of the staff who worked that evening," Coop said.

From his focused tone and energy, he seemed to have no similar yearning to take her right here on the musty file room floor.

"The chauffeur, whose name was listed as Richard Hampton, took longer to locate, but he was eventually questioned and let go. Two waitresses were never found. Neither were the jewels. When the police spoke to the hiring company, they discovered the women had used false identities. And since they were the only open leads and their trail grew cold quickly, the case was shelved here."

Lexie bit the inside of her cheek, a question occurring to her for the first time. "What was the exact date of the robbery?"

"December 31, 1951."

Lexie thought long and hard, recalling stories and information she'd heard over the years. Finally, something clicked.

"Yes!" She pumped her fist in the air.

"What is it?"

"I guess I was thinking 1950s, so it never dawned on me that my grandfather had an ironclad alibi. But in August 1951 he was drafted for the Korean War. I remember it was August because it's around Grandma's birthday."

Coop's eyes filled with understanding. "So he couldn't have been involved."

"Right!" Relief surged through her and she threw her arms around Coop's neck and pulled him into a kiss.

Coop responded and kissed her back, his tongue doing delicious things to her mouth, but he didn't let it last long. "We have more digging to do," he reminded her.

She reluctantly agreed and eased away, her body still humming. "Right. So . . . the chauffeur was exonerated after questioning and that leaves the two women."

Coop flipped through the aging papers, skimming hard to read handwriting, taking his time as he read the words on the pages. "Most of this is the following up of dead ends. Except . . ." He placed his finger on the paper. "Here. It says most of the party guests noted the two waitresses were flighty, disappearing for too long at a time, leaving guests without drinks or hors d'oeuvres. And they often congregated together, whispering instead of working. Like they knew each other well."

"Which wouldn't be surprising if they worked together often," Lexie pointed out, her stomach churning even as she didn't want to face why.

"Except . . . hang on. I remember reading something else in here . . ." Coop flipped backwards in the file. "Here it is. These two women were temps hired to fill in when the party list grew larger at the last minute."

Lexie swallowed hard. "Which puts us back where we started, asking ourselves how the necklace came to be in my grandmother's possession . . ."

"While your grandfather was stationed overseas." Coop placed a firm hand on Lexie's shoulder, as if bracing her for the blow.

A blow she'd already subconsciously taken as they'd worked through the question. "We can't possibly be thinking that she was one of the two women who were temporary help." She looked to Coop, praying he'd laugh at her assumption.

"For the sake of argument, let's say she was. Who could have been her accomplice?"

Lexie closed her eyes, fighting the truth that had been simmering just below consciousness. The other day she'd thought of her grandmother and her best friend, Sylvia, as Laverne and Shirley or Lucy and Ethel. Who else but Sylvia would Charlotte have had her head together with all those years ago while working a dinner party?

Who could have been her accomplice? "That's a rhetorical question," Lexie said to Coop, opening her eyes and facing reality. "The real question is, what are we going to do about it?"

CHAPTER TWELVE

With the Hot Zone Web design nailed down
and the implementation in Claudia's capable hands, Lexie spent a productive
Saturday working on Coop's Web site. He,
in turn, spent the day on assignment.
Though she worked out of her grandmother's place, Charlotte was not there.
She'd been asleep by the time Lexie had
returned home the night before and had left
before Lexie woke up.

Lexie appreciated the reprieve because she
hadn't yet figured out how she would handle
the discovery she'd made. No matter how
many ways she tried to spin things, she
always came back to the same conclusion.
Her grandmother and Sylvia had stolen
jewels from the Lancaster family collection.

Lexie massaged her temples in a continuing effort to keep a nagging headache at
bay. The shock and pain weren't so bad
when she was absorbed in design work, but

each time she took a break, the memory of finding out came flooding back. The woman she adored, idolized and looked up to was a *thief.*

How in the world had that happened?

And what did the revelation say about Lexie herself? She'd always found solace in the fact that even if she wasn't like the rest of her family, she could count on the comforting notion that she was like her grandmother — a free-spirited, happy, taking-life-as-it-came kind of person. But not a thief.

The doorbell rang and Lexie jumped up to answer it. She was surprised to see Coop standing on the other side, looking sexy as ever in a worn pair of jeans and a plain T-shirt. His muscles bunched beneath the fabric and the midnight blue accented his gorgeous eyes.

She wished he didn't always have that gut-twisting impact on her. The one that had her yearning to grab his hand and drag him to her bed. Or kitchen counter, whichever was nearest. If only she knew her grandmother was out for the whole day, she might actually do it, but she had no idea when Charlotte would be back.

So much for love in the afternoon, she thought wryly. "What are you doing here so early?" she asked him, her voice tame in comparison to her raging hormones and lust-filled thoughts. "I wasn't expecting you until six." When he was supposed to pick her up for the torture dinner at her parents'.

"I finished up my story early and I figured you could use a break from your thoughts." He tapped her temple with his finger.

She grinned, oddly pleased that he knew her so well. "You figured right. Although I have been doing great work on your site."

"Can I come in so you can show me?" He still stood in the hall.

"Sure. Sorry." She shook her head, embarrassed. "I'm just distracted. Come on in." She waved him inside. "But you can't see the designs yet. I want to surprise you with my genius."

He laughed, the sound doing nothing to ease the sexual awareness she was feeling.

"Did I ever mention how much I love your modesty?" he asked.

She tipped her head to one side, meeting his gaze. "Hey, when you're good at something you shouldn't hide it," she said pointedly, hoping he'd take the hint that she was talking about more than herself.

He dipped his head in acknowledgment. "Touché."

At least her point hadn't gone over his head, even if he chose not to get deeper into the conversation.

"So where do you want to go this afternoon? I want to get you out of this apartment and it's a beautiful day and this is just a crime." He pointed to the shades, drawn tight by her grandmother.

"I agree." She'd love to see some sunshine.

She had an idea about where they could go, but she bit the inside of her cheek, debating whether or not she wanted to share her special place with him. She worried that once she did, it would never be hers alone ever again. That she'd always associate it with him, even after he was gone from her life.

The thought caused a distinct lump to form in her throat, the panic practically choking her. She ought to be scared at how deeply she was coming to feel for this man, yet she couldn't stop the words from flowing out of her mouth. "Let me grab my bag and I'll surprise you."

"I love surprises." A pleased and seductive smile curved his mouth. "Lead the way."

No doubt about it, Lexie thought. Her special place would never be the same again.

Coop watched as Lexie stepped onto the small ledge and leaned her forehead against the window at the top of the Empire State

Building. He'd been here as a kid and again when covering a story or two, but a tourist site wouldn't be a place he'd normally choose to go to unwind. The line to get in, the wait, the crowds on the elevators . . . Definitely not for him.

But a funny thing happened once they reached Lexie's floor of choice. She led him to the windows and once they stood together, looking out over the beautiful skyline, all the noise, the chaos, the people around him seemed to disappear. He could appreciate why she came here when she needed solitude.

"Step up with me." She encouraged him to lean against the window with her.

"I'm not sure I want to feel that weightless sensation," he muttered.

"Chicken?" she asked.

With a resigned groan, he planted his feet on the ledge, his toes against the plate glass.

As if sensing his reluctance, Lexie reached out and clasped his hand firmly in hers. "Now look out," she said, softly, her fingers wrapping tighter around his.

He allowed himself to trust and did as she asked, taking in the incredible sight from a new and enlightening perspective. He felt as if he were flying over the city, free-falling without a safety net. And he loved it.

He tipped his head and glanced over, taking in Lexie's serene profile — this was the most relaxed he'd ever seen her and he had the sense that he was being given a glimpse into her heart and her soul. And somehow he *knew* she rarely shared this part of herself with others. It showed an incredible amount of trust — and that both pleased and scared the crap out of him.

"I hate that we have to leave," she murmured.

He squeezed her hand. "I know, but we still have some time." But even as he spoke, he realized that time with her wasn't something he could count on.

Lexie sat in the back of Coop's car, yielding the front seat to her grandmother. Charlotte talked to Coop nonstop, leaving Lexie alone with her thoughts.

She approached her family home with trepidation. She normally saw her parents at a restaurant and left immediately after dinner so she didn't have to prolong the agony or look for an excuse to leave. Tonight was different and not just because Coop was there to witness the dysfunction.

As they walked up the front path, Charlotte led the way, ringing the doorbell and entering as if she owned the place. "Hello! We're here!"

Lexie shot Coop an amused glanced.

He slid his hand into hers, his palm feeling warm and solid against her skin.

Footsteps sounded from the kitchen and her father strode into the marbled entryway. Of course he wore a suit and tie, making Lexie feel out of place in her bohemian summer dress. Not that she needed clothing for that. Coop's mere presence, in his khaki chinos and a pale-blue dress shirt, surprisingly put Lexie a little more at ease.

"You're on time!" her father noted, by way of hello.

"Coop drove us and he's prompt," Charlotte said proudly, as if she had something to do with that fact. "Sam Cooper, this is my son, Cary."

"It's nice to meet you, Cary." Coop extended his hand, while Lexie waited for the fallout.

"My name is Grant." Her father pinned his mother with an annoyed glare, which contrasted well with the embarrassed flush in his cheeks.

"Don't you listen to him," Charlotte said. "His given name is Cary Grant Davis."

"My legal name has been Grant since I turned eighteen," he reminded her.

This argument was as standard and expected as it was funny, and Lexie choked back a laugh.

"A pleasure, Mr. Davis," Coop said diplomatically, somehow keeping a straight face.

Lexie's father shook Coop's hand. "Grant will be fine."

Charlotte let out a snort. "My fanny, it's fine! Your father and I named you after Cary Grant in the movie, *It Takes a Thief*." Charlotte's voice took on a dreamy quality.

Grant rolled his eyes.

But Lexie was no longer amused at the byplay.

With the reminder of her grandmother's favorite movie, Lexie became even more certain of Charlotte's role in the jewel heist years ago. She just couldn't fathom why her grandmother would have done such a thing. Lexie still hadn't decided how to handle that knowledge. She wondered if Coop caught the movie reference, but he was still focused on Lexie's father.

"Come into the living room," Grant said and they followed him into a formally furnished area, complete with a grand piano — for show only — and a wet bar in the corner.

Lexie's mother, Caroline, waited for them, dressed as properly as her husband in a simple black dress and pearls. "I'm so glad everyone could make it!"

Her father made the introductions for Coop, while Lexie kissed her mother's cool cheek.

"Can I make anyone a drink?" Grant asked.

Lexie would have loved a stiff anything, but whatever she chose would meet with disapproval, so better to stay sober and on her toes. "Nothing for me, thanks."

Coop shook his head. "I'm fine, thank you." He obviously took his cue from her.

"Have something," Lexie urged.

"I'm having a martini. I'll make you one," Grant said before Coop could reply.

"You know, I read an interesting article online the other day," Charlotte said. "It said that rehab centers are seeing a rise in bankers who are admitted for alcoholism." Her naughty gaze fell on her son.

"Mother!" Caroline said, horrified.

Lexie's father turned a deeper red, but he said nothing, while Coop met Lexie's stare, wide-eyed.

She merely shrugged. If he wasn't used to her grandmother by now, he would be after tonight.

"Let's all sit," Caroline suggested. "Lexie, Mother, come and we'll catch up."

Lexie and Coop settled beside each other on the couch. Charlotte took Grant's favorite chair, which gave her a view of everyone in the room. After mixing drinks, Lexie's father joined them, sitting beside his wife on a love seat across from the sofa.

An old wall clock, which used to wake Lexie as a child, ticked loudly in the silent room. Lexie swung her foot back and forth until Coop settled his hand on her knee, stilling the nervous movement.

"Where are Margaret and Stan?" Lexie asked of her sister and her husband.

"She had an urgent meeting with the governor," Caroline said proudly.

Lexie's father nodded, beaming. "She has his ear."

"I hope that's all she has. Many successful women have been known to sleep their way to the top." Charlotte glanced down at her empty wineglass. "I'll have another, please." She extended her arm toward her daughter-in-law.

"You've had enough," Caroline and Grant said at the same time.

"Party poopers."

"So, Coop," her father said, ignoring his mother's outburst. "Tell me about yourself."

Coop leaned forward in his seat. "I'm the crime beat reporter for the *Daily Post.*"

"Impressive," Grant said, approval clear in his tone.

Lexie admired how comfortable Coop was in his own skin, even on meeting her parents, who eyed him with a combination of curiosity and wonderment. She clearly read the expression on their faces. How could such a fine man be with their flighty daughter?

"Lexie tells me you're president of Metro Savings and Loan," Coop said.

Smooth, Lexie thought, impressed. He'd obviously done his research, since she'd never told him specifically where her father worked. Lexie sat on her hands in an attempt not to applaud the fact that Coop had come prepared.

The two men had a brief discussion of business and economic issues, when Lexie's mother finally made her presence known.

She cleared her throat. "So tell me how you and my daughter met. Were you in Indonesia recently?" she asked, her tone as horrified as it had been when Lexie had announced her plans.

Coop, who hadn't removed his hand from Lexie's leg, gave her a gentle squeeze. At least he hadn't shuddered at the location of her last trip.

"Actually, we met in the city."

Before he could launch into an explanation of how they met over a garbage Dumpster, Lexie decided to use this conversation as an opportunity to gauge what her parents knew about her grandmother's necklace — and the older woman's shady past.

"I don't know if you saw the news, but Coop's a local hero," Lexie said proudly. She described his actions at the jewelry store and the ensuing reward.

"I didn't want to accept anything, but the woman insisted," Coop explained.

"And they showed the whole thing on the news. Grandma and I were watching and we realized that Coop's ring matched one of her old necklaces. I decided I wanted to buy it from him for her upcoming birthday." Lexie revealed her true plan to her grandmother for the first time.

"Why . . . I don't know what to say!" Charlotte blew kisses at Lexie from her chair. "You always were such a sweet child," she said, beaming with happiness.

"Which of your many *pieces* is it?" Lexie's father asked.

"The one that means the most to her because it was a gift from Grandpa," Lexie prodded, hoping her father remembered and could add some details to the story.

Grant choked on his martini. "Excuse me?

Lexie, are you sure? My father was never a gift-giver! In fact, he was more of a stingy bastard —"

"Cary Grant Davis, you take that back!" Charlotte said, jumping up from her chair.

Grant made a frustrated, growling sound. "Well, it's the truth."

Lexie had always known that her father's memories of his parent didn't match her grandmother's memories of her husband. Lexie had been too young to remember her grandfather as more than a big, booming man who'd loved her.

Charlotte pulled a tissue from inside her shirt and began blotting her eyes.

"Oh, brother." Grant eyed his mother, obviously annoyed with her theatrics. "I'm sorry," he finally said.

Charlotte sniffed. "Fine."

"Good. Now that that's settled, back to the necklace. Do either of you remember it? Because it has an interesting history," Lexie said. "It turns out that it belonged to a family named —"

"Oh, my heart!" Charlotte cried, rising and grabbing for her chest.

Lexie narrowed her gaze, unable to tell if her grandmother was faking because of the subject or really wasn't feeling well. Unwilling to take any chances, she rose from her seat and leaned close to her grandmother.

Coop followed, putting an arm around Charlotte's shoulders. "Have a seat," he said, gently leading her to the couch.

"Mother, are you okay?" Grant asked. Suddenly truly concerned, he too hovered over her.

"Should I call an ambulance?" Caroline already had a hand on the phone.

Lexie met her parents' worried gaze. "She told me she was just diagnosed with high blood pressure. Maybe her medications aren't working?"

Charlotte moaned and fanned herself with a magazine she'd picked up from the table.

Lexie's mother nodded and called 9-1-1, while her father rushed to the kitchen, mumbling about a baby aspirin and a glass of water.

Half an hour later, although her grand-mother claimed she was now fine, the paramedics insisted on taking her to the hospital. Protocol demanded it, since other things like a panic attack or acid reflux, could look like a heart attack. They needed to check her heart and Lexie agreed.

Many exhausting hours later, Charlotte was released, diagnosed with an anxiety at-tack. Grant wanted his mother to stay overnight so they could keep an eye on her. But when the older woman attempted to blame her son for upsetting her about her poor deceased husband, Lexie stepped in and, along with Coop, took her grandmother home.

"At least I saved us from eating Caroline's atrocious cooking," Charlotte said as they led her to her apartment.

Lexie rolled her eyes. "You took years off my life."

Charlotte shuffled down the hall in her slipper-looking shoes. "Well, can I help it if your father's a callous ass?"

Coop, who'd spent the entire night by Lexie's side, chuckled.

He'd been her steadying rock while the doctors took her frail-looking grandmother away in a wheelchair. In between reassuring her that Charlotte would be fine, Coop distracted her by asking questions about places she'd visited on her travels. More than once, Lexie caught distinct interest in his inquisitive look and pointed questions. Of course, she'd convinced herself that a man's mere curiosity was genuine interest once before.

Regardless, she owed Coop for staying with her. He could have gone home while she and her parents dealt with the hospital, but he'd insisted on being there for Lexie and making sure Charlotte was okay. No doubt about it, the man was a keeper.

Shaken by the thought, Lexie focused on her grandmother. She let them into the apartment and turned to find Charlotte standing behind her, looking tired and frail. "Grandma, please just get a good night's sleep, okay? We'll talk more in the morning," Lexie said, drained beyond belief.

Charlotte nodded and padded off to bed.

As soon as she heard the bedroom door close, Lexie dropped onto the couch with a thud. Her entire body ached, but nothing hurt as much as her heart at the thought of losing her grandmother.

Coop knelt beside her and brushed her hair off her face. "The doctor said she's fine," he said, reading her mind.

"But her blood pressure is still too high. She needs to have her medication regulated."

"And she will." His reassuring tone relaxed her, as it had all evening.

"Did you happen to notice that it wasn't Dad's comments that sent her over the edge — it was when I brought up the necklace?"

Coop nodded, having realized the same thing. He hadn't planned to bring up the subject, but now that Lexie had broached it first, he agreed. "She definitely didn't want to discuss it."

"Because she has something to hide and she knows we are onto her."

He caught the pain in her voice, but again couldn't deny the truth.

"If we confront her, will her blood pressure skyrocket? I mean, do you think we could bring on a heart attack or a stroke?" She rubbed her temples with both hands.

He wished he could think of something that would offer comfort or reassurance, but so far he hadn't a clue.

"Would you mind getting me some Tylenol from the medicine cabinet in the hall bathroom?" she asked. "My head's killing me."

"Sure thing." Grateful for something useful to do, he rose and headed for the bathroom to get the pills and then to the kitchen for a glass of water.

He returned a few minutes later to find that Lexie had already fallen asleep.

He placed the tablets and water on the table, then settled onto the couch beside her, unsure of whether to cover her with a blanket and leave her here, or move her into her room for a more comfortable night's sleep. For now he did neither, gently removing her glasses, putting them aside and settling in, content to listen to the sound of her breathing.

The low and steady in and out sound was at odds with the conflict raging on inside her. The grandmother she adored had a past she wanted to keep hidden, and the harder she and Coop pressured her to reveal the truth, the more they might jeopardize her health.

Unfortunately, Coop didn't know how to operate any way but honestly, by digging into the past. He had a hunch Lexie needed to know, too, for peace and closure, if nothing else. They'd agreed on that.

What to do with the information once they'd uncovered it? He had a feeling that decision was an explosive argument waiting to happen.

Charlotte paced the floor of her bedroom, waiting until she heard Coop leave for the night. Then she sat not so patiently on her bed, listening for the sound of Lexie's bedroom door closing, but she never heard the usual creak and slam. Finally, she decided to just go for it and padded softly out of her bedroom — past her granddaughter sleeping soundly on the family room couch — and headed for Sylvia's apartment.

She and her best friend and one-time partner had a lot to discuss. And they needed to formulate a plan. Obviously, Lexie and Coop were onto something. Charlotte wasn't sure what they knew — or how much — but a little knowledge was a dangerous thing. They could blow her carefully kept secret sky high. Charlotte couldn't have Coop revealing her cat-burglar past. She, Sylvia and Ricky had too much to lose.

If it was only up to Lexie, Charlotte knew that worry about her grandmother's health would keep her from digging further. But Coop, the reporter, wouldn't give up as easily, which meant the duo would stay on her tail.

Unless love for Lexie kept him silent. And Charlotte had no doubt the man had fallen for her granddaughter. She'd seen his concern at the hospital — not just for Charlotte, bless the man — but for a fearful Lexie, too. She wondered if he was aware of it yet. As for her granddaughter, she was already head over heels for the man, but poor Lexie was so scarred by that prick Drew, Charlotte feared Lexie wouldn't know a good thing when she was staring right at it.

Charlotte couldn't worry about matchmaking at the moment. She and Sylvia had something else to take care of first. Ricky, the cheating bastard, had items that belonged to each of them. The night of their last caper, Charlotte already had found the necklace, while Ricky had located the ring and the bracelet in another closet. They were supposed to meet outside, where he'd hand the bracelet over to Sylvia, completing the ritual of each of them coming away with a trinket for their trouble. But earlier that evening, Charlotte had given him another item to hold for safekeeping, one of both monetary and sentimental value. He'd never showed, disappearing and taking both items with him.

The no-good, rotten son of a bitch had Charlotte's wedding ring. And she wanted it back.

CHAPTER THIRTEEN

Lexie woke up in a cramped position on the family room couch, her neck crooked and aching, along with her head. The first thing she did was to check on her grandmother, but Charlotte was nowhere to be found. She called Sylvia's, but no one picked up the phone there, either. She'd just have to assume her grandmother was feeling more like her old self this morning and had gone out with her friend.

She showered, letting the warm water rush over her sore muscles, washed her hair and blow-dried it, then dressed and headed to the kitchen for some much-needed coffee. By the time she'd finished one full cup and started on another, she was finally beginning to feel human again.

She opened the newspaper, scanned the pages and when she came to the Bachelor Blog section, she groaned aloud. Apparently the Blogger's fame had spread to the suburbs because someone had told the Blogger that Lexie and Coop had been at the hospital last night. She'd long since given up having privacy when it came to her relationship with Coop. She just did her best to ignore the fact that anyone she passed could be taking notes and forwarding them to the Blogger. Lexie just hoped her grandmother was no longer the Blogger's source.

Between the caffeine and the reality check brought on by reading the paper, Lexie's brain began to function, too, and the events of last night came flooding back. From her parents' stiff demeanor to her grandmother's incident, the memories nearly caused her headache to return. Until she remembered that there had been something different about the whole miserable evening. Coop had been by her side, holding her hand when her parents' disapproval of her trip choices were mentioned, and keeping his reassuring touch on her shoulder throughout the ordeal at the hospital. She hadn't been alone.

And she'd been alone for most of her life.

Her cell phone rang suddenly, distracting her from what could have been a very risky thought process. She grabbed her Black-Berry from the counter by the coffee machine.

"Hello?"

"Hey, Lex."

At the sound of Coop's voice, her stomach fluttered with a warm, fuzzy alien feeling. "Hey, yourself."

"How are you feeling this morning?" he asked.

The vague memory of him leaning over her and removing her glasses flitted through her mind. "How long did you stay?"

"Long enough to watch you sleep," he said, his voice gruff.

"Oh." Swirling pools of desire circled inside her. "Sorry I wasn't good company."

"Says who?" He chuckled. "I like listening to you snore."

"Hey! I don't snore!"

"I say you do and it's pretty darn cute, if you ask me."

She smiled and hoped he was doing the same. "We need to talk some more." About her grandmother and the jewels.

"I know. Unfortunately, I have to work. A meeting I can't cancel. How about dinner tonight?"

She wouldn't mind having the day to work on her designs. Maybe she and Claudia could have an impromptu get-together as well. "Sure. Dinner sounds good."

"Great. How's our favorite almost octogenarian this morning?"

Lexie sighed. "I wish I knew. She was gone by the time I woke up. No note, either."

"Think she's avoiding you?"

"That's exactly what I think. She's afraid I'll ask more questions about how she really got the necklace."

Coop cleared his throat. "We need a plan."

Lexie nodded. "I agree. We can figure it out over dinner."

"My place?" he asked.

She remembered what happened the last time they had dinner at his apartment. So did her body, and a tingling arousal settled between her legs. She squeezed her thighs together to stop the sensation, but that only served to heighten the feeling.

"Lexie?"

"Your place sounds perfect," she murmured. Private, too. She doubted she'd survive the day anticipating what was to come.

"See you later, sweetheart."

Sweetheart. At the endearment, her mouth ran dry. "Later," she said, the words barely audible before he hung up.

She dragged a deep breath into her lungs. She had a long day ahead of her and wouldn't be productive if all she thought about were his rich voice and sexy hands.

Nope. She needed to work if she wanted those hours to pass quickly.

He was right. They needed a plan. But what would it be? Confront Charlotte and risk upsetting her? Or let it go, in which case the mystery would remain unanswered forever. The latter was unacceptable to Lexie, and there was no doubt in her mind that Coop would never agree to just pretend an unsolved jewel theft had never happened.

And if their digging confirmed her grandmother's guilt? Lexie closed her eyes, knowing in her heart that Coop the reporter couldn't possibly bury such a story. Right now they shared a mutual interest. Dig up the story, uncover the truth, figure out what had happened in the past. Afterwards? That mutual interest would be torn in two.

Clearly, the end was near. Sooner than she had hoped. In which case she had to make the most of the time that remained, which meant that when she saw him tonight, seduction first, discussion later.

Charlotte and Sylvia, scarves covering their red hair and Jackie O sunglasses perched on their noses, stood across the street from the Vintage Jewelers and waited for their prey. They'd already walked in and talked to Ricky's daughter. She'd told them that her father had gone fishing and hopefully would be back soon.

Ricky had never been a man who liked to get his hands dirty, and the story seemed suspicious. So they'd agreed to case the joint until he returned. On the off chance that, like them, he knew there might be trouble and was playing it safe. He might show up on off hours and try to sneak in without being noticed. They didn't call him a snake for no reason.

History had given him that name.

While watching for the man, Charlotte couldn't help but reminisce about how they'd come to this point. She and Sylvia had grown up together in the same poor Bronx neighborhood. Neither woman wanted to follow the traditional route of marriage and family in an era when that was the norm, which left them with no real means of support. They both took odd jobs to make ends meet, serving in local eateries, and yes, occasionally reverting to thievery so they wouldn't starve.

Who knew ancient history could come back to bite Charlotte in the butt this late in life?

Sylvia had met Ricky on a blind date when he was working part-time at a jewelry store. Later, he'd hired her and eventually he'd gotten the idea to rob from the rich to give to the poor — Ricky being the poor one. He must have sensed a kinship with Sylvia because he'd tapped her as his sidekick and she'd brought Charlotte along for the ride. Sylvia had always been in love with Ricky, but as soon as he'd laid eyes on Charlotte, he'd started viewing Sylvia as more of a friend. The unrequited-love business had always made for a risky partnership and friendship between the three, but somehow they'd made it work.

Until that fateful night when Charlotte had caught the two of them in bed. She'd stopped speaking to them both. A short time later, fate interceded in the form of her beloved Henry. She'd waited on his table and he'd asked her on a date. Being around him made her feel alive and happy, and Charlotte decided the time had come to live a *normal* life. She hadn't been able to conceive a child right away. Then came the draft and the Korean War.

Charlotte had been so bored and lonely that when Ricky showed up on her doorstep, begging her to go along for one last heist, she'd agreed. Along with Sylvia, whom he'd also found, they'd hit the Lancaster house. A place that Charlotte knew from her husband's days as their part-time chauffeur.

That part of the story she'd told Lexie had been real.

"I still don't see how such a low-down snake could have such a sweet, beautiful child," Sylvia said, pulling Charlotte's mind from the past.

She glanced up to see Anna step out of the store, probably for lunch. She'd had another young salesgirl with her and she was probably watching the shop.

"You didn't think he was a snake when you jumped into bed with him." Her mind had obviously still been in the past when the words slipped out, despite their agreement never to discuss their romantic history with Ricky again.

Sylvia straightened her shoulders, obviously upset. "That's the pot calling the kettle black, missy! You knew I had a thing for him and you lured him into your web anyway. Can you blame me for taking what was rightfully mine?" Sylvia asked, her face flushing, her voice rising.

Charlotte cocked an eyebrow. "Hell, yes, I can blame you, you shameless hussy! He was interested in me first!"

"Ladies, is there a problem?" A uniformed police officer asked, interjecting his authoritative voice.

"No, sir." Unless he counted her best

friend being a lying, cheating snake in the grass. "We were just discussing something that happened in the distant past," Charlotte said, sweetly.

"Apparently, we remember the situation differently," Sylvia added. Behind her glasses, Charlotte caught the frosty glare.

"You know how it is when time plays games with a person's memory. Especially with *age*," Charlotte explained.

Sylvia nodded. "And she would know, as she's a full year older than me, in case you missed the extra lines and wrinkles."

The officer shook his head hard. "All right now. I suggest you kiss and make up before this degenerates into a brawl," he said, laughing at his own joke.

"I can best her anytime," Charlotte said. "I've done it before and I'll do it again."

"As I recall, I had a hunk of your already thinning hair in my hands!" Sylvia retorted.

The officer sputtered, unable to formulate a coherent sentence.

Finally, he propped both hands on his waist, one on a baton, the other on his weapon. "Leave the past where it belongs and find something else to do." With a curt nod, he took off down the street.

Charlotte exhaled hard. "Well, that was close. Imagine if not one day after I landed in the hospital, poor Lexie had to bail me out of the hoosegow!"

"On that I agree with you," Sylvia said.

Both women knew Lexie was the reason Charlotte was in such a panic now. True, she wanted her ring back, but she'd lived without it for years. If given a choice, Charlotte would prefer that the whole thing stay buried and Lexie continue to look at her with stars in her eyes. Charlotte rarely felt guilty for her past anymore, but at the thought of her granddaughter finding out, Charlotte's heart nearly beat its way out of her chest. She'd lived a clean life ever since. She adored Lexie and Lexie idolized her. If she found out, would she ever look at Charlotte the same way again?

In an effort to avoid finding out, any time Lexie mentioned the ring, Charlotte distracted her, usually with well-timed words. She also gave the Bachelor Blogger whatever tidbits she could, both in an effort to encourage Lexie and Coop to stay together, and to distract them from the ring. But other than the photograph of them kissing, those two seemed oblivious of the Blog. And Charlotte couldn't focus on Lexie and Coop until she wrapped up her own troubles.

Last night, she would have resorted to faking a heart attack to avoid discussing the necklace, but she hadn't had to go that far. At the time, she hadn't known the difference between acid pain, pure panic and real heart trouble.

Charlotte glanced at her friend. "Instead of us arguing over the past, we need to figure out how to keep ancient history where it belongs!"

Sylvia slowly nodded. "You're right," she muttered. "Just promise me that you won't fall for Ricky's charm again. We have a good, solid friendship going and his reappearance can only mess it up."

Charlotte glanced at her wristwatch. "I don't want anything to do with him! I haven't since my beloved Henry!"

Sylvia paused, then tipped her head to one side. "Fine."

"And you? Promise you won't throw yourself in his arms at the first chance," Charlotte said, her own arms folded across her chest.

"Like there's room with that huge stomach?" Sylvia shuddered. "We have friendship, someone to talk to in the evening, have dinner with or see a movie. Why would I give that up for the likes of him?" She waved a dismissive hand toward the store.

"Then we understand each other," Charlotte said. "It's getting too hot out here.

Let's return around closing time and if we're not lucky, again tomorrow morning."

"Deal," Sylvia agreed.

But as they slowly made their way back home, Charlotte couldn't help wondering if Sylvia would be as immune to Ricky now as she claimed. She hoped so, because she really didn't want to spend her last few years without her best friend by her side.

After finishing the concept she had in mind for Coop's home page — going under the assumption he'd soon have more than one novel to offer the world — Lexie did something she rarely did. She went shopping.

If tonight was her last night with Coop, she wanted it to be a memorable one for them both.

She normally slept in any old T-shirt, so she wasn't familiar with frilly lingerie or the best place to buy it. The first store that came to mind was Bloomingdale's, a huge department store in midtown Manhattan. She left a note for her grandmother who still hadn't returned and headed for the store.

Stepping through the doors, Lexie was immediately assaulted by the overhead lights and assorted scents of cosmetics and perfumes. Overwhelmed was more like it. She began to walk around, feeling out of her element, and decided to ask someone where she could find the lingerie department. The faster she found and purchased what she wanted, the quicker she'd be out of there.

Catching sight of a salesgirl, Lexie stepped toward her.

"Excuse me, where is the lingerie department?" she asked.

"Intimate apparel is on four," the heavily made-up woman said, directing her to the nearest escalator with perfectly manicured fingernails.

"Thank you." Lexie turned in that direction, when she heard her name being called.

She spun around, surprised to find Coop's neighbor, Sara Rios, walking toward her. "I thought that was you!" Sara greeted her with a smile.

"Hi!" Lexie couldn't tear her gaze from the woman who once again, exhibited an entirely different persona from the hard-edged cop or the casually dressed woman she'd met before. Wearing a miniskirt, a ruffled tank, delicate sandals, a full face of makeup and her long hair flowing around her shoulders, Lexie probably wouldn't have recognized her even if she'd spotted her first.

"Small world," Lexie couldn't help saying.

"I'm a regular here. Days off and here I am." She spread her arms around her.

"I never would have imagined. Shopping really isn't my thing."

"Then what is?" Sara asked, while steering her through the store.

"Travel. I like to save my money so when I want to pick up and go, the cash is there," Lexie explained.

As they spoke, Sara would stop and browse at various cosmetic counters.

"What sort of places have you been?"

"Last month I went to Indonesia to see the area hit by the tsunami in 2004, then ended up in Darfur with some people I met."

Sara dropped an eye pencil in her hand. "So you're not what you seem, either. You have to be pretty brave to travel alone, and then to pick up and head to Darfur with strangers."

Lexie shrugged. She'd never thought of her traveling as brave. "The people I met were with an aid organization. They were safe enough."

Sara nodded. "So what started this love of travel?"

It was funny. Of all the people who'd questioned her about her transient lifestyle, Coop's friend seemed the most genuinely curious. Because of that interest, it was easy to open up to her.

"When I was younger, my grandmother would take me to local sites. Usually it was whenever life in my house got too intense," Lexie said, remembering. "At first it was local parks, places to escape. Later it was major tourist sites like the Statue of Liberty and then the Empire State Building."

"She sounds special," Sara said.

Lexie smiled. "She is." And probably a devious thief, she thought to herself. "Anyway, as I got older she encouraged me to travel and see the world while I could. I'd take these trips to amazing countries like France and Spain, and I'd realize what a breath of fresh air it was to be away from the pressure at home. Eventually, traveling just became a way of life for me. Something I craved and truly enjoyed."

"Sounds like life at home was tough."

"No more than for most people," Lexie said lightly, suddenly embarrassed that she'd spilled her guts about more than just travel. "Hey, I don't want to keep you, so it was great seeing you and I'll just go do my shopping."

She wanted to make a quick escape, but Sara's hand on her arm stopped her. "I'm sorry if I pushed. It's the cop in me."

Lexie shook her head. "Actually, you didn't. Something about you is just easy to talk to."

Sara grinned. "Ever hear the expression, *good cop, bad cop?*"

Lexie nodded.

"My ex-partner and I used to fall into those roles, and though I can be a hard-ass when I need to be, I can also be a good listener, which makes me perfect for the good-cop role. So, what are you shopping for? Because I'm just browsing."

Lexie really didn't want to share her mission with Sara. "I just need some lingerie," she said, vaguely, but even as she spoke, a heated blush rose to her cheeks. "I need something to wear to surprise Coop," she blurted out before Sara could accurately read her embarrassment.

A wide grin spread across the other woman's face. "Why didn't you say so? Mind if I tag along? I'm pretty good at picking out the racier things."

She wiggled her eyebrows and Lexie laughed. "Why not? I really suck at this shopping stuff," she admitted.

Sara had a way about her that put Lexie at ease, remarkable considering how uptight she'd made her feel in the beginning. Apparently, she kept her defenses high until she made a decision about a person, but once someone earned her stamp of approval, Sara let down her walls. Lexie only hoped Sara didn't live to regret her decision to help once Lexie and Coop's relationship ran its course.

The women shared lunch in the restaurant upstairs and by the end of the day, Lexie had a spectacular-looking lingerie set, which she hoped would knock Coop's socks off.

As they walked out of the store and onto the street, the heat struck Lexie immediately. "This was fun and I appreciate your helping me."

Sara smiled. "My pleasure. And now I'm going to go a step further with advice that goes beyond clothing."

A warning tingle ripped through Lexie. "I'm listening," she said warily.

"I come from a family of divorced cops. It's all part of the job, so long-term relationships really aren't my thing."

Lexie sensed a hint of sadness and regret in Sara's statement.

"Running away is something I understand better than most."

Lexie narrowed her gaze. "I don't run away."

She should have known she'd let down her guard too easily. Sara was yet another person who judged Lexie and her choices.

"I explained to you that travel has become a part of me."

"You did." Sara nodded, but didn't apologize for misunderstanding. "You also said the sightseeing and travel started as a way to escape tension at home."

"And it morphed into something greater. Something important to me. Why does everyone insist on viewing it as wrong?" Lexie asked, frustrated and upset. She'd suffered enough of this with her family. She didn't need it from a woman who was a perfect stranger.

But she was also Coop's closest friend.

Who's your closest friend? The question entered Lexie's mind uninvited, chipping at the defenses she'd built up over the years.

"All I'm saying is that sometimes we get caught up in a cycle that becomes impossible to break. And I'm suggesting you take a hard look at your life before you leave for wherever it is you decide to go next. Because the things that matter most to you might not be waiting when you return."

Wow. Now this was the Sara she'd first met. Hard-edged and intrusive. "Thanks for the advice," Lexie said stiffly.

Sara's penetrating gaze met hers. "I know you're mad now, but I hope one day you'll thank me for saying this."

"I doubt it." Lexie's fingers curled tightly around the shopping bag in her hand.

"We'll see. Enjoy your purchases," Sara said, turned and headed off in the opposite direction, leaving Lexie speechless and feeling blindsided by the unsolicited advice.

Somehow she pushed Sara's comments to the back of her mind and refocused on tonight. A combination of excitement and anticipation took over. Especially when she remembered she still had Coop's key in her purse.

Coop headed home from work, hoping for a few minutes to shower before Lexie arrived. He'd spent the last couple of hours sorting through the police blotter, deciding what stories would make it into the paper. Sometimes there were serious ones and sometimes, like today, he'd get the oddball crime. An upscale restaurant had hosted a collectors' meeting of the Fabergé Egg Society — who knew there was such a group? — where a rare egg had been reported missing. One minute the designer egg had been there, the next minute it was gone. All the members of the society, plus the waiters and staff of the restaurant, had been questioned, but there were no suspects.

A reward had been issued for the valuable antique. Since Coop had the room, he ran the piece and put the issue to bed.

Now he let himself into his apartment and immediately sensed Lexie's presence. Once again, he found himself overwhelmed by the rightness of her being here, waiting for him, and no matter how he fought it, he couldn't shake the feeling.

He tossed his keys onto the hall table and walked inside. The table was set with his mismatched dishes and he winced, taking in the lack of coordination along with the candles she'd had to have picked up herself, since he didn't own any. Chinese food cartons were also set out and still closed, waiting for them to enjoy.

"Lexie?" he called out.

"In the bedroom."

His mouth immediately went dry. He stepped closer and a seductive fragrance assaulted him in the best way. He inhaled again and the scent lured him toward the bedroom.

The door was partially closed, a ruffled dress hanging from the doorknob. His entire body went on red alert. He kicked the door open with the toe of his foot, drew a steadying breath and strode inside.

His dimly lit, normally masculine bedroom was also decorated with burning candles flickering seductively around the room, while Lexie lay in the center of the bed, a vision in skimpy red-lace lingerie.

She crooked a finger, a siren calling to him from across the room and all thoughts of Chinese food and showering fled. Coop couldn't think about anything except the woman waiting for him.

"This is a welcome surprise." He barely recognized his own voice.

"I thought you were expecting me."

He loosened the tie he'd been wearing and pulled it over his head, tossing it to the floor. As he continued to walk toward her, he worked on his shirt, opening the buttons one by one until he shrugged it off his shoulders and let it drop.

Lexie watched him with wide, eyeglass-free eyes, which darkened with every move he made.

"I never knew you were a frilly-lingerie kind of girl." He kicked off his shoes and rid himself of his socks, then unbuttoned his slacks. He hooked his fingers into the waistband and pulled off both pants and boxers in one smooth motion.

"There's a lot you don't know about me." Her voice dropped an octave, her gaze focused on his hard-as-a-rock erection.

He couldn't be sure, but he thought he thickened beneath that approving, hungry stare.

As he studied her, he wondered what was left to learn about Lexie, but he intended to find out. Sliding beside her on the mattress, he hooked his finger into the thin strap covering one shoulder and buried his face in her neck, inhaling her sweet scent and tasting her with long laps of his tongue.

She shuddered and tilted her head, encouraging him. He complied, laving his way up, taking soft bites of her flesh with his teeth, followed by long, soothing sweeps with his tongue.

Her entire body trembled at the gentle assault, while Coop couldn't believe how ready he was from just this simple taste. He paused long enough to devour the look of her, tousled and tempting, wearing seductive lingerie that revealed mere flashes of skin beneath the sexy material.

"I bought it for you," she said in a husky voice.

The admission nearly broke him. It humbled him. It also aroused him beyond belief. He wanted to bury himself inside her wet sheath, but she'd obviously put thought into this seduction and he wanted her to get more than a quickie out of it.

He cupped his hand around her face, turning her toward him. "And I appreciate it."

She smiled and stroked his cheek with her fingertips. "I've been looking forward to this all day," she said, then sealed her lips over his.

In the instant their mouths melded, things turned from gentle to urgent. She'd planned the seduction, but from the way her fingers dug into his shoulders and she pressed her breasts against his chest, rubbing restlessly, she obviously didn't want slow.

Neither did he. Coop dipped his head and pulled one tight, needy nipple into his mouth, sucking on the silken material, flicking at the tight bud with his teeth until Lexie whimpered aloud. She arched her back, pushing her breast deeper into his mouth. He roughly pulled at the fabric, exposing her breast and ripping the flimsy material.

"I'll pay for it," he muttered and sealed his mouth over her flesh. He flicked his tongue back and forth over her distended nipple and she groaned, thrusting her fingers into his hair, urging him on.

He tormented one breast until her entire body shook in reaction before exposing the other, licking, biting and soothing, taking himself to an incredible level of hot, clawing need.

They were both in sitting positions and she crawled on top of him, locking her legs around his waist and tilting her pelvis so her moist, damp heat sealed against his stomach.

No panties.

"God," he said on a guttural groan. She was so damn hot. He couldn't get enough and slid his hand between their bodies, easing one finger inside her.

Her inner walls clamped around him and he nearly exploded. In and out, he slid his one long finger, pleasuring her while kissing those luscious lips.

She wound her arms around his neck and eased herself backwards, giving him easier access. All the while she rocked against his hand, moaning, senseless, sexy words, urging him to give her more. With his thumb, he began to circle the sensitive outer bud and she cried out, so he deepened the pressure outside, continuing to thrust his finger in and out.

Her breath came in shallow gasps, her lower body moved on him, seeking deeper, more intense contact. Coop grit his teeth and swore to himself that he wouldn't come until he was inside her. He leaned forward and kissed her again, which had the effect of pushing his finger deeper into her body, pressing his thumb into direct contact with her clit.

Just when he thought he couldn't hold out, she screamed as her release washed over her, her body milking his hand while he wrung every last contraction he could from deep inside her.

Then he reached over and yanked open his drawer, pulling out a condom and barely getting it on, his hands were shaking so badly.

Lexie lay sprawled on the bed, eyes partially closed, legs spread wide. "Hurry," she whispered.

He leaned over her and thrust hard, fast and deep inside her wet sheath, knowing it wouldn't take much for him to come.

What he didn't expect was for her to join him.

But the minute he slid inside her, the union of their bodies woke hers up again. He met her gaze. Eyes wide, she watched him as he slid out, feeling every slick inch of her passage, then pressed deep once more.

Lexie bent her knees. "Again," she murmured, her gaze never leaving his.

He slid out, all the way this time, and her

eyes reflected her objection.

"What are you doing?" she asked.

He silenced her with a kiss, a hard, demanding, taking-everything kind of kiss. Then he spread her with his hands, positioned himself and again took possession of her body.

She cried out and he pushed deeper, wanting them joined as tightly as possible. Never wanting to leave her again. He levered himself up with one hand and began a steady pumping of his hips, possessing her. Owning her. As he moved deep inside, as his body curled tighter, release beckoning ever closer, Coop realized this was sex like he'd never had before.

This woman wasn't like any he'd ever had before.

Because he loved her.

Dammit. He thought he'd protected himself. Tried.

But as she met him thrust for thrust, giving of herself, all of herself, thought escaped him and a hot wave sent him over the edge, mind and body exploding, lost inside her.

And from the sounds she made beneath him, she'd done the same.

CHAPTER FOURTEEN

They'd had fantastic sex. Amazing sex. Sex like Lexie had never experienced before. She and Coop connected on so many levels, she actually *felt* the bond between them in bed as well as out. Half-dressed — she wearing one of his old T-shirts, he clad only in his boxers — they'd eaten the Chinese food and cleaned up the kitchen together.

They now found themselves back in his bed.

Coop leaned against the pillows, allowing Lexie to admire his tanned and muscular chest and the sprinkling of hair she'd felt against her skin. God, he was sexy.

He propped an arm behind his head. "I really need to get a full set of dishes," he said, completely unaware of the effect he had on her.

Lexie laughed. "I certainly can't criticize. I don't own any dishes at all."

"Good point." He set his jaw and his good

314

mood evaporated, the smile leaving his face at the reminder of her vagabond lifestyle.

While she was in the mood-ruining business, she decided she might as well launch into the discussion she'd been dreading. "So what are we going to do about my grandmother?"

Coop exhaled slowly. "You realize we need to find out the truth, right?"

Swallowing over the lump in her throat, she nodded. "I know." She'd already accepted that fact and had been preparing herself.

"I was thinking we ought to confront her directly." He raised a hand before she could object. "Wait. *Confront* is the wrong word. I think we should sit down with her, tell her what we know and ask her for the truth. No more dancing around the subject. I'm sure it'll be easier for her once everything's out in the open."

Lexie raised an eyebrow. "Really? This is a woman who's been keeping this secret over fifty years. I think she's a pro at hiding things by now. Revealing it will probably be the tough part."

Coop reached out and grabbed Lexie's hand. "Who are you more worried about hurting? Your grandmother? Or yourself?" he asked gently.

Lexie hated the question mostly because she already knew the answer. "Probably both," she admitted. "If my grandmother really did this —" and in Lexie's heart, she already knew Charlotte had stolen the necklace "— then where does that leave me?"

She asked the question that had been haunting her since the revelation in the police station basement. If Charlotte wasn't the person Lexie had always believed her to be, then what did Lexie have to hang on to?

Coop squeezed her hand tighter. "I think it leaves you as yourself — and that's someone you aren't yet comfortable with. That's why you've spent your life thinking that as long as you could model yourself after your grandmother, you could justify your choices and decisions," he finally said, summing her up pretty accurately.

His words pierced her heart and caused a painful ache in her chest. "Are you sure you're not a shrink?" she asked, laughing, so she wouldn't cry.

He grinned. "Minored in psychology in college. But that's not how I figured you out. I know it because I know *you*." He held on to her hand, imparting strength in his touch. "I met your parents, Lexie, and though you're very different from them, those differences don't make you a bad person."

"Really?" she asked, grabbing on to his words like a beacon of hope.

He nodded. "Hey, you inherited some good things from your parents."

"Such as?" she asked wryly.

His brows furrowed in thought. But not for too long. "Your work ethic for one," he said pretty quickly. "You worked hard at your Web-design business and made it a success, right?"

"Right."

"And you're innately honest. So are they — even if you don't always like what they have to say or the way they express themselves."

She nodded slowly. He did have a point.

"And maybe you can look at things from your father's point of view. It couldn't have been easy being as uptight as he is and growing up with Charlotte as his mother."

Lexie blinked, letting Coop's insightful words sink in. "I never thought about it like that." Never looked at the world from her father's perspective. "He probably felt as out of place with his mother as I do with him," she murmured.

"Common ground," Coop said, sounding pleased.

"Wow. Who'd have thunk it?" she asked, and her world spun a little bit on its axis.

"Hey. No matter how much you idolize your grandmother or want to view yourself as just like her, whatever she did fifty-odd years ago has no reflection on the woman you are today." He placed his hand beneath her chin and tilted her head upwards. "Promise me you'll think about that?"

How could she deny him anything? "Promise."

He smiled, satisfied. "While you're thinking, remember this. You are also a successful Web designer and a fantastic person regardless of how different you are from the rest of your family."

Warmth spread over her like sunshine on her skin. "Sounds as if you like me," she said, teasing him.

He met her gaze, his gorgeous eyes drinking her in. "I more than like you, Lexie," he said, his voice gruff with raw emotion.

Panic washed over her at the depth of feeling she both saw and heard. "So we're going to confront my grandmother. That's the plan?" she asked, deliberately changing the subject.

A flicker of disappointment flashed across his face before he quickly masked it. "Yes, that's the plan."

She nodded. "Good. So let's shower and do this." She slid out of bed.

Away from Coop, his touch and the feelings she didn't want to face.

"I don't know about you, but I'm getting tired of hanging out on the street corner like a common hooker," Charlotte said to Sylvia.

Charlotte peered across the street at the Vintage Jewelers. It was early morning and if they didn't see Ricky soon, Charlotte and her aching feet might have to call it quits. She wasn't as young as she used to be.

"I agree. It's hard to believe we haven't been propositioned yet. Kinda hard on the old ego." Sylvia adjusted her big-rimmed sunglasses.

"I think it's because nobody can see our faces behind the glasses and the scarves. On a good hair day, I'd have men lining up for a smooch." Charlotte glanced at her friend. "So would you," she added, trying to be nice.

Sylvia had never had Charlotte's looks. What she did have was a personality and a big heart. It was too bad she and Frank had never had kids. At least then she'd have a Lexie in her life, Charlotte thought.

"Look! That's him!" Sylvia pulled on

Charlotte's blouse. "The fat, balding man sneaking around the corner!"

He didn't go into the store entrance. Instead, he appeared to be sneaking around the side.

"That bastard. Is there a back entrance we missed?" Charlotte asked.

"I don't know. But at least we know he's back."

Charlotte nodded. "Now all we have to do is wait for his daughter to leave and we can ambush him!"

When the woman stepped out of the store at noon, Charlotte and Sylvia glanced at each other, locked gazes, nodded once and strode across the street, two women on a mission.

If Lexie didn't want to discuss anything serious, then fine. Coop wouldn't discuss anything serious. But that didn't mean the revelation he'd had earlier wasn't bouncing around inside him. And damn if he knew what to do about it.

After all, he'd gone and done the one thing he'd promised himself he'd never do again. He'd fallen in love with a woman who couldn't love him back or stay in town long enough to let life and love develop. What were the freaking chances he'd fuck up twice?

Pretty darn good, apparently.

At least he hadn't outright told her how he felt. He still had some dignity intact.

They showered — separately — and headed over to her grandmother's apartment. Coop drove. His mood permeated the car and neither one of them spoke on the way there.

Once at her grandmother's, Charlotte wasn't home.

"I swear the woman has radar," Lexie muttered, to herself. "Come. Let's check Sylvia's place."

He followed Lexie down the hall and waited as she banged on the other woman's door. Nobody answered.

"Of course not," Lexie said, her voice thick with frustration.

"Let's go back to your grandmother's." He took the lead and she followed behind him.

They sat at the kitchen table, staring at each other in silence. As a reporter, Coop had been in this position before, unable to find a person from whom he needed information, and asked himself what he'd do if Charlotte were any other source.

"We need to draw her out," he said,

answering his own question.

Intrigued, Lexie leaned across the table, chin against her hand. "How?"

He tried to ignore the inquisitive furrow between her brows, but found the tiny wrinkles cute. So were the freckles on her nose.

Damn.

He closed his eyes and attempted to focus. "We need her to want to talk to us."

"What if . . ." Lexie's voice trailed off.

Coop opened his eyes. "What? Say it." The only way they'd figure this out was to bounce ideas off each other.

She pursed her glossed lips. "Okay, I don't like this. But what if we take the necklace and leave a note in its place?"

"Then she'd have no choice but to come looking for us. It's brilliant! You're brilliant!" Coop said, excited with the idea.

At the compliment, pleasure flashed across her face and Coop rose from his chair to kiss her, but as reality dawned, self-preservation kicked in and he quickly lowered himself back to his seat.

She visibly flinched from his withdrawal. "Let me go see if I can find the necklace. Hopefully, she's not hiding it," Lexie said, dashing from the room. She returned seconds later with the necklace dangling from her hand. *"Ta da!"*

"Perfect. Now the note," Coop instructed.

She handed him the necklace, pulled paper and pen from a drawer and wrote her grandmother a ransom letter, propping it up against the fake fruit centerpiece on the table.

"Now what?" she asked.

"We head to my place and wait her out." Which Coop figured would be easier said than done.

If he and Lexie weren't having easy conversation, they certainly wouldn't be killing time by having sex. Which meant that until Charlotte showed up, they were in for an awkward, uncomfortable stretch of time.

Ricky couldn't believe the two old biddies had tied him to his chair with scarves they'd brought with them. They'd trussed him up with knots tighter than a Boy Scout's.

"What do you want?" he asked.

They exchanged incredulous glances.

Charlotte had propped her sunglasses on top of her scarf-covered head and he was able to look into her determined gaze. "I want my wedding ring. The one I gave you that night at the Lancasters so nobody would realize one of us had on a ring or any kind of outstanding clue," Charlotte said.

As if he needed the reminder. That had been his rule. One she'd forgotten during their last hurrah, so he'd pocketed the ring.

"And I want the bracelet!" Sylvia had lowered the glasses to the tip of her nose, looking at him over the rims like a librarian. "I'm sure you remember it. The one that matches her necklace from the Lancaster job. You were supposed to meet up with us and divide the loot and you never showed. Sneaky, no-good, lying bastard." Sylvia kicked his shin with an orthopedic shoe.

"Ouch! Dammit, settle down," Ricky yelled at her. "Let me go before someone comes into the store and finds you two idiots."

Charlotte shook her head. "Sylvia, you start there." She pointed to a set of drawers. "I'll look here." She sat down at his desk.

Together they began ransacking the back room and his private drawers and stashes in a futile search for their missing items.

He leaned back in his chair, relaxed despite the circumstances, because they wouldn't find what they were looking for. Ricky might have kept things like a hoarder, but the two items they'd come looking for, those he'd hidden in a safe place.

"Hey! I recognize this." Sylvia held up a brooch from one of their first heists. "I thought we agreed we'd only take enough so that we each ended up with one piece. To keep or sell if we needed the money."

Charlotte rose from the chair. "You mean to tell me you took other things from those jobs?"

Ricky remained stubbornly silent. He wasn't engaging these two lunatics in an argument and when he didn't reply, they went back to work, poring through every nook and cranny they could find.

Ten minutes later, they'd pretty well covered everything.

"Not here," Sylvia said, sounding defeated.

"I can't find them, either." Charlotte perched her hands on her slim hips — Ricky'd always had a thing for her slim hips — and strode over. "I want my wedding ring back and I want it now."

Sylvia reared her leg back for another kick.

"Whoa! No more kicking me, you old battle-ax!"

"Then tell us where our things are," Sylvia said.

Ricky shook his head. "How about a deal instead?"

"What kind of deal? And talk fast," Charlotte said, obviously realizing they might be running out of time before his daughter returned.

"You get my ring back from that nosy reporter *and* you make sure he and his lady friend back off their investigation of the ring. And of me. My daughter told me they've been snooping around, asking questions. Then we'll exchange goods." He smiled, knowing he still had the upper hand.

Sylvia glanced at Charlotte. "Think we can manage that?"

Charlotte muttered under her breath.

Ricky couldn't hear, nor did he care. He only wanted her to take the deal.

"Fine," she said at last. "But we're holding you to it. No weaseling out, disappearing or taking what's ours."

"Fine," Ricky said. "Now untie me."

"Wait. There's one more thing," Sylvia said, glancing at Charlotte as she always used to do, for the okay.

Charlotte shrugged. "Okay, why not."

"What's she talking about?" Ricky asked. "What'd you just agree to?" An uneasy feeling settled over him and while he was looking to Charlotte for answers, Sylvia kicked him again, harder this time.

"Oww!"

"Quit crying like a baby. And you'd better hold up your end or the next one'll be in the nuts," Sylvia promised before grinning at Charlotte. "*Now* we can untie him."

After all the excitement of the day, Charlotte needed a nap. Unfortunately, she also needed to formulate a plan. How in the world would she get Coop to give her the ring and agree to stop digging into the story? She doubted he'd do all that, even for love.

"Any ideas yet?" Sylvia asked.

"No, and stop talking. You're giving me a bigger headache than I already have. I need to think."

They walked into Charlotte's apartment and before she could ask her friend to go home so she could sleep, Charlotte caught sight of a note on the kitchen table.

"It's from Lexie. I recognize the handwriting," Charlotte said. She opened the folded paper and read aloud. "*We have your necklace. If you want to see it again, we want to see you.* There's an address below it," Charlotte said, figuring it was Coop's apartment.

She fell into the nearest chair, feeling every one of her seventy-nine years.

"Oh, no!" Sylvia said. "Now what?"

"I don't know about you, but I'm taking two Tylenol and then a nap. I know my limits and I've reached them today." She was exhausted; her brain was fried. And panic over what Lexie knew was threatening to overwhelm her. "We'll decide what to do when I wake up."

Sylvia nodded. "I'm exhausted, too. Nobody ever told me getting old was so hard."

Charlotte rolled her eyes. Sylvia always had been such a drama queen. "What do you say we meet up again later?" she asked over a yawn.

"Sounds good. By then maybe your brain cells will rejuvenate and you'll have a plan," Sylvia said, rising from her chair.

She always had the utmost faith in Charlotte to get them out of any jam. In the past, Charlotte had enjoyed the leadership role. Today, though, she just felt tired.

And old.

Lexie sat, legs crossed, on the large windowsill, looking out Coop's window at the view of the city below. Lights flickered in the darkness and she wondered how many people walking the streets were as conflicted as she was.

Coop had been holed up in the bedroom since dinner, working on his laptop. She assumed he was writing and not tapping out an assignment, but who knew? He certainly wasn't talking. And she could pinpoint the exact moment his mood and behavior had changed.

After he'd said, *I more than like you,* and she'd bolted like a scared rabbit.

She'd tried to work, pushing thoughts of her love life aside. She'd registered Coop's domain name and gotten his okay on the proposed design for his site. He'd beamed with pride when she'd showed him her work, his book cover a prominent feature on the home page. She'd used his newspaper photo as a placeholder, but he'd balked at the notion of having a professional photograph taken.

In fact, he'd sounded appalled. Lexie grinned, recalling the horrified expression on his face. But she wasn't finished trying to convince him. She'd spent some time accumulating Web site links of other famous authors who had causal photos on their pages. She planned to ambush him with them later. She could imagine readers seeing Coop's handsome face on his Web site. She knew she'd return over and over for a glimpse. He might not like that aspect of utilizing his photograph, but if it ultimately led to book sales based on his talent, then he ought to get used to it.

But once she'd focused on Coop and not just his Web site, she'd lost her concentration and found herself here at the window, staring out at the world, wondering why the emotional part of life had to be so complicated.

She was unable to sort out the waves of panic engulfing her at the thought of Coop developing real feelings for her. Was it that she couldn't trust in those feelings? Or was it that she was afraid those feelings would come with expectations for her to settle down? And would that be so bad? If Coop was the reason?

Sara had accused her of using travel to run away from problems at home. But Lexie couldn't imagine giving up her many sojourns around the world, feeding her mind and her soul with different cultures, images, sights and smells. Losing that ability would stifle her. So how could something that brought her such joy really be an escape? Besides, Coop understood how important her travels were, so would he really expect her to give them up completely?

She was afraid to find out.

Afraid she'd have to choose.

Afraid of leaving him.

And afraid of being asked to stay.

Lexie let out a huge sigh, no closer to understanding her conflict or coming to a resolution, when suddenly she heard the sound of someone playing with the lock on the front door.

CHAPTER FIFTEEN

Heart in her throat, Lexie headed for the front door.

Coop had also been on guard and came up behind her.

"Why isn't she knocking?" Lexie asked softly.

"Good question. I left the bolt undone, so let's see what happens." Coop paused a few feet away from the door, folded his arms across his chest and waited.

Lexie stood by his side.

After a few more minutes of listening to the sounds of someone playing with the lock, Coop reached out and yanked open the door.

A large, bald man stumbled into the apartment first, followed by Charlotte, then Sylvia. All three righted themselves and looked up, Charlotte and Sylvia with a guilty look in their eyes.

That was something, at least, Lexie

thought. "Grandma, what's going on? And who is this man?"

"My guess is that his name is Ricky Burnett," Coop said. "Am I right?"

"In the flesh." The older man stuck out his hand in greeting.

Coop shook it, though he looked at Ricky as if he had a screw loose in his head. "Living room. Now," Coop ordered the trio.

Lexie shook her head and followed them inside.

The visitors sat on the sofa, the two women on one side, Ricky Burnett on the other. Charlotte, to Lexie's relief, looked perfectly healthy, a glow in her cheeks.

"I want an explanation and I want it now," Lexie told her grandmother. "Start at the beginning." Lexie settled into Coop's recliner and steeled herself for whatever crazy story was sure to come.

Coop dragged a kitchen chair into the room, straddling it backwards. "And don't leave anything out."

The three elders each let out a put-upon sigh, but no one stepped up to speak.

"Let's start with why you didn't just knock on the door," Coop said.

When nobody answered, he turned his reporter's stare on Ricky. "Let me guess. You broke in once, figured it was so easy you'd do it again."

Ricky looked down at his khaki pants. "You changed the lock," the other man muttered.

Coop rolled his eyes. "Did you think I wouldn't? Better yet, did you really think we'd just leave the necklace out in plain sight so you could take it?" he asked, turning his pointed gaze on Charlotte.

"It was worth a shot," Lexie's grandmother said, a bit too defensively, in Lexie's opinion. "I'm actually just retrieving my own property."

That was open to debate. Her grandmother's audacity was not and Lexie clenched her jaw. "Let's not go there just yet."

Coop nodded. "So now that we've confirmed who broke in the first time, let's go back to how you three met. That's a simple enough question for all of you to tackle."

"I was born and raised in the Bronx, New York," Charlotte began.

Lexie shot her a warning look.

"Okay, fine." She folded her arms across her chest. "Sylvia and I grew up as neighbors in the Bronx, you know that."

"But at the time in question, I was set up with Ricky on a blind date. Later he gave me a job at the jewelry store where he worked," Sylvia said.

"I was the manager of the store," Ricky added.

Lexie nodded. "Better."

"It wasn't easy for women to get jobs back then. We were expected to marry and have babies." Charlotte's mutinous expression said it all on that subject.

"True. It wasn't the we-can-have-it-all attitude women have today," Sylvia added.

"And neither one of us was ready to settle down. There was just too much of the world to explore, things to do, people to meet," Charlotte said, her voice rising in excitement.

And sounding too much like Lexie, the world traveler, for Lexie's comfort, given the illegal, immoral detour the story was about to take.

"Go on," she said tightly.

"Well." Charlotte inclined her head. "Given that it wasn't easy for single women to find work at nontraditional jobs and sewing just wasn't my thing — I occasionally had to resort to . . ." Charlotte's voice trailed off, her cheeks flushed pink with embarrassment.

"Stealing," Lexie finished for her, her stomach cramping.

"It could have been worse. I vetoed prostitution," her grandmother said.

"Oh, God," Lexie said.

"Your parents wouldn't help?" Coop asked gently.

Of course, he didn't feel the same sense of betrayal that was coursing through Lexie at the moment. No question, her grandmother had made bad choices in her life and maybe she'd had her reasons. They'd find out. But to think Charlotte had lied to Lexie, of all people . . . it hurt worse than discovering there was no Santa Claus, Easter Bunny or Tooth Fairy. And hadn't Charlotte been the one to keep those illusions going as long as possible?

"Lexie, you have to understand, the world was much different then. It's one thing for you not to conform to your father's exacting standards. You can still go out and make your way, head held high. My parents washed their hands of me when I wouldn't conform to the standards of *society*. And that left me all alone," Charlotte explained.

Lexie met her grandmother's gaze, knowing how much Charlotte needed her to understand. It wasn't easy, but she nodded slowly, trying to imagine herself as an eighteen-year-old in not just an unforgiving family but an unforgiving society.

"My parents did the same," Sylvia said sadly.

"When all options run out, when you're hungry, you'll do just about anything," Charlotte said, her old eyes filled with the same determination she must have had back then.

"So what did you do?" Coop asked, filling in the silent void.

"I began to clean apartments. From there, wealthy families would offer me work serving during lavish dinner parties. I was grateful and it helped pay the rent on the hellhole of an apartment Sylvia and I shared."

"While I was lucky enough to have had Ricky hire me at the jewelry store," Sylvia said.

"See? I'm the good guy in this scenario," the other man said, puffing out his chest.

"Shut up!" Charlotte and Sylvia yelled at him in unison.

Lexie and Coop stared at each other, surprised.

Sylvia cleared her throat. "It was Ricky's idea for the three of us to use Charlotte's cleaning connections to vandalize big parties. He was also the one who made sure we spaced out the jobs so people wouldn't get suspicious. Does that sound like a good guy to you?" she asked.

Ricky frowned. "Isn't that just like a woman to shift the blame?"

The older women glared at him.

"Did Grandpa know about this?" Lexie asked, trying to put together the time line of her grandmother's life.

Charlotte shook her head. "Oh, no. No. You see, all the original jobs took place when I was eighteen, before I met your grandfather," Charlotte said. "Then the three of us, we . . . umm . . ."

"We broke up for a while," Sylvia supplied helpfully. "And your grandmother and I lost touch."

Lexie narrowed her gaze. She'd never heard about Charlotte and Sylvia losing touch with each other, but then again she hadn't known her grandmother had been disowned by her family or had worked cleaning houses, either.

"I met your grandfather a short time later, we fell in love and I accepted the traditional role I'd initially turned my back on," Charlotte explained. "But then Henry was drafted and I didn't have many friends. I was terribly lonely. Sylvia and I reconnected and that helped. But then this bozo contacted Sylvia for one last job." Her grandmother jerked her thumb toward Ricky.

"Hey, I needed the money!" Ricky exclaimed.

"And we were bored, I'm ashamed to admit." Charlotte glanced toward the wall, unable to meet Lexie's stare. The beginning robberies were because they'd needed money to live. This last one was pure fun and games, at least for the women. And that disappointed Lexie to no end.

Coop leaned forward, his arm braced on the chair. "How did you pick the Lancasters?" he asked.

"My dear Henry worked for them as a chauffeur. That much was true. But they were a pretentious family and didn't treat your grandfather well at all. He had told me about their eclectic jewelry collection, and how during various times he drove for them, the matriarch, as she liked to call herself, used to brag to her friends about how she didn't need a safe. She just spread the items throughout her various closets. So I suggested we find a way to hit their home. But that was the last job. I swear. Your grandfather came home and we lived happily ever after!"

Lexie closed her eyes and groaned. When she opened them, she snuck a glance at Coop, gauging his reaction to the story. He stared at the trio, clearly fascinated by the dynamic, the byplay, the history and reasoning behind it all.

"So now that you know everything, can I have my necklace back?" Charlotte asked hopefully.

"And what are you going to do with this information?" Ricky asked.

"Wait just a minute. I have a question first. We took the necklace because you've been avoiding me and any questions I had, but why did all three of you show up here now?" Lexie asked.

"Well, these old bats tied me up and demanded some goods back they think I still have," Ricky said before anyone else could answer. "I told 'em I'd give them what they wanted as long as they made *this* all go away. I can't afford for my past to get out. It'll ruin my business and destroy my daughter."

"Since when do you care about anyone but yourself?" Sylvia asked.

"People can change. I returned your laptop, didn't I?" he asked Coop.

Coop nodded. "You did. But you stole it first."

"It was a distraction, nothing more. I didn't want you to put two and two together and come up with the ring!" Ricky explained. "So what's it gonna be? Charlotte says you'll keep the past buried because you're in love with her granddaughter. That true, Mr. Reporter? If so, I'll give these two pains in the ass the pieces they're looking for."

Lexie's jaw dropped.

Coop's mouth ran dry. How the hell had this man verbalized something he'd never said aloud? How had Charlotte pegged his feelings when he'd only just admitted them to himself?

He glanced at Lexie who looked like she was about to faint. Considering the mere hint of him *more than liking her* had sent her running, he could only imagine what this declaration would do. If he chose to confirm it.

He didn't — at least not yet — and decided a good offense was the best defense. "What pieces would that be?" he asked Ricky, avoiding the statement altogether.

"He's had my wedding ring for the last half century!" Charlotte said on a wail. "Your poor grandfather died thinking I'd accidentally flushed it down the toilet while he was overseas fighting for his country." She sniffed, the exaggerated gesture not lost on anyone in the room.

"Hey! It's not like you're the queen of England. The damn thing isn't worth more than a washer."

"But it's *my* washer and I want it back!" Charlotte's voice rose.

"Grandma, calm down. It's not good for your blood pressure," Lexie urged the older woman.

Without warning, Sylvia stood, strode up to Ricky and kicked him in the shin. "That's for upsetting my friend. Oh. And did I mention I want my bracelet back? If Charlotte gets her Lancaster necklace, I want my bracelet from the same job." She adjusted her polyester shirt and reseated herself in her chair, crossing her ankles like a lady.

Coop couldn't write anything like the dynamic between these three older people. They were priceless, shameless and yet endearing all at the same time. The stuff of fabulous, fantastic fiction, he thought.

Coop glanced at Lexie. Even behind her glasses, he caught the little furrows in between her eyes and the concerned expression on her face. She obviously knew exactly what he was thinking. Or thought she did.

"Ricky, are you saying you have both ladies' items?" Coop asked.

"Maybe."

Lexie jumped up from her seat. "I've had enough. Do any of you remember that these items are *stolen?* Stolen. As in — aside from my grandmother's wedding ring — the necklace, Coop's ring and the bracelet don't belong to you!" She paced back and forth in front of the trio, chastising them under her breath until she finally paused. "Sylvia, you've been taking computer lessons, right?"

Sylvia nodded. "Yes, ma'am, and I'm pretty darn good!"

"And, Grandma, something tells me that you already know more than you've let on to me, correct?"

Charlotte glanced away. "Maybe."

"She's been coming to the Apple Store with me. But she loved the time you spent teaching her, and she didn't want to insult you by saying she didn't need your help," Sylvia said helpfully.

"I love our time together, too," Lexie said, her voice softening. "But we can spend it doing other things instead of you pretending not to understand my instructions."

Charlotte nodded, looking at her granddaughter with love.

"Okay, this is how it's going to be. You two computer-literate women are going to do research. You're going to find out who's still living in the Lancaster family, return the jewels and hope they won't press charges against an almost octogenarian and her cohorts who have learned their lesson. Right?" Lexie stared at each of them in turn.

They grumbled, but no one committed to returning anything. They did, however, focus on the last part of Lexie's statement.

"I'm not going to jail!" Charlotte cried out, grabbing her chest.

"Calm down," Coop said, recognizing the ploy.

"No more faking when it comes to your health!" Lexie exploded at her grandmother.

Coop rose and placed a calming arm around Lexie's shoulder. He admired the way she had held on to her temper and her emotions through this entire ordeal and he was about to make it even easier on her. "It's okay. I've actually done the research already and there's good news. First, the statute of limitations has run out and they can't be charged."

Everyone's shoulders slumped in relief.

"Coop, *thank* you."

Lexie's warm smile of gratitude settled inside him, expanding his heart even more. His feelings for her would be the death of him yet. "You're welcome. And second, the Lancaster family is gone. There are no direct descendants."

"So we can keep the jewels?" Charlotte and Sylvia asked at the same time.

Ricky kept silent. Coop knew the older man's only interest lay in hiding his past.

They hadn't broached that subject. Yet.

"No, you may not!" Lexie said. "Those items don't belong to you," she said, clearly exasperated.

Once again, Coop had done his research. "There is a foundation the family established in honor of Harold Lancaster that channels money into inner-city programs to keep kids out of trouble and provide scholarships to those who want a college education. If you sell the jewels, you can donate the proceeds to a good cause. At least that way the money will go where the original owners intended."

"But how are we going to publicly sell jewels without revealing how we got our hands on them in the first place?" Ricky said at last. Because his self-interest was finally at stake.

Coop had an idea. "Lexie, can I see you alone for a minute?"

Lexie shot the three a warning glance. "Behave!" she said, then followed him into the kitchen. "What's up?"

He brushed her hair off her cheek. "Are you okay?" Despite knowing she would trample all over his heart, he couldn't help but ask.

She nodded. "As long as I keep my breathing steady, I won't hyperventilate," she joked.

But he could see the strain and the disappointment etched all over her face. "It's almost over," he promised her, refusing to dissect that comment too deeply. "I was thinking that I can contact the Lancaster Foundation, tell them that I did some research on the ring in my possession and realized it belonged to them. I'll also tell them I was able to track down the other missing pieces and I'd like to give them back — with the stipulation that no questions be asked about where they've been because the previous owners agreed to an anonymous return."

Lexie paused in thought. "That might work," she said at last. "I can't thank you enough for keeping their names out of this."

"I'm doing it for you."

She visibly swallowed hard. "I know. And I appreciate that."

"I don't want your appreciation, Lexie. I want —"

"Well? Are you gonna leave us sitting out here all day?" Ricky bellowed from the other room. "These crazy women are threatening me."

Nothing personal would be accomplished right now, Coop thought, frustrated. Especially since Lexie appeared relieved at the interruption. And she hadn't picked up on the fact that Ricky had said Charlotte believed Coop was in love with her.

"Let's go give them the news," he said, walking out of the room without meeting her gaze.

He informed the trio, that if the foundation accepted the items without question, they'd be off the hook. But if they chose to make a big deal about where the jewelry came from, there was nothing Coop could do.

Lexie insisted on taking her grandmother and Sylvia home, thereby avoiding dealing with Coop and the unresolved issues between them.

Running away was something Lexie excelled at.

The next day Coop stopped by the Vintage Jewelers to collect the bracelet from Ricky. With much grumbling, the other man agreed to let Coop accompany him to the bank to get the item from the vault, along with Lexie's grandmother's wedding ring. With all three items now in his possession, Coop contacted the Lancaster Foundation and explained the situation to the president, who was overjoyed at the news. Coop handed the items over, officially ending his involvement with the ring.

What about his involvement with Lexie?

No easy answer there.

But he didn't contact her. She knew he had something to say to her. He knew she didn't want to hear it. She also had his Web site, which meant the ball was in her court. She'd have to come around or not.

That's the way it had to be.

Even if it wasn't the way he liked it.

He did call Charlotte, told her he had her ring and asked her to meet him so he could return it. Charlotte, of course, invited him over for dinner, but he declined. Since she'd waited over a half a century to get the ring back, she informed him he might as well hold on to it until the next time he saw Lexie.

"Wily old woman," he muttered.

With the mystery of the ring solved and no outside distractions, Coop spent the next few days at the office, doing his job covering the news. Concentrating wasn't easy but neither was going home to his empty apartment, without time with Lexie to look forward to.

"You're never going to believe this!" Amanda exclaimed, sitting down on the corner of his desk.

He glanced at the fashion editor. "Tell me," he said, not really listening.

"The Lancaster Foundation called me."

Coop's ears perked up. He lifted his gaze from the computer screen.

"I thought that would get your attention," she said, a pleased grin on her face.

Amanda had been annoyed with him since he'd admitted to her *off the record* that he'd returned the jewels, but refused to let her cover the news in her section. Coop understood. The fact that he'd uncovered jewels from a prized collection that had been missing for years would have been a big coup for her. For him as well, in his crime beat. He'd opted to protect Lexie and Charlotte instead. He couldn't have lived with himself if he'd revealed all and destroyed Lexie's beloved grandmother in the process.

But at night, he'd been pouring out the story onto the computer screen, a fictionalized version of events, names changed to protect the innocent, of course. It was his best damn work ever.

"Hey, wake up!" Amanda snapped her fingers in front of his face. "Where are you lately? Anyway, the jewels you returned? The foundation wants to auction them off. It seems the foundation is in desperate need of cash. They see the auction as a way to raise money and bring public awareness to their cause. And they want to give me exclusive, inside coverage!" she said, beaming.

"That's fantastic. See? Now you have your coverage, a better angle and you can forgive me for not letting you report on it in the first place."

"Not so fast."

Something in her tone caught his attention. "What do you want?" he asked warily.

"The foundation had a condition for giving me an exclusive." She met his gaze.

The steely determination he saw there unnerved him. "Just how does this involve me?"

"They'd like you, as in you, *the Bachelor,* to emcee the event."

"No. Way."

She clasped her hands together. "Please? Come on. I need you for this. You can bring whoever you want as a date," she said, obviously hoping to entice him.

"I'm not dating anyone," he muttered.

She raised an eyebrow. "So the Blogger rumors are true? It's over between you and Lexie?"

He clenched his jaw. He'd done his best to ignore the omniscient, seemingly ever-present Blogger who knew all his and Lexie's moves. But when someone threw the damn words in his face, he had to face it.

Just as he had to face the truth. "It's not over."

"Then invite her to the auction. And her grandmother for all I care! Just be there!"

"What do you know about her grandmother?"

She glanced away. "Nothing. I just heard our editor talking about the picture of the kiss, how the Blogger came by them. Please?" She clasped her hands together again.

Coop exhaled hard. "Oh, all right. I'll be there."

"And Lexie?"

He shook his head. Amanda was relentless. "Whether she comes or not, that's up to her."

All he could do was ask.

CHAPTER SIXTEEN

Lexie hated banks. She was pretty sure her feelings stemmed from childhood and *Take Your Daughters to Work Day.* She and her sister would spend the day with their father, older sibling Margaret competing for who could do any assigned task best, Lexie not even trying to win. She'd always wished she were anywhere else, preferably outdoors with the wind on her cheeks, breathing fresh air. Yet here she was, willingly standing outside her father's New York City branch.

She just couldn't bring herself to go inside.

Ever since her grandmother's confession, Lexie had been walking around in a fog, trying to find her place in the world. She'd made several trips to the Empire State Building, seeking answers in the clouds. In so many ways, her confusion made little sense. Whatever Charlotte had done as a young girl should have no bearing on Lexie as an adult. On the other hand, she had spent the better part of her life modeling herself after her grandmother. It wasn't that Charlotte traveled, so Lexie wanted to do the same. She hadn't. The ways in which she mimicked her grandmother were more subtle.

Charlotte lived life *her way,* no matter what anyone else thought. And that's what Lexie had admired so much. What she'd idealized. Or, to quote Coop, what she'd used to *justify* her life choices. But with Charlotte's revelations and her motives, at least for the last heist, being so self-serving, Lexie could no longer look at her own choices the same way. Again, it wasn't so much the similarities in how they lived their lives — there weren't many. It was the reasons behind them. Her grandmother's recent truths caused Lexie to look deeper inside herself.

Of course, it wasn't just her grandmother's past that was causing this self-reflection. It was Coop.

I more than like you, Lexie.

She still couldn't get those heartfelt words out of her mind. Or, to be even more honest, out of her heart.

While it wasn't a declaration of love — she knew she'd been keeping him from going that far — it meant more. Because unlike anyone who came before, Lexie had really let Coop in. He knew her better than she knew herself. Understood her family dynamic.

Wasn't he the one who'd pointed out that she and her father had common ground, when for years she'd believed there was none? So here she was, willing for the first time to reach out to her parent. To admit she'd been too stubborn for them to have had a relationship before — and to ask him to admit that maybe he'd been the same way. To see where they could go from here.

Lexie smoothed her white slacks and adjusted her silk short-sleeved shirt, both items a conciliatory nod to her father, showing respect for him and his place of business. As she drew a deep breath, ready to walk inside, she hoped he'd appreciate that she'd left her peasant skirts and multiple bangle bracelets at her grandmother's.

A few minutes later, cool air-conditioning making the hair on her arms stand on end, Lexie knocked once on the wooden office door.

"Surprise!" she said, and let herself into her father's office. She would have called ahead for an appointment, but she wanted to give herself an out in case she changed her mind.

"Alexis, this *is* a surprise!" He rose from behind the desk she'd always found big and imposing as a child. "What's wrong?" he immediately asked.

She didn't take the question personally. She'd never come here *just because* and, given the choice, she never came here at all.

"Is my mother okay?" he asked when she didn't immediately answer.

"She's fine," Lexie rushed to assure him. "I'm fine."

Confusion furrowed his eyebrows and she understood. He had no idea why she was here.

"I was hoping we could . . . talk."

"Of course." He extended his hand, gesturing for her to take a seat.

Lexie lowered herself into one of the big chairs, recalling how as a child, she liked to swing her feet back and forth until Margaret would remind her that ladies crossed their legs at the ankles and didn't fidget like boys. But the important thing now was that Lexie remembered enjoying something about being here — and wasn't that a shock, she thought wryly.

She drew a deep breath for courage before blurting out the first thing that came to mind. "I know I'm a disappointment to you," she said in a rush, before she could chicken out.

Her father jerked back, stunned at her comment. "That's a little harsh," he said.

Lexie shook her head hard. "Not really. It's the truth. I'm not like you, Mother or Margaret. I'm not focused or dedicated — at least not to your way of thinking. But I'm successful if you define *successful* as self-supporting. I'm able to save for the future and to take trips abroad and see the world. And I love what I do," she said, gaining steam and momentum. "I mean I really love Web design and the different clients I meet as a result of my job." A rush of adrenaline took hold as she described her life from her perspective.

"Alexis," her father said, his expression one of utter confusion.

"Wait, please. Just let me finish, okay?"

He nodded patiently. That, at least, was one of his virtues.

"I'm also honest to a fault. That's something you and Mom taught me and I'm proud of that. I don't overbill my clients, although of course I could. They have no idea how much time it takes me to design or update a site. But if someone hires me, they pay a fair price for my services. My assistant loves working for me because I pay her well and treat her fairly. And I expect the best, and as a result she's learning and growing as a designer. Again, I can thank you and Mom for instilling those qualities in me."

She glanced at her father, who ran a hand over his head.

"I'm . . . at a loss," he said.

"I know." She swallowed hard, searching for words that would explain. "I guess what I'm trying to say is that I might not have gone into your choice of professions or done things your way, but I'm a success just the same." She gripped the chair arms more tightly. "I'm well-rounded — more than you, if you don't mind my making that observation — I've seen more of the world. And I'm equally successful in my own right. Doing my own thing." Lexie drew a deep breath. "Can we agree on that?"

He paused and after what felt like hours, but was probably only a few seconds, he nodded slowly. "Yes, we can. I never thought of you or your life quite that way."

Lexie smiled. "I know. I'd like to say that I've also come to understand you."

He leaned forward. "How so?"

"Well, I think we have more in common than you ever realized."

"I didn't think we had anything in common, to be honest. So, please enlighten me."

Though his hands were folded on top of his desk, his posture stiff, his eyes and his expression were open. Curious. Inviting, even.

Lexie took great hope in those signs. "We both know what it's like to grow up in a home where it's impossible to meet the expectations of your parent and disappointment permeates everything you say or do," she said, her heart pounding hard in her chest.

"I suppose we do," he said at last. "I never looked at it that way." He looked as stunned as he sounded.

Neither had she, until a wise man pointed it out to her. "I'm sure it wasn't easy growing up with Charlotte as your mother," Lexie said, then bit the inside of her cheek, nervous about how he'd respond.

But he nodded in agreement. "Though she married my father and settled down, she never quite did things the same way as the other mothers. From the way she dressed to how she acted, it always made me uncomfortable. I felt different from her and different from the other kids. So I never wanted to bring anyone home. And the more outrageous she acted, the more uptight I became."

Lexie stared wide-eyed. She'd hoped for

understanding. She'd never expected him to open up to her in any way. To let down those walls she'd never been able to breach as a child and allow her a glimpse of himself.

"It was the same for me," she said softly. "Except in my case, the more rigid the rules and expectations, the harder I rebelled. The more I wanted the freedom to be me. The more I needed to be accepted for who I was and what I wanted." She forced the painful words from deep inside her.

"Something I never gave you," her father finally acknowledged. "Because I saw too much of my mother in you and I'd told myself I was finished living with flighty ways and unexpected behavior." He cleared his throat. "But you . . . you reveled in your similarities to your grandmother. In fact, sometimes it felt like you were rubbing my face in being just like her."

"I was," she admitted. "I loved being like Grandma because it meant I wasn't alone. That I wasn't a bad person because I was different from you, Mom and Margaret." She swallowed over the lump in her throat, unsure if it was caused by the pain from the past or the possibilities now offered in the future.

"I remember how hard it was for me, growing up and being so distinctly different from my mother. I can't believe I didn't see I was doing the same thing to you."

In his voice, Lexie heard how difficult the admission was for him to make. But in doing so, they'd crossed a divide Lexie never believed was possible.

"I think I could have made your life a little easier, too," she said, laughing.

He smiled, but quickly sobered. "The question is, where do we go from here?" he asked awkwardly.

Lexie drew a deep breath, the answer obvious at least to her. "How about we go forward?" she suggested.

Her father stood and rounded the desk.

Lexie rose from her seat and met him halfway, giving her father the first heartfelt hug she could remember.

And she knew she had Coop to thank. Not that he knew it. Telling him would come later.

Assuming he still wanted to hear it.

Lexie arrived back at her grandmother's to find Charlotte trying on clothes, parading through the apartment. Sylvia sat in the living room, offering her opinion on a ruffled, magenta-colored dress that clashed with her hair.

"This is my favorite!" Charlotte exclaimed. "What do you think?"

Sylvia narrowed her gaze. "The ivory one suits your skin tone better," she said, glancing at Lexie with a quick wink.

"What's the occasion?" Lexie asked, settling into a chair.

Charlotte twirled in her dress — as well as she could twirl at her age. "We're all going to a gala for the Lancaster Foundation."

"Excuse me?"

Sylvia reached for a glass of water, taking a sip before explaining. "It seems they're auctioning off the jewels to raise money and they're throwing a big shindig."

Lexie narrowed her gaze, focusing in on the two ex-thieves who'd just happened to once own said jewels, preparing for the occasion. "How did you two wangle an invitation?"

Charlotte smiled, beaming from ear to ear. "From the master of ceremonies, of course! Your favorite bachelor and mine, Sam Cooper." She imitated a drumroll for emphasis.

Lexie's stomach curled at the sound of his name. "Coop invited you?"

Charlotte bent down, leaning closer to Sylvia. "I think she's jealous," she said in a stage whisper.

Despite the idiocy of it all, Lexie flushed.

"I am not."

"Well you shouldn't be, because you're invited, too!" her grandmother said.

Once again, Lexie's stomach flipped. "Did Coop come by?" she asked, pathetically hopeful.

Sylvia shook her head.

"But this lovely invitation came in the mail with a handwritten note." Charlotte pointed to a large invitation on the coffee table.

Lexie lifted up the envelope and scanned the preprinted address. "Hey, it's addressed to me!" She shook her head at her grandmother.

"Yes, but the note inside says there are enough tickets for all three of us — by name!"

"Something you wouldn't have known if you hadn't opened my mail," Lexie chided.

"Minor details. Do you like this dress?" her grandmother asked.

The two women had certainly bounced back from the revelation of their caper and losing the jewelry.

"Honestly? I prefer ivory on you as well," Lexie said diplomatically.

"Okay, ivory it is. Would you like to borrow this one?" her grandmother offered.

Lexie nearly choked. "No, thank you."

"Don't tell me you aren't going! I know

you, Lexie Davis. You've been avoiding Coop ever since you captured the three of us."

Lexie rolled her eyes. "What is it with people and that word *avoiding?*"

"If the shoe fits, dear," Sylvia said.

"It's always the quiet ones you have to watch out for," Lexie muttered. "I'm going to my room." She rose and turned toward the hall.

"Are you saying you *aren't* avoiding Coop?" Her grandmother planted her petite body directly in Lexie's path.

Experience told her if she didn't deal with the question directly, she wasn't getting past. "I was and now I'm not. Satisfied?"

"Not yet. What are you going to wear to the party?" Charlotte pulled a tissue out of her cleavage and blew her nose. "Buy yourself something new. Something eye-catching. Expose your boobies," she said when she'd finished.

"Oh, brother. You two stay out of trouble." Lexie darted around her grandmother and headed for the safety of her room.

She lay down on her bed, hands beneath her head and stared at the ceiling. She needed more than a new dress, though she'd definitely go through the pain of shopping to look good for the event.

She needed to talk to Coop before the gala. She couldn't say what she wanted to in a public place. And she couldn't handle seeing him with everything still unsettled between them.

But she'd tried to reach him after leaving her father's only to get his answering machine at home, the recording on his cell and his voice mail at work. Even if he didn't want to speak to her, he wouldn't avoid her. Which meant he was busy on a story.

She didn't leave a message because she wanted to hear his voice and gauge his reaction when she called. She didn't want him to have time to think or cover his feelings.

So she'd just have to keep trying.

A teenager turned up missing, consuming the cops and the press for the better part of a week. By the time Coop found himself with downtime, he was dressing for the auction and he'd barely slept in days. He thought he'd been eating, but he couldn't remember. Though the child had been found alive, he didn't want to think about the psychological damage that had been done to her in the interim. He'd been living, breathing and eating that news for too long as it was.

At least the auction, as much as he was

dreading it, would take him away from the horrific story he'd been covering. It helped that he wouldn't be alone there. He'd invited his family to the event. Matt and his wife were busy, but his father had surprised him by agreeing. Not only had he gotten someone to cover the bar, he'd also invited a date. A widow he'd been seeing on the side.

Coop was happy for the old man. At least one of them had a love life that seemed to be on the upswing.

Coop also had a date. On speaking to the foundation people, they'd told him they were hiring guards to keep an eye on the items being sold. Charlotte's pieces were only a part of what was on the block and they needed at least two security guards. Knowing that Sara liked to take outside work, he'd tipped her off and she'd applied for the job. She'd extended the information to Rafe Mancuso, her ex-partner, and with Coop's recommendation and their references, they'd both been hired. Coop and Sara were going to the event together.

Coop showered and changed into a rented tuxedo, realizing only when he glanced in the mirror to do his tie that he'd forgotten to shave. He had a few days growth of beard covering his face, but a glance at his watch told him he had no time to worry about it now. The show couldn't start without him.

Lexie and company arrived half an hour early at the Upper East Side town house where the Lancaster Foundation was hosting the auction. It wasn't that she wanted her grandmother and Sylvia to have extra time to drink, but she did want the opportunity to get Coop alone if she could.

The town house décor took her breath away, from the beautiful marble floors to the intricate pillars and mirrors around her. There was a large room for the showing of the auction items; that was where cocktails would be served. During the early hours, people could view the jewels and their tag number for identification during the auction. Invitations had gone out to the elite of Manhattan and Lexie recognized some impressive society people trickling in. Her grandmother and Sylvia were in the cocktail room, presumably on their best behavior.

Lexie waited in the main hall. For at least the third time in as many minutes, she smoothed the sparkly silver dress over her hips. She wasn't a woman comfortable in glitzy outfits and between the fitted dress that ended at the knee, and the high heels the salesgirl had talked her into, Lexie was way out of her comfort zone. Especially since the lady who'd helped her at the makeup counter at Bloomingdale's suggested she wear contacts to better show off her eyes.

Because the woman had been complimentary and not critical, and since she'd made so many other big steps this week, Lexie had taken the address of a store around the corner that specialized in contact lenses. She still wasn't used to not having her eyeglass frames to fiddle with from time to time.

All in all, she didn't feel like herself tonight, but at least she looked as if she belonged. That in itself was an accomplishment, Lexie thought.

She leaned against a large, marble pillar and sipped from a champagne glass, the bubbly liquid bypassing her empty stomach and going directly to her head. Minutes ticked by. If she stood here nursing this drink much longer, she'd be punch drunk before Coop even arrived.

Finally, just when she was about to give up and go looking for her grandmother, she caught sight of him. She'd never seen him in formal attire and the man in a well-fitting, elegantly cut black tuxedo, took her breath away. The exhaustion etching his features did nothing to detract from his sexy appearance and the razor stubble darkening his face merely enhanced it.

Then she realized he wasn't alone. A beautiful blonde wearing a loose yet extremely sexy three-quarter-length gown stood by his side.

Nausea washed over Lexie.

She wanted to turn and run, but the blonde noticed her first and treated Lexie to a brief wave and recognition finally took hold.

Sara, Lexie realized, nearly weak with relief.

The other woman tugged on Coop's arm. She whispered something in his ear, then pointed Lexie's way.

He glanced over and met her gaze, his eyes widening as awareness dawned.

She was still shaken and the nervous feeling in the pit of her stomach didn't disappear as the couple strode closer.

"Lexie," he said, his voice gruff, devouring her with his darkened gaze.

"Coop." She barely recognized her own voice.

"Lexie, I almost didn't recognize you!" Sara exclaimed, pulling her into a friendly hug.

"I definitely didn't recognize you!" Lexie

stepped back and admired yet another change in the multifaceted cop.

Sara leaned closer. "Don't tell anyone, but I'm working security." She stepped back and subtly patted her thigh. "Gun beneath the dress," she whispered.

Which explained the loose material, Lexie realized. And also clarified that she and Coop were not together on a date. Lexie's rapidly beating heart finally began to slow to a more normal pace.

Sara glanced back and forth between the two. "I am going to make myself scarce and check in with my employer. See you later." She waved and disappeared, leaving Lexie and Coop staring into each other's eyes.

"Hi there," she said, feeling ridiculously silly.

"Hi, yourself."

She swallowed hard. "You're a hard man to track down."

"I didn't know you were looking." He never took his gaze from hers.

She shrugged. "I didn't leave a message, but . . . I'm here now. Early. For you."

He braced his arm against the pillar behind her. "Really."

She nodded.

"Why?" he asked. "What do you need to talk to me about, gorgeous?"

Her throat grew parched. With him so close, his familiar scent surrounding her, sensual awareness enveloped her completely. "We left things unsettled."

"And?"

He was putting this all on her, not that she blamed him. "I've done a lot of thinking since I saw you last. About things you've said and done. And about myself and what I've learned." She licked her lips and tasted champagne. "I visited my father," she blurted out.

His eyes opened wide. "Now that's a surprise."

She couldn't agree more.

"What happened?"

"We made some headway, thanks to you."

Silence descended between them. Lexie's head was swimming with words she wanted to say, but her feelings overwhelmed her and she couldn't get her thoughts straight.

"What else?" he finally asked, his voice deep and compelling.

"I missed you," she admitted, the words costing her pride everything but her heart nothing.

Progress, Coop thought.

"I missed you, too."

"And —" she began. Then paused.

His heart stopped completely as he waited.

"And I more than like you, too, Coop," she said, drawing a deep breath. "I love you."

Finally.

He grinned. "I love you, too."

He dipped his head and sealed his lips against hers. She separated from him only long enough to place her champagne glass on a nearby table before returning to wrap her arms around his neck and kiss him back.

And if he thought he'd imagined those three little words, she said them again, over and over with her mouth, her tongue, her lips until without warning, she eased back, resting her forehead against his.

"I'm not finished," she said, her voice hoarse.

"Then don't stop."

She laughed. "I meant I'm not finished talking."

He placed his hands on her hips and nodded in understanding. "We can talk later." Right now he needed to be alone with her, not standing here in a public place.

"There's a coat closet that's not in use during the summer," she said, reading his mind.

"How did you know what I was thinking?" he asked, amused but not surprised that she knew him that well.

"I already told you I came here early. I had time to scout around," she said, eyes gleaming in anticipation.

"Show me." He glanced at his watch. "Quickly. There's only twenty minutes before I have to check in."

And he intended to make good use of each and every one.

Coop grabbed Lexie's hand. She led him around the corner, through an empty hall to a two-part door that would open on top for a coat check. "This is it. I heard the staff say they'd leave it unlocked in case anyone needed to store things in here." She turned the knob and the door swung open wide. "Voilà," she said, stepping inside.

He flipped on the light, kicked the door closed, locked it and reached for Lexie once more.

He couldn't tear his gaze from her beautiful face as he pulled the hem of her dress high enough for him to cup her feminine heat in the palm of his hand.

Lexie leaned her head back and groaned. "God, I missed you."

He pulled at her panties, helping them down her long, sexy legs and easing them over those fuck-me high heels before tucking her underwear into the pocket of his jacket.

"You take my breath away," he said, kissing her cheek, her jaw, her neck.

"You're pretty hot yourself. Especially this." She rubbed his scruffy face with her palm.

Coop could look into her eyes forever, but he was aware of the minutes ticking by. He needed to finish this before they were missed. He slid his hand between their bodies and with his thumb, massaged her outer folds, finding her so good and wet. She arched into him, allowing him access and he eased one finger deep inside. Her body clenched around him, surrounding him in slick heat.

Lexie cried out, so he sealed his lips over hers, silencing her as he aroused her further, sliding his finger in and out of her slick passage. She panted in his ear, urging him harder, deeper and he complied, while also drawing circles over her clit with his thumb. Her body shook and he pressed harder against just the right spot until she was bucking against his hand.

Lexie impatiently reached for his trousers, her hands shaking as she attempted to open them.

"Easy," he whispered. "Let me." He released the button, yanked down the zipper and when the pants fell to the floor, he freed one foot, giving himself leverage.

He placed his hands on her hips, about to lift her onto him when reality set in and he muttered a raw curse.

"What's wrong?" Lexie asked, surprised.

He met her gaze and she saw regret and real pain in his eyes.

"No protection."

At one time, Lexie would have called a halt. But this was Coop, the man she loved. Trusted.

She felt an unexpected smile curve her lips. "Well, you're in luck because I'm on the pill." Fully aware of how huge her words were, she cupped his erection, teasing him until he let out a groan.

"Lexie . . ." The words sounded like part warning, part plea.

"I'm safe, Coop. Tested yearly. The last time just happened to be when I was home in June. There's been nobody else for a long time."

"That's not it. If you're suggesting it, I trust you."

"Same here, so what's the problem?" she asked.

His curious eyes stared into hers. "I'm wondering why I'm just hearing about the pill now."

Always the journalist, questions came out even at the most inopportune times, Lexie thought, loving him even more for it.

But she shook her head, drawing her hand up and down his hard shaft. "Do you really want me to answer now?" She spread his come over the head of his penis with the pad of her thumb.

He grasped her hips, lifting her into the air until she locked her legs around his waist. Once she anchored herself, Coop backed her against the wall and Lexie closed her eyes, guiding him with her hand, helping him lower her body onto his rigid shaft.

She was hot for him. Wet. So wet and so horny. She'd missed him, wanted him and she'd just admitted she loved him. Now she needed him, too.

He seemed to know it, staring at her as he filled her slowly, lovingly, completely. And she felt him, naked, bare inside her body.

Really felt him — unlike anyone who'd come before. And she couldn't imagine anyone coming after. She grabbed his hair in her hands and pulled his face to her, kissing him hard. He kissed her back, but he was multitalented and he tilted his hips and thrust harder. Deeper than he'd ever been before.

Lexie moaned, rocking her body against him, grinding together. He eased out and thrust back in deep, in and out, in and out, taking her higher with every slick stroke until her legs began to slip.

Before she could right herself, the change in position rubbed her body against his, bringing her suddenly closer to orgasm. She shuddered and let out a raw moan.

"Hang on," Coop said, shifting so she could rewrap her legs around his waist.

But he also must have understood what the last position did to her because the next time he drove deep, he tilted his hips to match that last angle of penetration. His body connected with hers in that perfect way and the stars collided behind her eyes. He repeated the motion over and over as his body rocked hard against hers, taking her higher. And higher.

She cried out and he covered her mouth with his and took her up and over the edge, his hips bucking harder and harder until he came on a low groan, pumping into her again and again, wringing every last drop of her orgasm before his movements finally stilled.

She wasn't sure how long they stood like that, wrapped in each other's arms, trying to catch their breath. Finally, awareness came back to her.

She breathed in deep and smiled. "Coop?"

"Hmm?"

Clearly words were still beyond him.

"Come with me to Australia," she said, the words shocking her the minute they'd escaped.

CHAPTER SEVENTEEN

In silence, Coop pulled on his pants while Lexie adjusted her dress.

"You have something I need," she said stiffly from behind him.

He pulled her underwear from his jacket pocket, fingering the soft material before handing the pair back to her.

Her words hung between them. "I don't know what to say."

She redressed, pulling her panties back on. "Then do what my parents taught me and don't say anything." Her voice was tight with hurt and disappointment.

Had she really expected him to drop his entire life and head off on one of her journeys? he wondered.

Then again, she wasn't asking about a single vacation and they both knew it. There was too much between them to think she was referring to a one-shot deal. This was a serious commitment issue they were facing here.

He placed his hands on her shoulders, forcing her to face him. "Lex, I have a job, here. I can't just pick up and take off whenever the whim strikes," he tried to explain.

"Oh. So your *I love you* came with the expectation that I'd suddenly want to give up everything in my life and settle down?" she asked incredulously.

He set his jaw, seeing stalemate all over this argument.

"It sounds like yours came with the opposite expectation. That I'd pick up and run at a moment's notice."

Her eyes filled, causing his stomach to cramp.

She forced a cavalier shrug. "To quote you, 'That's what I do.' And you knew that."

Yeah, he had.

She wiped at her eyes. "Just like I knew you'd write my grandmother's story, one way or another."

"And you're okay with that?"

She shook her head. "I still don't know. But I've made my peace with it. Because it's part of who you are. I could see that story lit a fire in you and it would be good for your writing. So, yes, I'm okay with that."

He blew out a deep breath. "Lexie . . ."

She fluffed her hair with one hand, but she still looked as though she'd been thoroughly kissed, and more.

"I have to admit I didn't think it through before I asked you to go with me, but now that I have, it's a good idea. You could write. Free from the draining confines of the news, you could explore the world and see the colors!" Excitement tinged her voice and that pink flush colored her cheeks as she shared her reasons with him. "Imagine what that would do for your creative process."

Her words excited him. They also scared the crap out of him at the same time.

He raised an eyebrow. "Would the creative process pay the bills?" he asked more defensively than he'd meant to.

"Would it hurt to find out?" she shot back.

His head began to pound. A drink before this damn auction might also be a good idea.

Coop glanced at his watch. He was supposed to check in with the Lancaster Foundation people half an hour before the start of the auction. He was already late.

"Don't let me keep you." She jerked away. "I'll leave first. I need to stop at the restroom anyway to freshen up." She headed for the door, storming through it without looking back.

"Well, that went well," he muttered, feeling like an uncaring ass.

But, really, had she expected him to uproot his entire life just for her?

Why not? He expected her to alter her entire being to stay home for him. He might not have said as much, but by refusing her outright, he'd implied it.

He didn't have a solution, but he had an auction to emcee. He wondered if Lexie would stick around for the event or take off, leaving him to face this crowd alone. If their fundamental disagreement was anything to go by, it was something he ought to get used to.

Lexie headed directly to the ladies' room. She found herself sitting in the powder room, head in her hands, trying to pull herself together before dealing with the outside world — her grandmother and Sylvia, the crowd in general and, yes, Coop.

For a few brief minutes she had everything she could ever want and then in typical Lexie style, her impulsiveness had destroyed any chances at a future. Of course she wanted Coop to travel with her, but she could have approached him with the idea in a way he could have handled. Instead, she'd ended up alone.

Well, then. Her body still tingling from sex in a coat closet of all things, she stood and glanced in the mirror. "Just great. Look at me," she muttered, staring at her bare lips and messed-up face.

"Can I offer you some makeup?" Sara strode over.

"I didn't hear you come in."

The other woman shrugged. "Here I am."

"Ditto."

"What happened?" she asked, opening her gold purse and pulling out an array of makeup products.

"Too bad I didn't think to bring any with me. Thanks." Lexie forced a smile and began repairing the damage both her own tears and Coop's beard had done to her face.

"I'm a good listener," Sara pushed.

Lexie sighed. "I didn't run away, if that's what you think. In fact, it was just the opposite. I asked Coop to come with me to Australia." She met the other woman's gaze in the mirror.

Sara let out a slow whistle. "You've got guts."

"But not many brains. I scared him to

death." She patted concealer beneath her eyes and applied some blush to her cheeks.

"I'll just bet you did. Coop's such a creature of habit it's almost scary. He likes what's comfortable."

"Then how do you explain his attraction to me?" Lexie asked, choking back threatening tears.

She'd promised herself she'd never let a man hurt her the way Drew had. Well, she'd certainly kept that promise. Falling for Coop had caused her far worse pain than Drew ever could. Because she loved him so much more.

Sara shook her head. "There's no explaining chemistry. I ought to know."

Curious, Lexie glanced at her. "Sounds like you're talking about one person in particular."

She shrugged. "We're not discussing me, remember? We're talking about you. And Coop. When I warned you not to hurt him, I never considered the possibility that he might do a number on you. I'm sorry."

Lexie raised one hand in the air, letting it helplessly drop to the ground. "The course of true love never runs smooth."

"Is that what this is?" Sara asked.

"It is for me. And Coop said the same thing. Until I blew it."

Sara's eyes opened wide. "You don't walk away from love. Unless you're in my family," she said, laughing. "Lexie, what is it you want from life, if you don't mind my asking? I mean where do you see yourself five or even ten years from now?"

She shrugged. "I don't know. I've never looked that far ahead."

Sara glanced at her watch. "Auction starts soon. I have to go, but can I offer you a suggestion?"

Lexie nodded.

"Think about it. Before it's too late."

Coop waited a few extra minutes to get himself under control before walking out of the coatroom. He stopped in the men's room before checking in with the foundation people, who briefed him on his role. They'd hired an auctioneer, so all Coop had to do was read descriptions from notecards and let the professional do his thing.

He caught sight of Amanda mingling with potential bidders, looking beautiful as always, and practically salivating at the prospect of being the only journalist in the room. He waved and continued scanning the crowd.

Sara walked into the room, her eyes alert as she strode around. To all the world she appeared to be looking for someone. To Coop, she was surveying the guests, making certain everyone belonged. Seemingly satisfied, she headed for the bar to order her standard club soda with a twist of lime.

Coop's father stood off to one side along with his date, Felicia. Coop admired the woman with his dad, a brunette who appeared larger than Coop's petite mother, but who wore the same expression his mother had around the old man. A look of adoration.

Jack Cooper had obviously met someone who cared for him. And if Jack had brought her here, he obviously felt the same way. Coop was happy for him, and headed over to meet the woman who'd finally woken his father out of his long coma.

During the introductions and conversation, Coop looked around for Lexie, wanting nothing more than to share this momentous occasion with her.

But she was nowhere to be found.

"Where's your lady?" Jack asked, reading his mind.

"Sara is by the bar," Coop said, being deliberately obtuse.

Jack glanced at the ceiling. "Did I really raise him?"

Felicia laughed. "Maybe he wants to keep

his private life private. I'll go freshen up," she said diplomatically.

Coop shook his head. "Please stay."

His father shot him a look of gratitude.

"Look, Lexie's here. We just had a disagreement and she's probably taking a minute to compose herself," Coop admitted.

"Are you still being stubborn? Insisting you can't be with a woman who loves to travel?"

"She asked me to go with her." Coop's head still spun from the question.

"That's great!" Jack met his gaze before realization dawned in his eyes. "You said no. Son of a bitch."

Coop shook his head. "How did I become the bad guy? I have a life here. A steady, successful job. An apartment."

So why did he feel so empty? How could all the things he'd valued suddenly not be enough?

"If you're lucky enough to find love, you don't run away from it," his father insisted. And to Coop's surprise, he hooked his arm through Felicia's.

Coop glanced around the banquet room, the glittering chandeliers and the elite of society surrounding him, but he only had eyes for one woman. Who was destined to drive him crazy.

"Do you think it's normal that she doesn't have a home to call her own?" Coop asked, keeping his voice low but firm.

Jack shrugged. "Doesn't mean she can't. Or that she won't down the road. So she doesn't have a home. Did you offer her yours?" his father asked.

He hadn't. Not in those exact words. Coop reeled at the realization. "We both assumed it could only be all one way."

"Hmm. I wonder why you wouldn't want to run off with the girl of your dreams. Let me think. You'd have more time to write. And no excuses if you failed," Jack said, rubbing Coop's face in the one thing he knew his son could not handle.

"Not now," Coop warned him.

"Then when? Do you really think I give a damn that you couldn't be a cop because of a bum shoulder? Or that your marriage bottomed out because your wife couldn't be faithful? None of that's a reflection on the man you are, but you're too damn stubborn to see it."

Coop massaged the back of his neck. He heard his father. He even acknowledged that the man had a point. So maybe it was time to rethink his future.

■ ■ ■ ■

Lexie knew Coop had a job to do tonight. He didn't need more personal drama before the auction and she needed time to think. So she headed for the jewels. She wanted to take a look at the pieces of the set her grandmother and friends had kept hidden for years.

To her surprise, it was hard to get near them. For items Lexie had always considered ugly, they sure were attracting a lot of attention. Which was a good thing for the foundation, she thought, since it probably meant someone would bid on them. Too bad she couldn't afford to buy the necklace back for her grandmother, but the jewels were worth more than the price of a house. Who knew?

She hadn't seen her grandmother and Sylvia yet, and hoped they were staying out of trouble. The town house was spacious and they could be walking around or in the ladies' room.

She glanced around. Waiters were serving champagne, taking drink orders and returning with requests. Lexie accepted a glass of bubbly and strode around, waiting for an opening to get closer to her grandmother's necklace.

She looked at the guests, wondering if she was mingling with the rich and famous without realizing it. A pretty blonde, who looked like a news anchor on television, walked by in a red dress Lexie absolutely adored.

She caught Lexie staring and smiled.

"Do I know you?" the other woman asked.

Lexie laughed. "I thought you looked familiar. Maybe from TV? The news?"

The other woman shook her head. "You flatter me. I'm actually a behind-the-scenes kind of woman. Amanda Nichols, fashion editor at the *Daily Post*."

Lexie's eyes opened wide. "Oh! You work with Coop. I'm Lexie —"

"Lexie Davis, I know. From the paper. The Bachelor Blog mentioned you," Amanda said.

Lexie rolled her eyes. "Don't remind me."

"I think the Blog is kind of sweet. In a matchmaking sort of way." Amanda smiled. "Anyway, are you having fun tonight?"

"I am," Lexie lied. She wasn't about to burden a stranger with her problems. "I was hoping to get a look at the jewelry being auctioned off before it's gone for good."

Amanda nodded. "I think I can help you with that." She grabbed Lexie's arm and brought her around the side of the table. "Excuse me," she said, pushing past people who were talking but not really looking at the items.

Lexie finally had her one last opportunity to see the ring and the necklace that had brought Coop into her life. It still seemed odd to her that the necklace her grandmother had worn with her housecoat was now being sold for a small fortune.

She shook her head, amazed before turning back to Amanda. "Thank you. I really was curious about them."

The lights above began flashing and a voice on the loudspeaker announced that the auction would begin in five minutes.

"Ma'am, I have your drink," a waiter said, speaking to Amanda as he arrived with a glass of red wine on his tray.

Amanda shook her head. "I'm sorry but I didn't order anything."

He cocked his head to one side. "Well, someone ordered red wine. I thought it was you."

"I don't drink red. Lexie? Would you like it instead?"

Before she could answer, a woman carrying a tray filled with champagne tripped and fell into the man holding Amanda's supposed drink. The red alcohol spilled all over

Amanda's beautiful dress, while the other waiter's glasses full of champagne also fell to the floor, crystal shattering and champagne splattering everywhere.

Amanda jerked back, stumbling into the jewel-laden table before righting herself.

"Here, let me help." Lexie knelt down for the pile of napkins that had also fallen to the floor. As she bent lower, she saw the waiter reach out and snag the ring from the table and slip it into his pocket.

She blinked, absorbed what she'd seen and immediately stood and called out. "Security!"

The waiter froze.

"That man took the ring!" Lexie yelled.

He turned to run, realized he was surrounded and the next thing Lexie knew, he'd grabbed her, yanking her against him. Something sharp pricked the skin on her neck.

He had a knife.

And he had her.

Coop spotted Charlotte and Sylvia in the crowd. He hadn't seen the women yet this evening and he wanted to say hello.

They noticed him as well and waved.

He inclined his head and made his way across the floor.

"Ladies, don't you two look beautiful tonight," he said to them.

They both blushed and fluttered their eyelashes, pleased with the compliment.

"Thank you! I wanted to wear my magenta dress but Lexie and Sylvia thought this dress did wonders for my skin tone."

"The other dress made her look like a Spanish hooker," Sylvia explained.

Charlotte glared at her.

"Well, it's the truth!"

Coop laughed. "You made the perfect choice for the evening," he assured Charlotte. "So. Have you heard anything from Ricky?" he asked the two women.

They eyed each other warily.

"No," they finally said at the same time.

Coop nodded, satisfied. He'd figured the other man would stay out of their lives and vice versa to keep their past history under wraps.

"Have you seen Lexie?" Charlotte asked.

Coop shook his head. Not since the coat closet, but he doubted her grandmother would appreciate what had transpired in the other room. He knew she'd been hurt by his reaction to her question and he was worried she'd left the gala alone.

Instead of telling her grandmother that, he said, "I was just about to ask you the same thing. I'll go see if I can find her before the actual auction begins."

"We'll come along," Charlotte said.

With the older women hooked on to either one of his arms, Coop strode through all the people milling around.

"I'm so excited to see where my necklace goes," Charlotte whispered. "I hope it's to someone special. Oh, there's Lexie!" Charlotte pointed a few feet away, to the crowd near the auction items.

Coop turned and his gut cramped at the sight of her in the low-cut silver dress, his body immediately remembering hiking the hem over her waist and thrusting inside her. Then he'd let her walk away.

What kind of idiot was he?

Charlotte raised her hand to wave at her granddaughter.

A second later, chaos broke loose.

Glass shattered.

Lexie screamed.

Coop, Charlotte and Sylvia pushed through the crowd, getting to Lexie in time to see a waiter, one hand around her waist, a knife to her throat.

He wondered if he was dreaming, but clearly he wasn't. Nausea swamped Coop as he took in Lexie's panicked expression and the knife in the man's free hand.

Amanda came up beside him. "One minute we were talking, the next . . . chaos!" she whispered.

Coop glanced around for Sara and found her slowly making her way past stunned guests, but the undercover security guard was too far away to do any good. Rafe, her ex-partner, slowly circled from the other side of the room, but he wouldn't get near the guy in time, either.

And there was no way Coop could reach Lexie before the other man panicked and thrust the knife into her throat.

"He's got the ring," Lexie called out to Coop.

"Shut up!" He pricked her skin with the tip of the blade. A small trickle of blood oozed down her neck.

Coop swallowed but his mouth was bone dry. "Just how do you think you're getting out of here?" He stepped toward them, his hands in the air, trying to buy time.

"Who the hell are you?" the waiter asked.

"I'm with the lady you're holding. Now just relax," Coop said to the man, attempting a step forward.

Lexie's wide-eyed gaze never left his.

"Stay there!" the other man yelled.

Coop drew to a halt. He couldn't turn and call attention to Sara or Rafe, but he hoped they'd had time to move in closer.

"I'm just gonna walk out of here," the waiter explained, never moving the knife. "And nobody's going to stop me." He pulled Lexie along with him as he made his way toward the exit door.

Lexie teetered, tripping in her high heels.

"Faster!" the waiter yelled.

Coop lost years off his life. He couldn't believe he'd found a woman like Lexie, only to lose her forever. If he'd agreed to go to Australia, she wouldn't have been alone, an easy target.

The man reached the exit at the same time Sara approached from the other side. But before she could act, the guy shoved Lexie hard, forcing her to twist her ankle and hit the floor, while he bolted up the stairs without looking back.

Sara slipped her gun out from beneath her dress and took off after him.

Coop knew Rafe would go after her, so Coop ran for Lexie and knelt down, pulling her into his arms. He breathed in her familiar scent, grateful she was alive and well and shaking in his arms.

"You're okay, sweetheart," Coop promised her.

Lexie drew in a deep breath, believing it because Coop's strong arms reassured her.

He'd faced the guy with the knife for her, too.

"Are you sure you're not aiming for your cop brother's job?" she said, forcing a laugh.

"Been there, tried that," he said.

Surprised, Lexie lifted her head and met his gaze, at the same moment Charlotte threw herself over Lexie.

"I almost lost you and that is not okay!" the other woman wailed, her thin arms feeling especially frail.

"I'm fine. I swear. But I think you're squishing Coop to death." Lexie tried to make light of the situation but they all knew the man could have slit her throat.

Lexie almost gagged at the realization.

She, Coop and her grandmother stood up.

Coop kept one arm around Lexie, the other around Charlotte. Sylvia stood beside them wringing her hands despite Lexie's continued reassurance that she was fine.

"Well, you certainly know how to liven up a party, young lady!" Jack Cooper said, walking over.

Lexie hadn't realized his father was here.

"I'm okay, Mr. Cooper."

The other man frowned. "It's Jack. And this is my . . . lady friend, Felicia," he said, gesturing to the woman who stood by his side.

Lexie smiled at the other woman, and since there was no way around it, decided more introductions were in order. "Grandma, this is Coop's father, Jack, and his friend, Felicia. Mr. — Jack, this is my grandmother, Charlotte Davis, and her friend, Sylvia."

"Nice to meet you," Charlotte said.

"Me, too," Sylvia added.

"The pleasure's all mine, ladies."

The duo remained silent.

Lexie narrowed her gaze. The two women must be shook up for them not to fawn all over Coop's father.

"Dad, have you heard any news about Sara?" Coop asked his father.

He shook his head. "She's a trained professional. She'll be fine," Jack said. But he held Coop's gaze too long, and Lexie realized the situation was still serious.

Before she could ask questions, the police burst through the doors. While the cops herded people into groups for questioning, paramedics arrived and insisted on checking Lexie over.

For the first time, she put her hand to her neck and realized there was blood there. She blinked, suddenly dizzy.

"I'll stay with you," Coop said.

"We're just going where it's quiet," the

man with an emergency kit said, gesturing across the room.

Lexie smiled at Coop. "I'm okay. You find out what's going on and where Sara is. Gran, you and Sylvia come keep me company." Lexie figured the other women wouldn't want to let Lexie out of their sight.

Coop reluctantly stepped back and headed toward the commotion across the room.

She let the paramedics lead her to a quiet corner and a short time later, the man had bandaged Lexie's neck and checked out her ankle.

Coop joined her just as she was pronounced fit, to a hovering Charlotte's relief.

"Did they get the guy?" Lexie asked Coop.

"Not yet," Jack said, joining them, real worry in his voice. "The waiter must have been expecting someone to follow him because he ambushed Sara on the rooftop. Rafe was a split second too late and the guy's holding her hostage."

Lexie gasped.

"Rafe's trained SWAT and they called in the full team," Jack said to reassure her.

It didn't work and Lexie shook her head, frightened for Coop's best friend.

"I'm not sure I can handle much more," Charlotte said, drawing Lexie's attention to her grandmother.

As much as Lexie wanted to stay with Coop until this ended, she knew she had to get Charlotte and Sylvia away from the excitement and stress.

"Come, Grandma. Let me take you and Sylvia home," Lexie said, wrapping a reassuring arm around her grandmother's shoulders.

"You're a good girl. Let me go talk to Sylvia," her grandmother said.

Coop met Lexie's gaze. "I'd take you all home, but I have to cover this for the paper."

"I know. And Sara is your best friend. I understand. I'd stay, too, but . . ." She tilted her head toward the older women.

"You need to get them out of here. And you need to rest. I'll come by as soon as I can," he promised.

"Okay," she said, not wanting to further upset her grandmother with the real question on her mind.

To what end? What was the point of Coop coming over when he'd already made it clear he wasn't interested in the lifestyle she had to offer?

Sara's question rang in Lexie's ear. *Where do you see yourself five or even ten years from now?* she'd asked.

Maybe it was time Lexie figured that out.

CHAPTER EIGHTEEN

Lexie didn't sleep much. When the image of the crazy waiter grabbing her with a knife didn't keep her awake, the memory of sex in the closet with Coop did. Along with his accurately spoken words.

Had she really expected him to leave his life behind for her wandering lifestyle?

And wasn't that the crux of it? For as much as she loved to travel, it was time she faced facts. She was twenty-nine years old with a successful career, a substantial bank account, an aging grandmother and not much else to call her own.

When Charlotte was gone, what would be left? And when Lexie looked down the road, is that all that she wanted for her future?

She shook her head, realizing that Sara, a woman she'd just met, had nailed her dead-on. She had been running. Not facing the fact that her grandmother was growing older and so was she. She didn't have to give up her love of travel, but it was time to grow up.

Lexie showered, dressed and headed for the kitchen. Her grandmother was already sitting at the table, still in her robe.

"Are you okay?" Lexie asked.

Her grandmother nodded. She didn't jump up to greet Lexie as she usually did. "But I should be asking you that question."

"I'm fine." She placed a hand on her neck. She'd replaced the too-big bandage with a small Band-Aid. It was just a nick and would heal in no time. "That was too much excitement last night." Lexie poured herself a cup of coffee and added more into her grandmother's cup before joining her at the table.

"I could have lived without the man and the knife," her grandmother admitted.

She looked old.

And tired.

Lexie covered her weathered hand.

"Have you heard anything from Coop?" Charlotte asked.

Lexie shook her head. "Not yet . . . wait." She ran to her room to check her phone, returning with it in her hand. "Dead."

Charlotte frowned. "You're really going to have to lose that nasty habit of forgetting to charge it."

"I know." She placed the useless phone on the table.

"Wouldn't he have called here if he had news?" her grandmother asked.

"I doubt he'd want to wake you this early. Did you check for the newspaper yet?" Lexie asked.

With a shake of her head, Charlotte rose and walked into the hall, opened the door and returned with the paper. "I was too exhausted this morning to do much of anything. Here." She slid it across the tabletop. "Tell me what you find out."

Lexie pulled off the plastic wrap and scanned the front page. Sure enough, there was a short article with Coop's byline. She only hoped he was hard at work and not at the hospital waiting for news about Sara.

Lexie read quickly, relief pouring through her. "Looks like Sara's ex-partner intervened and got Sara out safely," Lexie said, relieved. "But she injured her knee. *Reinjured,* it says. Oh, they use the word *career-threatening.* I feel awful!" Lexie knew how much the other woman loved being a cop.

"Oh, that poor child," Charlotte said. "We'll have to send her flowers!"

Lexie smiled at her grandmother's thoughtfulness. "Absolutely."

"What about the waiter?"

She continued reading. "Sara's partner, Rafe Mancuso, was seriously wounded, but his injuries aren't life-threatening. Wait! Listen to this. According to the police, the waiter in question turned out to be the same man in a recent string of other snatch-and-grab robberies at major events and collectors' meetings throughout the city. An eyewitness identified him as the man driving the getaway car at the last incident where he struck and killed an innocent bystander!"

Charlotte sucked in a shocked breath.

"It says the suspect — the waiter — knew if he got caught last night he'd be charged with murder in that case, so he panicked, grabbed me and made his escape," Lexie said, lowering the paper.

"Oh, my."

Lexie nodded.

Together, they sat in silence for a few minutes, digesting the news.

"I need to talk to you," Lexie said at last.

"And I need to talk to you." Her grandmother looked up, a serious expression on her face.

Lexie gestured with a sweep of her hand. "Age before beauty." She laughed.

Her grandmother chuckled. "Fine. I'll go first. You're a fool if you let Coop go. And no granddaughter of mine is a fool."

Lexie exhaled long and hard. She also nodded. "You're right."

"I am?" Charlotte sounded stunned.

With a shrug, Lexie said, "Of course. I'd be a fool to let Coop go and I'm no fool. I am, however, a woman in transition."

She went on to explain to her grandmother how she'd blurted out the suggestion that Coop go to Australia with her — omitting the part about sex in the closet. "I never even took his feelings or his life into consideration. I just blindsided him. And myself, since I never planned on asking him. It just happened."

"He didn't take it well, hmm?"

Lexie rested her chin in her hand. "Nope. We hit a stalemate and we both retreated to our separate corners. Then the gunman grabbed me and my life flashed before my eyes. My empty life." She picked up a paper napkin and began shredding it to little bits. It wasn't easy to admit her failings and it helped to have something else to concentrate on.

Charlotte leaned back against the cushion of her chair. "If your life is empty, there's a simple solution. Fill it up! I had a full life, but it would have been even fuller if your grandfather had lived. Or if I'd let myself love again," she said, her tone wistful and sad.

"I'm sorry."

Charlotte shook her head. "Don't be. I made my choices. But if you learn nothing else from me, learn this. Live each day to the fullest. Make sure when you're my age and look back, you don't have any regrets."

Lexie smiled. "You're a smart woman, Grandma."

"Tell me something I don't know. Now what did you want to say?" Charlotte asked.

Lexie glanced at the coffee she'd yet to drink. "To fill the emptiness, I need to make some changes." She drew a deep breath. "And as much as I appreciate your giving me a place to return to, it's time for me to find a home of my own."

Her grandmother's eyes opened wide. "My baby bird is finally leaving the nest." Charlotte clasped her hands to her chest. "I thought the day would never come."

"You aren't upset? But what if you need me?"

Charlotte waved her hand, dismissing the notion. "Isn't that what those computer lessons were for?" she asked, a naughty smile flirting across her lips.

"Which ones?" Lexie asked, wryly. Rising from her chair, she pulled her grandmother into a hug, savoring her familiar and comforting scent and feel.

Life without Charlotte as a safety net loomed before her. Instead of being scary, though, it was an exciting prospect.

"So where does Coop fit into this new home of your own?" her grandmother asked.

"I'm not sure." Lexie met the older woman's inquiring gaze. "But this decision is about what's right for me. No matter what he decides."

Charlotte smiled. "I'm so proud of you!"

As always, her admiration and acceptance warmed Lexie's heart. "What can I say? I learned from the best."

"You most certainly did."

Lexie dumped her untouched coffee into the sink, rinsed the mug and placed it in the dishwasher. "I need to go out for a little while."

Charlotte pulled the lapels of her housecoat tighter. "Where to?" she asked.

"Where I always go when I need to think."

Lexie had plans to make for her future. Whether or not Coop wanted to be part of those plans was up to him.

Coop got no sleep. He'd put the early edition to bed, and then gotten started on the afternoon one. He'd called Lexie's cell a few times in between, only to realize that she'd probably forgotten to charge the damn thing. And 6:00 a.m. was too early to wake Charlotte.

In the moment the waiter held the knife to her neck and the times he'd had to relive it since, Coop knew he couldn't live without her. If it meant traveling around the world, so be it. At least he'd have her by his side. Maybe giving up his job *would* free his creative spirit. He sure as hell hoped so because after his savings ran out he didn't know how else he'd pay the bills.

He showed up on her doorstep, flowers in hand, to find out Lexie wasn't home. Charlotte had been happy to accept the flowers, however.

"Where can I find her?" Coop asked.

"Where she always goes to think," Charlotte said.

"Are you being deliberately cryptic?" he asked the older woman.

She pinched his cheek. "Certainly not. I'm telling you what I know. If you're as intelligent as I think you are, finding her shouldn't be a problem."

Coop rolled his eyes. "I'm going!" To the only place in the world he thought she might be.

■ ■ ■ ■

Lexie settled herself on the floor, her back to the glass windows overlooking the city. Because it was raining outside, the landmark was relatively empty, not many people interested in looking out over soupy fog. Lexie didn't care. She knew she was high above the clouds and that was enough for her.

She turned on her iPod and stuck her headphones in her ears, then focused on the real estate section of the paper. There were so many choices.

Apartment or house.

The city or the suburbs.

Rent or buy.

Her heart beat faster at the thought of having her own place at last. Things to come home to. Knickknacks with meaning. Pictures. Books.

"Excuse me, but you realize this isn't a public library," a muffled voice said.

"I know," Lexie answered without glancing up.

"It's not a coffee shop, either."

Lexie frowned. "I can't be in your way. There's an entire set of windows for you and there's no view to look out at anyway!"

Someone kicked at her feet.

"Hey!" She glanced up, intending to give the annoying person a piece of her mind, and looked into a familiar set of gorgeous blue eyes. "Coop! What are you doing here?"

But even as she asked, her pulse sped up because he knew this was her special place.

"Why do you think I'm here?"

"Looking for me?" she asked hopefully.

He nodded, his gaze warm.

"How's Sara?" she asked. She'd been worried about the other woman all morning.

"In a lot of knee pain. Pissed off about potentially not being able to return to full capacity. And in a foul mood. But both she and her partner are going to be okay and that's all that matters," Coop said. "Mind if I join you?"

Lexie gathered her things, freeing up the space beside her.

Coop settled on the floor next to her, back against the window, his long legs stretched out in front of him, his thigh touching hers.

The heat traveled straight to the pit of her stomach, settling low. "How did you know where to find me?" she asked.

He turned his head, meeting her gaze. "Your grandmother told me you went to the place you always go to think."

She couldn't help but smile. "Good thing

you know me so well."

"I'd say so, or else I'd be wandering the city."

He still hadn't shaved and she ran her hand over his scruffy beard.

"Like it?" he asked.

She grinned. "I do."

"Hey, can I ask a favor?"

She nodded. He could ask her for anything and she'd likely agree.

"Either buy an extra cell phone or learn to charge your battery. In the *future,* I can't not be able to get in touch with you," he said, his voice husky and gruff.

The future.

Her heart skipped a beat at his use of the word. "I think I can manage that."

"Good. So what made you come up here? What's going on in that beautiful head of yours that you need to think about?" he asked, picking up the paper she'd been reading.

Embarrassed, Lexie wanted to snatch it back. Instead, she curled her hands into tight fists, waiting for his reaction.

He studied the page, his eyes narrowing in confusion. "It's the *New York Times* Real Estate section."

She swallowed hard. "I've heard it's the most comprehensive."

"Is your grandmother looking to move?"

"No." Lexie bit the inside of her cheek. "I am."

Confusion darkened his gaze. "I don't understand."

Lexie drew a deep breath. "I'm looking for a place of my own. An apartment or maybe a house. I'm not sure. I'm also not sure if I want to stay in the city or explore something more suburban. Although that might be too ordinary for me, at least at first." She knew she was rambling, but until she'd made her point and he understood, she couldn't relax.

"Lexie, if you're looking for a place of your own because you think that's what I want —"

She shook her head. "This has nothing to do with you. Well, that's not exactly true. If it weren't for you I probably wouldn't have taken a hard look at my life. But I'm doing this for me. It's time I stood on my own, don't you think?"

Coop was dizzy and the altitude had nothing to do with it. "That depends what you mean by standing on your own. If you can do that with me by your side, then, yes, I think it's time. And you don't have to settle down for there to be an *us*. I was wrong insisting that you had to give up what makes you you."

She met his gaze, but said nothing.

So he continued. "You're special, Lexie. I always knew that. You brought that vitality into my life and believe it or not into my work. My writing work. And that's what matters. The crime beat will exist without me. I want to travel and see the world through your eyes."

She blinked back tears "Why? What changed in the last twenty-four hours?" she asked, obviously not yet convinced.

"You have to ask?" He cupped her cheek in his hand. "I almost lost you. In the minutes that guy had a knife against your throat, I got a glimpse of my life without you. And I realized what an idiot I was for letting you walk away."

A tear trickled down her cheek.

"Hey. I didn't mean to make you cry." He pulled her glasses off before they could fog up, and brushed the moisture from her cheek with his thumb.

"It's just amazing to me that you care so much about me," she whispered.

It was so wrong that she still didn't think he could love her for who and what she was. "I don't just care, Lex. I love you. I said it last night but I failed to follow up. I love you and I will spend the rest of our lives

412

making sure you know I mean it."

She smiled, the genuine, open grin he'd fallen hard for the first time they met. "What if I still want a house?" she asked. "I wouldn't give up travel completely, mind you, but I'd have a home base. What do you think?"

If she needed to stand on her own before she could commit to him, he'd hate it but he'd accept it. Anything she wanted or needed to be whole. "I suppose I could be persuaded to drive out to the suburbs to visit."

"No." She scrunched up her nose. "What if I wanted *us* to have a house? Together. I noticed that you talk the talk about having your own place, but you don't even have matching sheets or dishes. We could start together and build. From scratch."

"A place of *our* own." He needed to repeat the words to believe them.

She nodded. "So when we did travel, *we'd* have a home to come back to."

"And when we weren't traveling?"

She shrugged. "We'd work . . ."

"And have a family?" As soon as the words were out, Coop held his breath.

Eyes wide, she absorbed the question. And then she nodded.

"You're sure?" he asked.

"Yes." She grinned. "Yes. Absolutely." Then and there, Coop had the answer to all the dreams he'd never known he'd had.

Lexie couldn't stop smiling. She had never let herself think about real love, family or permanence. Never believed she wanted it or could have it for herself.

Everything had changed with this one man. "Want to know why?" she asked.

"Yeah, I do."

She couldn't stop touching him and she caressed his cheek.

His eyes deepened with every touch. "If I'd known how much you liked the beard, I'd have grown it sooner."

She laughed.

"Now tell me why you're sure about a home and a family with me."

Lexie's mood sobered. "Because you give me the security I never had. You give me a reason to want to be home."

He brushed his lips over hers. "That's funny because you give me the freedom I was always afraid to take or trust in. And you believe in me, which helps me believe in myself."

He leaned in for a deeper, emotion-sealing kiss, but she broke it off quickly, remembering a question she'd had from last night.

"What did you mean last night when I

made that joke about your looking to take over your brother's job as a cop? You said, 'Been there, tried that.' "

He groaned. "I had to quit the police academy because of an old sports injury. It felt like I'd failed and let my father down. Then with the divorce, I failed at marriage. The only thing I didn't fail at was being a reporter."

She finally understood so much more about him. "So when I asked you to go away with me, expecting you to leave everything behind, you felt like I was taking away the one thing you did well."

A horrified look crossed his face. "Hey, I hope I do more than that one thing well."

Grinning, she patted his thigh, her hand dangerously close. "Trust me, there are many things you do *very* well," she reassured him, nuzzling her face against his.

"What a pair we make," Coop said.

"I like it."

"You do realize the irony, right? My dad's a cop and your grandmother's a thief."

"Ex-thief."

"Semantics," Coop said and pulled her into a long, deep kiss that held the promise of today, tomorrow and the future, which had never looked so bright.

EPILOGUE

THE DAILY POST
THE BACHELOR BLOGS

Our latest bachelor quit his day job for love. Sam Cooper's heart is spoken for, ladies. But, luckily, there's a new heroic bachelor in the city. Rafe Mancuso stepped in and saved one of New York City's Finest last night, getting injured in the process. I can hear you all swooning now.

Amanda Nichols, fashion editor at the *Daily Post,* was there live covering the Lancaster Auction. She asked the hostage negotiator how it felt to save a damsel in distress. Mr. Mancuso, not realizing he'd been stabbed, answered from the heart — "Just doing my job. With the added perk of rescuing a gorgeous cop with a killer bod," before passing out from his injuries.

Could romance be brewing between this hero and the lady he saved? Or is the field clear for the other women of our city? Only time — and the Bachelor Blogger — will tell.

ABOUT THE AUTHOR

Carly Phillips started her writing career with the Harlequin Temptation line in 1999 with *Brazen,* and she's never strayed far from home! In 2002 Carly's book *The Bachelor* was chosen by Kelly Ripa for her Reading with Ripa book club, making it the first romance to be chosen by a nationally televised book club. Carly has published thirty books, and, among others, she has appeared on the *New York Times, USA Today* and *Publishers Weekly* bestseller lists. An ABC soap opera addict, Carly lives in Purchase, New York, with her husband, two teenage daughters and two frisky soft-coated wheaten terriers who act like their third and fourth children. You can find Carly online at www.carlyphillips.com; www .plotmonkeys.com and www.myspace.com/ carlyphillips.